INDEPENDENCE

Also by Kaitlyn Andersen

Reliance
Disobedience

INDEPENDENCE

Book Three of the
Reliance Trilogy

Kaitlyn Andersen

Heliosphere®
BOOKS

San Diego

INDEPENDENCE
Book Three of the Reliance Trilogy
Heliosphere Books®

Library of Congress Cataloging-in-Publication Data

Names: Andersen, Kaitlyn, 1986- author.
Title: Independence / Kaitlyn Andersen.
Description: San Diego : Heliosphere Books, [2023]
| Series: The Reliance trilogy ; book 3

Identifiers: LCCN 2022060049 (print) | LCCN 2022060050 (ebook) | ISBN 9781937868758 (trade paperback) | ISBN 9781937868956 (epub) | ISBN 9781937868963 (kindle edition)

Subjects: LCGFT: Science fiction. | Novels.

Classification: LCC PS3601.N436 I64 2023 (print) | LCC PS3601.N436 (ebook) | DDC 813/.6--dc23/eng/20230112

LC record available at https://lccn.loc.gov/2022060049
LC ebook record available at https://lccn.loc.gov/2022060050

This is a work of fiction. Names, characters, places, and events either are the products of the author's imagination or are used fictitiously. Any resemblance to actual persons, living or dead, corporations, or other entities, is entirely coincidental.

Heliosphere Books are published by Endpapers Press, a division of Author Coach, LLC.

Heliosphere Books is a registered trademark of Author Coach, LLC.

This book is dedicated to all those who stand up and fight for what's right while the rest of us sit at home and write books about them.

And to my daughter, River; my love, my light, my life, and without whom this book would have been finished a cycle earlier.

ONE

"I warned you," Finn No Last Name growled. Her gloved hand shoved the hybrid formerly known as Supersonic against the cold, interior wall of *Independence*. These days, the Xandar woman went by her given name, Sasha, rather than the speedster nickname she'd adopted in the Dome, the gladiatorial arena where she and a whole host of other hybrids had fought to the death for the entertainment of Reliance nobility. The toes of the female's boots scraped against the floor as her feet fought for purchase. The girl tried to say something, but she barely got out more than a hoarse croak of residual air escaping her lungs.

Her right hand came up to slap weakly at Finn's exposed forearm, where her long-sleeve shirt had ridden up. At the contact, Finn fought to block out the buzzing in her ears and the accompanying rush of memories that demanded her attention. She loosened her hold slightly, grimacing in annoyance. Finn's own abilities allowed her to take, or "siphon" memories from others via physical contact. As an odd side benefit, she retained information with preternatural accuracy.

She usually made a point to keep her distance, fearing the swarm of memories that rushed her when her bare skin touched another's. Controlling what she saw when contact occurred was like isolating a drop of water within a vast ocean. Her time in the Dome had taught her a level of control over her ability to siphon memories from objects that she'd never dreamed possible, but her ability to siphon them from *people* was still mediocre at best.

Finn especially feared siphoning memories of the Dome from this hybrid and the others Shane Montgomery and his crew had rescued little more than two weeks ago.

If she saw their memories, she knew she would see *him*.

The mere thought of seeing AJ Montgomery again, even if only through memories, made her heart race with panic. Finn slammed Sasha's head against the wall, forcing a shock of dark hair to come loose, and her hand to fall to her side. As soon as she did, Finn brought her face close to Sasha's, hissing out her next words through clenched teeth. "Say his name again," she ordered.

Sasha's eyes began to bulge as the skin covering her face became a dark shade of red tinged with purple. The girl wheezed once, then twice, but no words made it past her pale lips. The sounds of approaching booted feet echoed down the hallway and Finn dimly registered someone's gasp of alarm.

"What are you doing? Let go of Sasha!" a gruff shout sounded from a few feet away. Finn's glare harshened and her grip tightened slightly hearing the concern in Shane's voice when he said the girl's name. "Dammit, Finn!" he yelled again when she didn't move. "Let her go!"

Finn turned her head a few inches. Just enough to let her eyes slide over to the ship's captain, Shane Montgomery. His elegant, yet rugged features looked out of place alongside Conrad, his adopted brother, who always looked ready for a fight, and their leader and Finn's former mentor, Grim.

The captain's green eyes were wide with alarm as he ran a shaking hand through his messy blond hair and looked to Grim for help. The giant, red-skinned, horned Khaleerian ignored the human in favor of meeting Finn's gaze unflinchingly. Though he didn't seem particularly distressed by the scene in front of him, his black eyes flitted between her and the dangling Xandar hybrid meaningfully.

The message in them was clear: *Put her down, Dhala,* she could practically hear him thinking.

Finn's free hand tightened into a fist, and she released a deep breath of frustration. She couldn't bring herself to look at Conrad. The small part of her that still cared feared the judgment and horror she knew she would see in his hypnotic, blue eyes.

There had been a time when she'd called Shane a friend and ally. His brother, Conrad, had been even more than that. Not long ago, she thought perhaps she'd been falling in love with the ebony-skinned hybrid. Now, the two men were just painful reminders of what she had become, and the little brother that had been lost in the process.

Finn held Grim's stare and released Sasha from her grip. She finally tore her eyes away when the girl dropped to the ground and slumped against the wall. She sucked in air and the dark-red blotches slowly began to fade from her face. Finn continued looking down at her in disgust as she watched the life return to the hybrid's darting brown eyes.

"Finn?" Conrad's low rumble washed over her, but she shook it off like a chill and ignored him.

The calm measure of her voice belied the rage swirling deep inside of her as she willed the hybrid on the ground to meet her gaze.

"You don't get to say his name," Finn told her flatly. "Ever."

The female nodded so vigorously, her enhanced speed blurred her movements and made the action almost difficult to track.

"I . . . just wanted . . . to apologize." Each utterance looked as though it pained her, but Sasha didn't seem deterred.

She never got the chance to finish. Without another word, Finn turned her back on the girl. Not sparing any of them a glance or a wave goodbye, she walked silently past Shane, Conrad, and Grim.

Waves of auburn hair that had come loose during the struggle fell into her face as she went, and with a look of frustration, Finn pulled the mass back into a ponytail and tightened it. As she turned the corner and made her way deeper into the ship's center, her fists clenched and unclenched, and her nails dug into the palm of her hand through the material of her gloves.

She forced her fingers to uncurl and stretched them as she quickened her pace. She made it farther than she expected before the sound of footfalls, followed by Conrad's voice, reached her.

"Finn, stop." The sound of his heavy boots against the deck slowed behind her as he called out.

Undeterred, she increased her speed and kept walking in the opposite direction. She'd been ignoring him for weeks, but Conrad seemed incapable of taking the hint.

She'd only made it a few feet when Finn abruptly halted mid-step and her muscles froze on the spot. One minute she'd been making her hasty retreat and the next her body and its movements had become locked in stone. Her feet felt as though they had been weighed down and secured to the floor with cement. She knew from experience that no matter how hard she tried, she would never be able to budge on her own. Stalling her movements, Finn bit out a growl of frustration.

As a half-Merlidian, Conrad had the enviable ability to manipulate energy molecules to move objects and people with his mind. The stubborn lout had resorted to using his powers on her. She knew if she turned, she would see his eyes glowing from the exertion.

"Why won't you just leave me alone?" she hissed angrily.

"Because 'alone' is the last thing you should be right now," he answered quietly.

As he spoke, she felt him release her; her body jolted slightly from the sudden freedom. But still, she didn't turn to face him.

"Are you addicted to pain?" he asked. Is that what this is?"

"What are you talking about?" Her back remained to him, her hands clenched and her shoulders tight.

"I'm the reason AJ is dead," she whispered, and finally half-pivoted in Conrad's direction, but refused to make eye contact. A tense silence filled the space between them.

Two weeks before, Finn had embarked on a reconnaissance mission to Aquarii, taking along Conrad and Shane's kid brother, AJ. The troubled boy had been through hell in his short cycles, having spent most of them imprisoned and tortured by the Reliance.

Somehow, despite his initial hatred of Finn, the boy had learned to trust her. He'd even become a friend. Together, they'd trekked to the planet with Nova, a doxie pilot and acquaintance from Finn's past as a thief on the Mud Pit. Once on Aquarii, they'd discovered the Dome: an arena where groups of enslaved hybrids were forced to compete in an exhibition of games pitting them against one another in a fight to the death . . . in front of a crowd of thousands.

All of this for the mere entertainment of the Reliance upper caste.

Before they could report back to Shane's ship, *Independence*, Finn and AJ discovered Nova had betrayed them to the Reliance, as well as given up the coordinates to *Independence* and Shane's crew of rescued strays. Shane and his crew managed to escape, but Finn and AJ hadn't been so lucky. As the Dome's newest prisoners, they'd been forced to compete in the deadly games along with the other imprisoned hybrids.

Though Finn had been made to participate, she refused to take a life, making her an easy target for the other fighters. Because of this, she and AJ had formed fast alliances with some of them, and made deadly enemies out of the rest. On their final day in the Dome before the skies opened up and Grim, Shane, and the rest of his crew came to their rescue, Finn had failed to protect her friends. Gray Matter, an odd-looking hybrid of unknown origins who could predict future outcomes of events, had died saving Finn's life.

After that, she'd been forced to watch on, powerless to intervene, as her enemies killed AJ. Something had changed in Finn irrevocably as she'd watched the light leave AJ's eyes. In the melee, a switch seemed to flip in her brain . . . one that could never be turned off.

A long time ago, she'd been a prisoner of the Reliance. They'd forced her into slavery as a small child and sold her to Alistair Adams, a prominent chancellor on Aquarii. During her torture at the hands of the chancellor, an accident had forced her to do the unthinkable. She'd killed her only friend, a little girl and fellow prisoner named Sophie. The act had proven so traumatic that Finn had blocked out the memory, along with all her others. She'd escaped to the Mud Pit, her mind a blank slate by the time Grim had found her.

She hadn't even been able to remember her own name.

All those traumatic memories had come rushing back during her involuntary stay on *Independence* with her estranged older sister, Iliana. Time, and the gentle coaxing of Conrad, had convinced her to let go of her guilt.

Until it all came back that day in the Dome.

That day, she had become the merciless killer she'd feared she'd always been. She'd spent her life atoning for the sin of taking Sophie's life, even going so far as taking a vow never to kill.

In an instant, she'd broken it.

After taking out her opponents one by one, Finn had then turned her rage on the chancellor and the Reliance soldiers protecting him.

Unfortunately, Conrad had hauled her away before she could watch the light leave her tormentor's eyes.

"Finn," Conrad whispered, grief filling his voice, "what happened to AJ wasn't your fault."

Finn knew he truly believed what he said; he'd been saying it repeatedly since she'd returned. She felt a mocking laugh bubble up in her chest and scoffed.

"*I'm* the one who brought Nova here . . . I *trusted* her. *I'm* the one who took AJ with me to Aquarii. He never should've been there, Conrad." Finn felt the walls of her chest constricting with pain. "He was just a kid. *I* put him in danger, and *I* couldn't protect him."

She saw movement in her periphery as Conrad inched closer.

"No, Finn. *You* were in an impossible situation. *You* did everything you could to keep him safe."

She could hear the tenderness in his voice. There was a time when that tenderness would have been her undoing. Now, it just fueled the inescapable anger bubbling up in the pit of her stomach.

"What about Viper and Rock?" she bit out harshly.

"The hybrids that tried to kill you . . . that killed AJ?"

"Viper wasn't trying to kill me then. We'd already seen the ship. She knew we were being rescued and she'd stopped attacking."

"Finn—" his murmured interruption barely phased her. She had to make him understand that the woman he was fighting for didn't exist anymore.

"I didn't kill her because I had to," she continued, relentless in her bid to make him understand. "I killed her because I *wanted* to. The same with the chancellor and those soldiers."

Finn finally turned fully and met his gaze. His dreads hung freely around his chiseled face and his blue eyes glowed brightly with emotion. They searched hers intensely, as though looking for something.

"Finn—"

She refused to let him speak. Her measured stare held his as she finished,

"I'm going to kill them all, Conrad. Even if I die trying, I am going to take the Reliance with me."

She didn't give him a chance to respond. Instead, she turned and strode down the corridor and around the corner. Her steps didn't take her far before another voice interrupted her.

"Is everything okay, Finn?"

She turned to see a child emerge from the shadows. *Tiri.* She twirled a white-blonde curl around a small lavender index finger. Her other hand fidgeted with the hem of her shirt. The child's grass-green eyes were somber. Seeing her so hesitant and unsure, it nearly killed Finn to maintain her stiff posture and detached expression.

Finn gave the girl a sharp nod but didn't speak. She studied Tiri carefully. She had gotten taller since Finn had last seen her, making her limbs look willowier than ever.

She had made several attempts to visit Finn over the last two weeks, even making multiple failed endeavors to use her telepathy—or mind-snooping as Finn liked to call it—to get a response from her friend, but to no avail.

Finn had shut the girl out completely.

Tiri was most likely the galaxy's only salvation, given her unique Aquariian heritage and abilities, but she'd also been Finn's friend. The first one she'd made on the ship. The only problem was . . . Finn couldn't stand to look her in the eye anymore.

She couldn't look any of them in the eye.

Weeks ago, when Isis had told Finn about Tiri and her ability to heal and grow plant life, her mind had reeled with the implications. For a galaxy full of people dependent on the government for their oxygen, the little girl was a much-needed miracle.

Finn's head turned left then right to scan the hallway around her. Slowly, the realization dawned on her that the tiny savior of their galaxy was walking around the ship without anyone to protect her. What was Isis thinking letting the child out of her sight? The Aquariian healers who had sacrificed their lives to bring Tiri into the world had named Isis the precious child's protector. And where was she now?

Finn's thoughts began to spiral as AJ's pale face filled her mind. She couldn't lose Tiri too. The thought was unbearable. She took a step toward Tiri and grabbed her around the bicep.

"Where's Isis? You shouldn't be off wandering by yourself. It's not safe."

The little girl winced at the harshness in Finn's tone.

"I heard arguing," she muttered sheepishly.

"Your quarters are on the other side of the ship, Tiri, so the only way you heard anything is if you were out roaming where you're not supposed to be . . . or you were mind-snooping." The lingering anger from her altercation with Conrad intensified at the thought of Tiri sifting through her thoughts. She didn't want Tiri anywhere near her mind. The things she could see and hear from the Dome alone would scar the child for life. Battling her growing fear and anger, Finn forced her mind to blank and prodded her with a sharp hiss. "Well, which is it?"

Rather than cower under the intensity of Finn's gaze, Tiri's small frame straightened, and her green eyes narrowed. She pulled roughly from Finn's hold, her eyes shooting fire as she did.

"I know Isis told you about me . . . about what I can do."

Finn swallowed the lump in her throat and crossed her arms over her chest.

"So?"

Tiri studied her for long moments. Her round eyes still burned with anger, but the girl's shoulders sagged slightly.

"I know you're only being mean to me because you think you're protecting me."

Finn's hands came to rest on her hips, and she looked at Tiri with a challenging glare meant to incinerate.

"And how exactly do you know that?"

Rather than admit to mind-snooping on Finn's thoughts, Tiri's mouth set in a stubborn line and her gaze sharpened. After a few tense beats of silence, she whispered, "What happened to AJ isn't going to happen to me."

Finn's muscles locked. Her chest burned with the emotions she'd tried to bury there, and the sound of pumping blood filled her ears. She felt hot tears rising and forced them back down with a will she hadn't known she possessed. Taking a step closer to the child, she bent down and whispered back in a carefully measured tone.

"I'm going to say this one last time: stay out of my head and stay away from me."

Despite the desperate aching in her chest, Finn locked gazes with Tiri for a moment longer, allowing her words to sink in. Ignoring the determined glint in the little girl's eyes, she stood to her full height and walked away.

Tiri didn't follow.

TWO

Finn shot up in bed. Her indigo eyes opened to complete darkness, tears streaked her face, and a silent scream hung from her lips. Visions of the Dome and AJ's bloody body haunted her every time she closed her eyes to sleep. She ended up staying awake most nights, but the fatigue from the last two weeks—coupled with her altercation with Conrad— must have finally overwhelmed her.

On the floor beside her bed, a large figure snored softly. Thick, multihued hair spread out around her head in a halo of browns, reds, and golds, and deadly claw-tipped fingers were resting interlaced atop her furred chest. Since she'd saved Enyo, a half-Sirian, from enslavement, the lupine woman had taken it as her solemn duty to protect Finn. Every night she slept on the floor of their shared room, protecting her savior even in sleep. It had been this way even before Finn's rescue from the Dome.

Finn silently rose from the bed. Afraid to disturb Enyo, she bent slightly at the hips and tiptoed around her. Finn monitored the rise and fall of Enyo's deep, even breaths for a moment before creeping her way to the door.

"I don't know why you bother sneaking out, *N'Goza*." Enyo's whisper reached her across the room before she could take another step.

Finn rolled her eyes.

"For the same reason you pretend to sleep through it . . . it's *polite*."

"You would wake any Sirian worth her claws." She could hear the smile in Enyo's voice as she responded to the gentle reprimand. Enyo paused before adding in a more serious tone, "Be safe, *N'Goza*."

Finn waited for Enyo's breathing to deepen once more before turning away.

Once she'd made it out into the hall, she straightened her posture and walked with steady strides to the room four doors down. She entered without knocking. Like hers, this room was dark, save for a small lamp on a steel desk he always left on for her. The glow washed over the room's massive occupant where he lay on the bed. Her gaze took in his long limbs as they spilled over the edges of the mattress. His eyes were closed, and the hard lines of his face were soft, almost peaceful.

Finn made her way to the side of his bed and sat down on the floor. Without opening his eyes, Aedan flicked out a wrist and tossed her a blanket and a pillow. She caught them with ease and spread them out on the floor, before settling herself within the new makeshift bed.

Aedan opened one eye and glanced down at her.

"Another nightmare?" he asked quietly. Finn swallowed hard and nodded. Both of his eyes opened, and the dark orbs studied her as he ran a large hand over his bald head. "The chancellor or AJ?"

Finn wrapped her arms around her knees and studied the charcoal-colored skin covering Aedan's feet. It was so dark, it took on a blue hue in certain lights. A half-Solidarian who could control and manipulate fire, his thick, dark skin could withstand high temperatures.

Finn forced herself to focus and answer Aedan's question.

"AJ," she whispered.

Aedan sat up and the blanket covering him fell to his waist, revealing a thin white shirt stretched tight over his muscular torso. When she'd first met him in the Dome, his mere presence and size had intimidated her more than she'd cared to admit at the time. He'd been fighting and ruthlessly killing in the Dome for many cycles—surviving longer than any other hybrid prisoner ever had—and there'd been a sharp intelligence in his gaze that unnerved her even more than his practiced silence.

No one had been more shocked than Finn when the giant became one of her most-trusted allies in the Dome.

"Blaming yourself won't bring him back." Aedan's gruff voice pulled her from her thoughts.

"I know."

"Yet you still do it," he persisted.

"I liked it better when you didn't talk," Finn muttered quietly, as her eyes flitted away from his gaze.

She needed the guilt; she *needed* the pain. It was the only thing keeping her from tipping over the edge into oblivion. This newfound thirst for vengeance gave her a purpose and a reason to stay alive. She went to sleep and woke up with AJ's name on her lips so she wouldn't forget.

A long time ago, she'd let herself forget Sophie.

She'd pushed the memories so far down, allowing herself to erase her only childhood friend and the brutal end she'd faced at Finn's hand until they'd all but disappeared.

She would *not* forget again. Instead, she fed the rage coursing through her bloodstream.

"I understand, Finn."

She looked back up at Aedan when he spoke and some of the tension left her shoulders. He did understand. As a child, the Reliance had hunted him. When they'd finally found him hiding with his human mother and siblings, they'd captured Aedan and forced him to watch as they murdered his entire family.

After that, he'd burned every last soldier and their barracks to the ground, before being captured again and ultimately thrust into the Dome.

"I know you do," she whispered.

"Tell me the plan," he urged gently. "You always sleep better after you do."

It was a simple plan, one she had decided on weeks ago as she'd watched AJ's coffin ejected into space.

"We're going to kill them all."

"Killing them won't bring the boy back," he reminded her as he always did.

Finn swallowed the emotion clogging her throat and took a deep breath.

"No, but it will still feel *really* good."

Aedan's mouth formed a half smile, but his eyes remained serious.

"Yes, it will."

AJ.

Finn woke with a start. As the echoes of her latest nightmare faded, her eyes adjusted to the waning darkness and she saw a wall of fur. Finn felt herself smile as she took in the width of Enyo's back resting mere inches from her face. As had become her habit, Enyo had given Finn privacy as long as she could before joining them sometime in the early morning hours.

Stubborn Sirian, Finn thought affectionately.

Before she could wake either of her companions, static sounded in the air as the ship's overhead comms activated. Moments later, they heard Shane's voice echoing around them.

"Everybody up and ready in ten; we've got a crew meeting in the rec room."

He repeated the message twice more before disconnecting.

Finn sat up and exchanged a glance with Aedan and Enyo. Moving to stand, Finn offered him a small smile.

"Gotta change. See you in ten," she called out, as she moved to the doors. Aedan nodded sleepily and rubbed a hand over his bald head. Finn glanced at Enyo where she sat on the floor. "Are you coming?" she asked the female. Eyes still partially closed, Enyo offered her a groggy nod and waved her away with claw-tipped fingers.

As they had all learned over the last few weeks . . . Enyo wasn't exactly a morning person.

Finn's eyes still twinkled with humor when the doors opened before her, and she promptly bumped into the wall of Conrad's muscular chest. She stepped back until her spine hit the now closed doors and craned her neck up to meet his gaze. His dreads were pulled away from his face and the emotion in his blue eyes quickly morphed from surprise to anger.

"You weren't in your room," he bit out through clenched teeth by way of an explanation.

"No, I wasn't," she returned, stating the obvious.

He studied her intently as he took a step forward and closed the small distance that separated them. She inhaled his scent and forced herself to ignore the resulting racing of her heartbeat.

"Back off, Conrad," she snapped at his chest, not daring to look up and get trapped in his knowing stare. She wished he would just leave her alone. Pushing him away these last few weeks had been a special sort of torture, however necessary it was.

Their paths, once so intricately intertwined, had diverged. She couldn't take him with her where she was going; she'd already lost too much. Somewhere, in a place deep within her brain she refused to acknowledge, she knew one thing: for the rest of her days, however short they may be, she'd always wonder what could have been.

"Look at me, Finn," Conrad demanded.

"Conrad, I need you in the rec room," Shane's deep voice interrupted the moment between them, and Finn just barely fought back a sigh of relief. She peered around Conrad's shoulder to see the ship's captain watching them. His green eyes narrowed as he seemed to quickly pick up on the tension. He held the handle of a steaming metal cup in his hand and his dark-blond hair was still wet from a shower.

The trio stared at each other silently for several long moments. Before anyone could say anything, the doors at Finn's back opened. She lost her balance and stumbled backward. Big hands steadied her shoulders from behind.

Conrad's eyes hardened as he watched Aedan's fingers squeeze Finn gently before letting her go.

"Problem?" Aedan asked in a terse grumble.

Conrad's hands tightened into fists at his sides and the muscles of his jaw nearly spasmed from clenching it so hard. His glowing eyes filled with hurt for the briefest of moments before he turned away from them and stomped down the hallway without a word. The sounds of his steady footsteps echoed around them until they receded.

Aedan moved out of the doorway to stand next to Finn. Shane watched them, his eyes hard and expectant.

"Are you going to fix this?" Aedan asked her quietly.

She knew what he meant. Conrad and Shane obviously thought there was more to her relationship with Aedan than platonic friendship. She should've been offended by the casual assumption, but she was too busy realizing she could use this misunderstanding to her advantage. She didn't bother looking up when she bit out a harsh, "No."

She'd been looking for a way to push Conrad away for good. Fighting his pull had become increasingly exhausting and she feared she was close to giving in someday soon. Maybe now, with the giant standing between them, he would finally move on and let her go. It hurt more than she thought it should for someone who felt so dead inside.

In the silence that followed her refusal, Finn looked up to find Aedan glaring at her. She fought not to shrivel at the sight. She was saved from further discussion when the doors opened again, and Enyo nearly walked into them.

Her tawny eyes were half-closed, and a mass of tousled multihued hair had fallen over one.

"I thought the meeting was in the rec room," she grumbled in annoyance.

Shane's head swiveled from left to right, taking in the odd trio as his blond brows shot so far up his forehead they almost disappeared.

"I'm confused," he muttered.

"Aren't you always?" Enyo bit out sarcastically. As she looked up to see if her barb landed, she noticed the aluminum mug filled with steaming liquid in Shane's hand and unceremoniously snatched it from his grasp.

"I'm taking this."

Before the befuddled captain could riddle them with questions, Finn grabbed Aedan's hand with one arm and Enyo's bicep with the other and pulled them to her room. She shuffled them through the doors and took one last look at Shane's bemused expression before they shut.

THREE

B y the time Finn, Enyo, and Aedan made it to the rec room, the rest of the crew had already gathered there. Finn's eyes widened and she took in the scene before her. The once spacious area was now crowded with people . . . aliens, humans, and hybrids alike. The normally empty couches and chairs spread throughout were now all occupied and the holoscreens mounted to the walls flashed with images of the Inner Rings.

A news segment occupying the upper, right-hand corner suddenly grew, overtaking the rest of the screen. Finn saw herself, as well as the faces of Grim, Iliana, Conrad, and Shane Montgomery, the captain, projected as red and gold words flashed below them.

Wanted: Dangerous Disobedients.

Last seen in the Inner Rings.

Do not engage.

Highly dangerous and unstable.

By storming the Dome to rescue Finn and the others, the Disobedience had compromised their anonymity. Finn cursed under her breath and looked around.

Shane and Conrad stood shoulder to shoulder by the pool table, wearing serious expressions that clouded their handsome features. She was careful to avoid eye contact with either brother.

Finn's older sister, Iliana, watched her from her seat on a metallic stool at the flashing neon bar. The courtesan wore an emerald-green, silk wrap dress that clung to her curves, and her long, fiery red hair hung in loose curls around her shoulders. Her indigo eyes looked worried as they regarded Finn, but then again, they always did these days.

The sisters had hardly spoken since Finn's rescue from the Dome, and she knew the growing silence between them deeply bothered Iliana. Before she'd ended up fighting for her survival on Aquarii, things between the two had finally been improving. Iliana had spent countless hours training her younger sister how to use her Teslan abilities and, over time, they began to return to the casual sibling banter and affection they'd known as children. The gaping crevice between them began to lessen until it all but disappeared.

It had returned tenfold in the last two weeks.

Madam Califax occupied the stool next to Iliana. Finn still couldn't believe the proper, little woman who had hosted a Reliance ball celebrating the Arcturians and their rule was actually a spy for the Disobedience. The senator's wife had only recently joined them on *Independence*, after using her considerable Reliance contacts to help them escape the Dome.

She held her plump frame rigid with her hands folded neatly on her lap. She wore a metallic-gold wrap dress with red jewels sparkling along the long sleeves and high collar. Her brown hair had been pulled away from her round face and secured with ruby-colored pins. Madam Califax peered around the room, her intelligent eyes taking in the conversations around her.

The prim, older woman and beautiful courtesan painted an odd picture in their fancy garb compared to the rest of the crew chatting casually around the pool table.

Finn heard Tiri's laughter and briefly glanced over at the small girl where she stood at the far end of the room with the ship's Aquariian healer, Isis, and a half-Merlidian girl named Carrow they'd rescued from the Dome. Like Conrad, the child could manipulate energy and move objects with her mind. Naturally, the two little powerhouses had become fast friends and seemed practically inseparable these days.

As if feeling her gaze—or perhaps reading her thoughts—Tiri's wide, green eyes briefly met Finn's and filled with sadness. Finn felt it like a punch in the gut and her eyes darted away quickly.

Shane cleared his throat and the rest of the room fell silent at their captain's subtle command.

"Thank you for coming. The Luminary has an announcement."

Shane motioned to the giant, red-skinned Khaleerian entering the room, ducking his massive frame to avoid hitting the doorframe. He came to a stop a few feet to Shane's left. Grim's dark eyes scanned them slowly and lingered on Finn for a moment before moving on. Flashing shades of neon reflected off his shiny, dark horns.

"We are entering Tuathan's orbit. We will prepare to land in two hours, at which time we will be leaving the ship. Pack your things and be ready."

"Home sweet home. You're going to love it." One of the ship's pilots, Jax, leaned forward in his seat and ran a hand over the fish marking on his cheek as he shot the others a rueful smile.

He and his twin sister, Lex, were squeezed tight on either side of Axel. The massive Khaleerian hybrid had folded into one of the couches near the pool table. His light-brown hair had been buzzed short, putting his horns on full display. The twin pilots wore their usual uniform of white shirts and tan suspenders on their lean frames. Both had recently dyed their hair—Lex in two poofs atop her head and Jax in short spikes shooting out from his scalp—a bright shade of periwinkle. The color complimented their dark complexions and amber eyes.

"I thought Tuathan was a drone planet," a breathy voice called from the back of the room.

Finn didn't recognize it and quickly turned her head to see who the voice belonged to. The remaining three rescued from the Dome stood together—away from the rest of the group—with their backs against the wall.

Finn's eyes briefly landed on Sasha, the Xandar hybrid, and took in the angry, purple fingerprints on the girl's neck, before quickly moving on to study her two companions, one male and one female. She hadn't bothered learning their names. They had been newer additions to the Dome, having only been imprisoned there for a day before their rescue. They'd been trying to kill each other the last time she'd seen them. From the way they stood together now, it seemed as though all had been forgiven.

The male was a half-Saosin with broad shoulders, tan skin, and silver hair that fell into his dark, gray eyes. His deadly talon-tipped wings were pinned to his back by a thick, black harness. The female was a half-Chihiri with plum-colored skin covered in iridescent scales, and dark, piercing eyes. She brushed several long, dark braids behind her shoulder and watched Grim expectantly. The oddly breathy voice obviously belonged to her.

Chihiris were known to possess unique vocal cords that could reach octaves beyond both human and alien hearing with varying effects on the different races. Some alien races could become entranced by the sound, while others were repelled or even injured by it.

Grim spared the female a cursory glance before answering. "It *is* a drone planet."

The Khaleerian did not elaborate, apparently deciding no further explanation was needed. Finn knew very little about the small planet on the outskirts of the Outer Rings. However, she did know that a drone planet was the absolute last place they should be looking for sanctuary. Planets like Tuathan had been deemed inhospitable when the Arcturians first established their tyrannic reign over the galaxy. They'd become—more or less—unoccupied wastelands the Reliance monitored with drone technology.

"You said we had allies on Tuathan. We're on the run," Finn hissed, unable to remain silent. "Why the hell would we go to an empty planet monitored by the Reliance?"

The room crackled with electricity as its occupants fell into a loaded silence and waited to see how the Luminary would respond to her insolence. Finn fought an eye roll.

Grim's head turned slightly, and his dark gaze met hers. His expression was unreadable.

"We will prepare to land in two hours, at which time we will be leaving the ship," he repeated slowly. "Pack your things and be ready."

Finn's eyes narrowed as she shot a glare at the man she'd once trusted above all others. He'd been a mentor and caregiver for many cycles before she'd realized everything she'd ever known about the Khaleerian had been a lie.

Movement rustled around her as the crew began to speak again in low murmurs. The tension slowly leaked out of the room as they took their dismissal like a pack of obedient dogs.

Enyo and Aedan remained by her side as she continued to glare at Grim and waited.

"*Dhala* . . . a word?" Grim glanced meaningfully at her protectors.

She gave a quick nod of dismissal to Aedan and Enyo. Though they looked like they wanted to argue, the two of them swallowed their protests and left.

She was alone with Grim for the first time since her rescue from the Dome and neither one seemed willing to be the first to speak. Finn squirmed as the silence continued to stretch between them. She could feel a lecture coming. The air was thick with it. Her stomach flipped uncomfortably in anticipation, and she silently cursed herself for the weakness.

She remembered all too well what it had been like to be his student. Before the illusion of him had been shattered by his lies, Finn would've rather burned alive than disappoint Grim. It wasn't that she feared punishment. He never lost his temper with her, never yelled . . . not once. Yet it was his silent reproach that was somehow worse than any punishment he could dream up.

Despite her best intentions to remain dispassionate and detached, her chest burned with anxiety. It seemed that the desire to please him and avoid disappointing him at all costs was more ingrained than she'd imagined.

Grim's eyes did a final sweep of the room before resting on her. She noted that they appeared calm rather than annoyed as she'd expected.

"How are you?" he asked quietly.

"Wha—" she stammered in confusion. "What do you mean?"

"You look tired," he told her, frowning.

"You always say that." She responded automatically with their practiced banter before she could stop herself.

Grim's dark eyes smiled sadly as he assessed her features. Not missing a beat, he replied, "That is because it is always true."

A wave of cold washed over Finn at his words. She couldn't do this with him. She couldn't pretend things were like they used to be. Not while AJ was dead and floating in a box out there somewhere. Finn's hands turned to fists and she clenched her jaw. It took a moment, but she shut her feelings down.

"What is waiting for us on Tuathan?"

Sensing the shift in her, the smile left his eyes.

"Trust me, *Dhala*," he urged quietly.

"That ship crashed and burned a while ago, remember?" When he didn't say anything, she threw her hands up in frustration. "If you didn't keep me behind to tell me what we're doing on Tuathan, then what do you want, Grim?" She turned her back on him and started pacing back and forth.

"Before you went to the Dome, you and I made an agreement. You completed your end of the bargain and now I have completed mine."

He watched her as she continued to pace, waiting for realization to dawn on her.

Finn's head snapped around, her eyes open wide, and then she smiled.

"You found him?"

Grim led Finn, Enyo, and Aedan to one of the cargo bays deep within the belly of the ship. Only Finn and Grim were aware of the reason for their trek, however. Weeks ago, Finn had agreed to the fated reconnaissance mission on Aquarii on the condition that Grim find a Sirian soldier named Argo. Finn had learned—through an accidental trip into Enyo's memories—that the Sirian soldier was Enyo's half brother and the person responsible for Enyo's enslavement and the slaughter of her people.

And Grim had found him.

If she weren't so angry with him, she would marvel at Grim's proficiency.

Was there anything he couldn't do?

They reached the bay doors and Grim motioned the others inside. It didn't take her long to find Argo's large figure; he had been chained in the corner. At the interruption, the Sirian soldier's canine snout chuffed and sniffed at the air, his dark-gray fur bristled, and he let out a low growl.

It was nothing compared to the menacing snarl Enyo released as she took in her half brother's hunched form. Her nails elongated until they became like small blades at the tips of her fingers. Her tawny eyes—glazed from her rage—snapped to Finn and her head tilted to the side as though in question.

"You should be dead, you mutt bitch!" Argo roared, enraged.

Aedan moved forward, most likely to beat the Sirian sense-less, but Finn stayed him with a wave of her hand and waited for Enyo to look at her.

"I can't make you forget," Finn said quietly. She watched Enyo's eyes soften as she seemed to remember the request she'd made of Finn weeks ago. Finn motioned to the giant

Sirian still growling at them from the corner. "This was the best I could do."

Enyo smiled, exposing her fangs as she watched her half brother strain against his chains.

"What do you want to do with him?" Grim asked as he leaned casually against the wall of the ship and crossed his large arms over his chest.

"Unchain him," Enyo ordered.

"You wish to let him go?" Grim's eyes widened in surprise and he pulled away from the wall. Listening in, Argo released deep rumbles of laughter.

"You heard her, release me!" the Sirian soldier yelled.

Enyo nodded to Grim when he again looked to her with disbelieving eyes.

"I will not kill a chained man," she told him.

Understanding filled his gaze and he smiled in approval. He grabbed the end of the Sirian's chains and released them. Argo thrust the restraints off and straightened. He flexed and the holes in his torn uniform revealed patches of his heavily muscled, fur-covered chest and arms.

Fangs bared and claws out, Enyo circled her half brother.

"What are we doing?" Aedan's eyes tightened with tension and he looked ready to intervene. Finn stayed him with her response. "We're watching."

The three of them moved back as Argo ran his claws down the wall of the bay. The metal screeched. He met Enyo's eyes and sneered.

"Our mother said your name before she died. Did you know that?"

Enyo cried out in rage and lunged at her half brother. Jumping through the air, she landed with her feet on Argo's chest and her hands on either side of his head. She sank her claws deep into the meat of his shoulders as her jaws snapped at his neck.

Argo let out a roar of pain-laced fury and grabbed Enyo by her thick mane. He threw her across the bay, ripping her claws from his flesh and sending a spray of blood onto the floor. Enyo's back connected with the opposite wall and she dropped to the floor. Barely taking time to recover, she was back up on her feet again. Her eyes narrowed to feral slits and she sprinted at Argo.

Finn winced as blows from both sides landed.

"What the *hell* is going on?"

Finn glanced back to see Shane and Conrad storming through the doors behind them and wondered who had ratted them out. The captain's eyes held a comical mix of horror and confusion as he took in the violence before them. With a helpless expression, he turned to Grim.

"What are you doing? Stop them!"

Grim's eyes flitted briefly to Shane before returning to the fight. Growls and grunts sounded as claws tore into flesh. Enyo landed a kick to Argo's throat and he stumbled. He bit out a cough and struggled for breath before lashing out wildly with his claws.

Shane turned to Conrad. "Can you stop them? Lock them down or pull them apart?" Conrad nodded and his blue eyes began to glow, but before he could do anything, Grim's low growl froze him on the spot.

"Do. Not."

Conrad's eyes narrowed with anger as he checked his power. Finn didn't turn away from the main event, but had heard Grim's warning.

A howl of pain filled the air as Enyo pinned her half brother, straddling Argo's chest. His breaths heaved in and out as they stared at one another. He bared his fangs and his eyes burned with pain. In one fluid motion, Enyo slashed Argo's throat. Blood gushed from the wound and the light slowly left his gaze. He died staring into his half sister's eyes.

Covered in gore and chest heaving, Enyo climbed to her feet and stared down at her kill. After a moment, she brought a hand up to her ribs. They had already begun to swell beneath her fur, but a subtle hunching of her shoulders was the only acknowledgment she gave to the pain. She shot Finn a small, tight smile and turned, limping past the rest of them. Aedan pulled away from Finn and walked close to the Sirian's side, ready to offer his support should she need it.

"*What the hell was that?*" the captain demanded. Shane's angry eyes focused on Grim and contempt he couldn't quite hide leaked into his expression. The Khaleerian held his stare unflinchingly but remained silent.

Shane was a far cry from the stoutly loyal follower he'd been up to that point. As a staunch defender of "the Luminary" and his lies, the captain had always chosen to trust in Grim rather than doubt . . . like Finn.

However, it seemed as though he'd finally been pushed beyond his limits.

Without speaking, Grim put a large hand on Shane's shoulder and led him away. The captain's face was thunderous, but he allowed Grim to steer him out the door. The Khaleerian seemed oblivious to Shane's ire as he led him through the doorway and out of sight.

That's an interesting development. Finn pondered the cracks beginning to form in Shane's blind loyalty to Grim.

Conrad shifted on his feet next to her, interrupting her thoughts.

Suddenly realizing she'd been left alone with the giant she'd been avoiding—and Argo's dead body—Finn's stomach sank, and she moved her feet for a quick getaway. Conrad's tight grip on her arm prevented her from getting far. With a tug, he turned her fully and forced her to meet his gaze.

His blue eyes glowed angrily. His dark dreads hung freely around her face and jaw and she forced herself to ignore the familiar scent of oil and mint that had once served as the anchor for her abilities, helping her to not lose herself in the memories she siphoned from others.

He looked ferocious and formidable. He also looked like he wanted to shake some sense into her.

"Are you going to explain?" Conrad motioned angrily with his free hand at the leftover carnage in the cargo bay.

"Someone's going to have to clean that up," she pointed out dispassionately. When she didn't say anything else, he gritted his teeth in frustration and squeezed her arm tighter. With a glare, Finn yanked herself free from his grasp and took a step away from him. "That was Enyo's half brother. He's the one who turned Enyo in to the Reliance and had her people slaughtered."

"Yet that doesn't explain why he's dead on the floor of our cargo bay," Conrad bit out harshly.

Finn straightened her shoulders and locked eyes with him. "Actually, I think it does." With that, she turned and walked out the door, away from the smell of blood and gore. Conrad followed her into the corridor. He reached out and grabbed her by the arm, turning her back toward him. She yanked her arm free, but stopped and faced him, fire in her eyes.

He continued to stare down at her, but after a moment his gaze softened, and his voice got quiet.

"This isn't you, Finn."

Her stomach clenched in anger at the unmistakable tenderness in his tone. Her heart began to pound with the force of it and the blood rushed in her ears. She tried to focus on the man in front of her, but all she could see was AJ's face . . . his smile. She saw him lying lifeless in the dirt. She saw the wooden box floating in the blackness of space . . . *alone.*

A buzzing filled her ears as the corridor came back into focus. Conrad watched her carefully, studying her in a way she found unnerving.

"*That* was justice," she hissed. His eyes widened at the vitriol in her tone. "*That—*" she threw her arm out and pointed at the door to the cargo bay, where Argo's body rested, "*is* who I am . . . whether you want to see it or not."

He stood still for a long time. Then, without warning and at a speed that left her reeling, he came at her. She hadn't been expecting it and his movements forced her to back up. She narrowly avoided tripping on her own feet. He didn't stop until her spine hit the wall and they stood chest-to-chest.

His eyes burned with intensity and anger as he leaned down. "You want to go down this road, Finn? You want to pretend you don't care about anything but revenge? Fine."

It took a moment for his words to sink in. His warm breath on her cheek distracted her and she had to fight the urge to sag into him. She remembered all too well what it felt like to be wrapped in his strong embrace. A pang of longing hit her so hard and fast, she almost gave into it . . . Almost.

Instead, she got angry.

Finn gritted her teeth and leaned the weight of her body into him in an attempt to push him back. "Get away from me," she bit out in frustration when the giant hybrid didn't budge.

Conrad placed his hands on the wall on either side of her head and his face dipped closer while his eyes—glowing with the strength of his emotions—bore into hers.

"You want to shut down because you can't deal with what happened to AJ?" he growled. At the sound of his name, Finn's veins filled with fire and her muscles went rigid. If Conrad felt her growing tension, he ignored it. He moved his hand from the wall to tenderly brush a strand of auburn hair from her face and her breath caught in her throat. "Do what you have to do," he continued in a whisper. "Be who you need to be. I've already told you I can take it, so keep pushing me away all you want . . . I'm not going anywhere."

A few months ago, before the Dome, those words would have been Finn's undoing.

Now . . . she was on a path he couldn't follow, and behind every kind word and tender vow was his stubborn refusal to acknowledge it.

Finn shoved against his chest in fury, knocking his hand away from her face, and causing him to stumble back in surprise.

Why wouldn't he just give up? She was the reason his brother was dead for the Gods' sake. Maybe the stubborn oaf really was a glutton for punishment. She didn't understand how he could look at her, let alone want to be with her.

Even if *he* could get past it and forgive her, Finn couldn't.

She needed him to give up.

"That will be kind of awkward with Aedan sleeping in my bed, don't you think?" She wanted desperately to snatch the words back as soon as she said them, but the blow had already landed. Conrad's head recoiled back slightly as though she'd slapped him. The glow dimmed from his gaze as he stared down at her. He searched her face—for what she didn't know—until the glow completely dissipated, and his face shut down. He let out a breath of defeat and released her.

Her chest burned with pain and her legs felt numb. Was he finally giving up? The idea filled her with despair. This is what she'd wanted, so why did it feel like her stomach had filled with stones and her heart was slowly breaking?

He studied her for a long, uncomfortable moment before speaking through clenched teeth. "This is about the Solidarian?"

Finn was so startled by the question, she forgot to keep the glare fixed on her face.

"Yes," she said quietly. As she spoke the lie, she nearly winced at the hitch in her voice. Finn took a steadying breath. She needed him to believe he'd lost her . . . he'd never let her go otherwise. "*Aedan* was there for me in the Dome, Conrad," she whispered. He understands what I've been through. I can talk to him. I *do* talk to him. We've become very . . . close."

His gaze dropped to her hands. Finn realized they were shaking and worried her lower lip.

A nagging sensation of guilt began to spread from the pit of her belly to her throat, as though she'd just taken ten shots of dragon's breath simultaneously.

"Right," Conrad bit out. She winced at the coarseness in his voice.

"Right," she murmured, hands still shaking. She made a hasty exit on wobbly legs, leaving Conrad in the corridor outside in the cargo bay.

He didn't follow her.

FOUR

Her heart ached the entire way back to her quarters, even as she told herself she'd done the right thing. It sounded halfhearted at best. Fortunately, she wasn't given much time to think on it. By the time she got to her quarters, she barely had time to pack a bag and get to the bridge before *Independence* began to make her descent. Every member of the crew had strapped into their seats in preparation for the landing. The already tight space buzzed with nervous energy. The ship's twin pilots were uncharacteristically serious.

Not nearly recovered enough from her most recent inter-action with Conrad, Finn sat between Enyo and Aedan and employed her new tactic of avoidance. She did her best to keep her eyes forward and focused on the planet coming into view.

While Finn had been busy destroying her relationship with Conrad, Enyo had found time to visit Isis for some healing. The normally stoic Sirian appeared completely at ease, and the ghost of a smile flitted across her face when Finn caught her eye.

At least I did something right today. Her eyes drifted to the main viewport.

It appeared to be nighttime on this side of Tuathan. Darkness shrouded the ship as the air cleared and the planet's terrain slowly came into view.

Finn sucked in a breath as her eyes adjusted to the low light and she took in the smooth ripples of shadowy water. Endless waves of dark purple as far as the eye could see lapped beneath *Independence* as she continued her descent.

The ship made no signs of slowing down.

"All drones within twenty kilometers are experiencing unexpected updates," Lex chirped through a smile. "We're clear to land."

Enyo's calm demeanor slowly started to fade as Lex's words sank in. Her claws dug into the arms of her seat and her tawny eyes shot to Finn.

"Land where?" the Sirian whispered in alarm. "You need land to *land.*"

In wholehearted agreement with her, Finn's eyes sought out Shane and Grim. She didn't know much about Tuathan's landscape, but she had to assume there were better places for their ship to touch down than in the middle of a vast ocean. She felt Aeden tense next to her and shot the Solidarian a sympathetic—albeit increasingly nervous—smile. Both Solidarians and Sirians spent their lives in humid, rocky terrain, and her companions most likely had little experience with large bodies of water.

Given how the Arcturians and the Reliance tended to dispatch all of the colonized planets' flora, fauna, and natural resources, it was hardly surprising.

A sense of growing unease rippled through the bridge as Jax and Lex carefully brought them down lower and lower until the ship's underbelly hovered just above the swirling, murky water.

Aedan's hand clenched the sides of his seat as he glanced over at Finn and bit out under his breath, "You trust those two not to kill us all, right?"

She fought not to show the panic she felt. *Not really.*

Finn's head shot to the right, searching out Grim. His black eyes caught her stare immediately, as if he'd been waiting. As though he fancied himself invincible, the giant Khaleerian hadn't even bothered strapping in for the landing and stood near the pilots with his large, red arms folded at the chest. He offered Finn a reassuring nod and she could almost hear him in her mind saying, *"Steady,* Dhala."

She took a calm, steadying breath and released it. The force of it blew hair one shade from fire away from her face. As much as she hated to admit it, she was grateful Grim still had a knack for helping her stay centered. Holding his stare for a moment longer, Finn leaned over as far as the unforgiving straps of her seat would allow to whisper to Aedan.

"Whatever the plan is, I think we're going to be okay."

Aedan kept his jaw locked and his eyes forward.

"I hope you're right," he muttered.

Me too.

The ship hummed as the twins took her lower. Jax reached out a hand and his sister took it. The fish markings on their cheeks began to glow and Finn braced.

She'd seen the same thing happen once before, when they'd been trying to outrun the Toad after the job on Cartan. No one actually *enjoyed* dealing with the disgusting power broker—his unfortunate nickname being all too accurate—but eventually, everyone did. Jax and Lex had done the very same thing just before the ship had come to life, her various wires and controls snaking around the twin pilots and sending *Independence* into hyperdrive. Finn had almost died then, and she wasn't looking forward to a repeat performance.

The silence in the ship became unbearable as they hovered above watery oblivion and waited to see what the twins would do. Just when Finn felt sure the bridge would implode from the tension leaking out of the impatient passengers, the twins' markings glowed even brighter and the waves undulating before them erupted into the air and onto *Independence*. Once they settled, Finn realized something had emerged from the water beneath them. Between the dark and the violent sprays of water that accompanied its ascent, it was almost impossible to make out. Finn blinked a few times.

"Is that what I think it is?" Aedan whispered next to her.

Finn squinted and sucked in a surprised breath as her eyes took in the scene before. A giant, cylindrical platform had risen from the sea. With a loud groan, it finally settled a few feet below *Independence*. The surface of the structure was more than big enough to accommodate two ships the size of *Independence*.

"*Mienkomman,*" Enyo muttered what had to be a Sirian expletive under her breath.

Finn found her eyes moving of their own accord until they landed on Conrad. Dark shades covered his bright blue eyes, and he wore a shirt and pants that were a few shades darker than his skin. As if sensing her stare, his head moved a quarter of an inch and he looked right at her. His jaw tightened as he looked from her to Aedan then away again.

Her gaze moved to Iliana where she sat strapped in next to Shane and Madam Califax. The trio appeared to be perfectly at ease as they patiently waited with their eyes forward . . . for what, Finn had no idea.

The sound of waves crashing mingled with the low hum of the ship as they waited to see what would happen next. The twins sat with their heads bent, hands still entwined and cheeks glowing brightly. Suddenly, a massive groan rent through the air and Finn sucked in a breath as the center of the platform opened up before them. The pilots carefully positioned the ship over the gaping hole left in its wake.

"We're not going down there, are we?" Sasha called out to no one in particular. The speedster had a death grip on the arms of her seat.

As if in answer to her question, the platform beneath them began to rise again. It climbed until it gently connected with *Independence*'s underbelly, barely jarring the ship in the process. Lex and Jax let go of the controls and leaned back, the glow fading from their cheeks as the platform and *Independence* began to descend. When the top of the ship became level with the water's surface, the top of the platform slid closed above them, shrouding them in darkness. Suddenly a low hum sounded, and lights went on all around the ship. The water encircling them shimmered, and with the extra light Finn realized a hard-light projection surrounded them on all sides, protecting them and forming an underwater elevator of sorts.

It was the same tech used to create the Dome.

Finn's palms began to sweat, and her heart beat a furious rhythm in her chest. Next to her, she felt Aedan tense.

What the hell is this?

They weren't given any time to process as the platform beneath them began to descend. Finn tried to quiet the triggered memories of the Dome and the roar of the cheering crowd that filled her head until it was spinning. She slammed her eyes shut and her hands clenched into tight fights as she waged war with her mind.

Finn kept them closed for long minutes that nearly stretched into an hour. She didn't open them again until she heard someone gasp.

Her gaze shot forward at the sound. Finn inhaled sharply as she took in the underwater metropolis before her at the bottom of Tuathan's ocean. An entire city filled the dozens of domes dotting the sea floor as far as the eye could see, interconnected by a system of tubes all made from the same hard-light projection tech.

Independence finally completed her descent. They settled for a moment and then were pushed into motion again by what appeared to be a giant conveyor belt beneath them. They traveled easily through the hard-light tubes. No one on the ship uttered a single word as they were carried along the bottom of the ocean floor and into the nearest dome. They finally came to a stop inside what appeared to be a docking bay. A few other smaller ships of various makes and models sat to the far right of the bay. Large, black doors stood to their left.

The silence had stretched on so long that they all jumped when Lex's high-pitched squeal echoed through the bridge around them.

"Welcome home!" she cried enthusiastically.

The ship's outer doors opened, and the stern ramp lowered to the floor of the bay.

Lex, Jax, Shane, Conrad, Grim, Iliana, Madam Califax, Tiri, and Isis all unstrapped from their seats and moved to depart from the stern of the ship. Finn and the rest of them followed, still slightly dazed from all that had transpired.

"You didn't mention your home was at the bottom of the sea!" Enyo growled angrily at the twin pilots.

The Sirian's tawny eyes shot fire, but Jax was busy guiding Axel off the ship and Lex hardly seemed to notice. Her dark brow wrinkled slightly and, as she shrugged her shoulders, her periwinkle braids swayed around her shoulders.

"I could've sworn we mentioned it," she muttered with a conspiratorial grin.

Finn snapped. Between the memories of the Dome and the descent to the bottom of the ocean that took at least ten cycles off her life, she'd finally had enough. She turned her glare on Grim where he stood at the bottom of the ship's ramp and waited until he gave her his eyes.

"Where in the hell did you take us?" she yelled.

"Welcome to Tuathan."

They all turned at the sound of the deep, smooth voice and found a man standing in the now open doorway to their left. He had a creamy, light-brown complexion with a fish marking on his cheek, identical to the ones the twins sported. His long, silvery dreads hung below his shoulders. Some of them had been adorned with shimmering, multicolored beads. Dark-gray robes draped his powerful body.

He entered the bay and made his way to their ship. Though he appeared to be in his fifties, he moved with a confidence and purpose that came with age and experience. His slightly stiff movements were nearly imperceptible, but they were enough for Finn to take notice.

The stranger came to a stop next to Grim. Though he was a large man, he appeared small standing next to the massive

Khaleerian. He reached up a hand to slap Grim's shoulder, as a warm smile broke out on his face.

"It's good to see you again, my friend," he stated warmly. His amber eyes took in the rest of the group and lit up when they came to rest on Tiri. "It's even better to see *you*, little one."

The child—with one hand wrapped in Isis's and the other entwined with little Carrow's—beamed.

"Hi Zekiel!" Tiri chirped with her big smile still firmly in place.

"And who do we have here?" The man called Zekiel leaned down to ask as his smile fell on Carrow.

The dark-haired little girl was even smaller than Tiri and painfully shy—not surprising given all she'd endured in the Dome. Rather than meet the new stranger's eyes, Carrow hid behind Tiri as though trying to disappear. Zekiel gave Isis a knowing look, the warm smile never leaving his face. Atop his head was a beautiful cascade of dreadlocks, each adorned with multicolored beads. His amber eyes were striking, as was the fish-shaped mark on his light-brown face.

"This is my new friend, Carrow," Tiri said, oblivious to Carrow's discomfort. "She's half-Merlidian just like Conrad." The girl's anxiety seemed to make the runes on her body shimmer.

"It's a pleasure to meet you, Carrow," he said gently. "Any friend of Tiri's is a friend to all Tuathans." His voice lowered an octave in a mock whisper as he said, "You know, Cynthia and some of the others have prepared pastries to celebrate your return. Perhaps Isis would like to take you to the mess hall to get some while I show the others around."

Finn didn't think it was possible, but Tiri's face lit up even further. She turned to Carrow excitedly, nearly knocking the girl over in the process.

"Wait until you try Tuathan pastries, Carrow. Can we go, Isis? Please?"

The tension that had set up residence in Isis's shoulders since AJ's funeral finally eased a bit and she let out a relieved exhalation. Her silver eyes warmed on Zekiel before falling to the little girls at her side.

"Of course. As long as the Luminary agrees." The Aquariian healer looked to Grim for approval and the large Khaleerian nodded. Tiri barely waited for his head to stop moving before she sped off in the direction of the doors, followed closely by Carrow, then Isis.

"Can we go too? We can show the others around." Lex motioned to the newer additions to the crew. The half-Saosin, the half-Chihiri, and Sasha looked from Grim to Zekiel with uncharacteristically eager expressions on their faces. Given how long they'd been in the Dome, the idea of fresh-baked pastries had to be too much for them to pass up. Grim rolled his eyes before nodding and Lex took off with the others in tow.

Zekiel watched them go before turning back to the rest of the group and clapping his hands.

"How about that tour?"

Finn tried to keep her mouth from hanging open as Zekiel led them out of the bay and into the heart of the underwater dome-like structure. The outer walls, floors, and ceilings were all made up of the same hard-light projection tech, so that everywhere she looked she found dark-purple water surrounding her on all sides. Creatures big and small swam around them outside, illuminated by the bright lights within each structure. Tall seagrass the same iridescent blue as Grim's eyes swayed back and forth, providing shelter to the organisms foraging in the rocky sand beneath them.

She followed at a distance, sticking close to Aedan and Enyo, while Grim, Iliana, Madam Califax, Conrad, and Shane kept pace with their guide.

"Each of the sectors is connected by a pathway of tunnels. We have sectors for residences and medicine. The sector we're in right now serves as the hub of our city. We have the mess hall," he motioned to the spacious room filled with tables, chairs, and a large kitchen in the back. Finn noticed Tiri— the remnants of pastry clinging to her chin—chatting away at a table in the corner with Carrow, Isis, and several other people she didn't recognize. The strangers all had the same fish markings on their cheeks as Zekiel and the twins.

"Where does the food come from?"

"Phytoplankton, zooplankton, some fungi thrown in for fun." Finn couldn't quite hide her disgust and she knew he saw it when his smile widened and he said "We can replicate flavors with various spices we have engineered, and our chefs use a lattice oven to replicate form and textures. Of course, Isis and Tiri tend a garden above to fill in the gaps. Down past the mess hall are quarters for the handful of us that live here on site, as well as a few training rooms, equipment storage, and the secondary docking bay."

He continued to lead them down another hallway, stopping near a doorway at the end.

"This hall holds our tech rooms," Zekiel commented as he motioned them inside.

The vast space above them was filled with holoscreens. Dozens of Tuathans sat in front of monitors displaying coordinates, additional video feed, and a myriad of other things Finn didn't recognize. They watched the screens, speaking quietly into comms and downloading data onto holopads. "From here we can monitor the drone feeds on planet, as well as any other drone feeds the Reliance may be using throughout the Union of the Planets."

One of the Tuathans looked up briefly and noticed Conrad. He wore his dreads in a style similar to Conrad's—tied up and away from his face—though his fell almost to his hips, far below where Conrad's hair reached. The Tuathan shot him a dazzling smile and rose to clap him on the back affectionately. Shane and Iliana broke away from the group to speak with some of the workers in low whispers, while Madam Califax studied several of the monitors from a distance.

All of them seemed perfectly at home in this strange underwater city . . . a place Finn hadn't known existed until about an hour ago. They obviously spent a lot of time here and yet no one had thought to mention it.

More secrets. Her hands tightened into fists at the thought.

"Zekiel and his people control the drone feed on planet, allowing us to come and go without Reliance detection," Grim explained. "Tuathan serves as a central meeting place for disobedients."

He glanced meaningfully at the others, once again reading her mind in that unsettling way he'd always done since her childhood.

He motioned to the screens around them and Finn felt her eyes go wide as she finally took in the images on the holoscreens nearest to her. She could hardly believe what she was seeing. One of the screens to the left showed real-time images and a video feed of her adopted home planet, the Mud Pit. She could even see the inside of Grim's tavern, the Dirty Molly. Doc, the bar's co-owner, chatted animatedly with patrons as he poured drinks.

The screen next to it showed soldiers and a few wealthy members of the Reliance walking down the streets of Aquarii. By all appearances, things had gone back to normal on the planet since the Dome's destruction.

All of that suffering erased as though it had never happened.

The fiery rage that had set up residence in the center of her chest since AJ's death bubbled and swirled inside of her like a pot boiling over.

Seeming to sense her disquiet, Enyo and Aedan closed in on either side of her, offering comfort with their nearness. On a deep inhale, Finn forced herself to tear her focus away from the feed to Aquarii and take in the rest of the screens around her.

She saw live feeds of every planet under Reliance rule.

If what Zekiel and Grim said could be believed, the Tuathans had a direct line to everything the Reliance did.

"You can control what they see?" Enyo asked with disbelief furrowing her multihued brow. Zekiel gave a quick nod of ascent.

"How is this possible?" Finn blurted out before she could stop herself.

Zekiel turned to her then and did a top-to-toe scan of her with a serious expression on his lined face. He seemed to be fully taking her in for the first time and Finn's skin itched under the scrutiny. She fought against the urge to fidget as he completed his assessment. His kind smile returned in full as he met her eyes for the first time.

"We finally meet, Finn No Last Name." His head swiveled to Grim then, completely missing the look of shock on Finn's face at his statement. "She is exactly as you described."

Grim's eyes warmed slightly with pride, stunning Finn even further.

Grim had talked about her?

Zekiel returned his attention to her.

"To answer your question, Finn, the Tuathan people are technopaths."

"What does that mean exactly?" Aedan cut in quietly.

"It means that we are able to psychically perceive and interface with technology."

"The Tuathan people thrived on this planet before the Arcturians arrived," Grim growled as he mentioned the golden gods. "The planet's large nickel core and strong electromagnetic fields enhance their abilities and allow them to operate on a much more advanced level than any other planet. They were well on their way to building their own Utopia."

"Then why do you live in hiding?" Enyo asked Zekiel.

The Tuathan brought his hands together in front of him and shrugged.

"Because war has no place in Utopia. The Arcturians arrived prepared for a fight when they entered our galaxy. Their weapons far outmatched anything my people had at the time. We simply had no desire or need for destruction."

"The only thing the Arcturians were missing was the kind of tech necessary to unite all the planets under one rule and ensure compliance," Grim added.

"Yet, when they came to Tuathan," Zekiel continued, "They discovered everything they could possibly need. It was a massacre. They wiped out my people . . . stole our tech and planet for themselves. Those who weren't killed were enslaved . . . forced to use our creations for their will. Fortunately, a small number of survivors managed to escape. They created this sanctuary."

"The te—tech they used to create the Dome was yours?"

The way she choked on the words, Finn's question sounded more like an accusation. She felt Aedan tense next to her but kept her eyes on the older Tuathan. Something like pain flashed on Zekiel's face.

"I'm afraid so, though it was never intended to be used for such a foul purpose." He paused to hold her stare. "We are all very sorry about what happened to you and AJ."

Finn flinched at hearing his name and she clenched her hands at her sides, her fingernails digging deep into the palms of her gloves.

Being the mediator at heart, Shane took one look at Finn's tense posture and glassy eyes and swiftly returned from his conversation with the workers on the far side of the room. He immediately waded in. "The Tuathans want to take down the Reliance just as badly as we do."

Finn's body remained locked tight as she turned to the captain of *Independence* and addressed him in a low voice filled with hatred. "*No one* wants it more than I do, Shane."

"Enough," Grim chastised firmly, shooting Finn a meaningful glance. "We need to focus on the enemy, not on our feelings. There is no more room for distraction from our end goal."

He motioned with his head for Iliana, Conrad, and Madam Califax to rejoin their little group. They had already been watching the scene with wide eyes and were quick to follow the Luminary's orders.

"That end goal being to take down the Reliance for good?" Enyo asked, her face skeptical and her tone somewhat sarcastic. Knowing what she did about Finn's rocky relationship with the Khaleerian, Enyo refused to treat him with the same deference the rest of the crew did.

"Yes," Grim said emphatically. His eyes narrowed slightly in annoyance at being questioned, but he said nothing further.

"How?" Finn asked him.

Her eyes pleaded with her former mentor. She wanted more than anything for him to answer. Making the Reliance pay was all she'd been able to think about since AJ's death. She wanted it so badly, she thought about it constantly. Revenge was the only thing that mattered to her and if Grim had a way to help her reach her goal, she needed to know what it was.

The Khaleerian's eyes softened on Finn. He looked almost apologetic as he said, "Now is not the time for that discussion. All of us will meet tomorrow to talk about next steps. For now, I suggest you all get settled."

Grim was not the apologetic sort and seeing the emotion plain as day, rather than his normally stoic expression, for the third time in as many weeks piqued Finn's curiosity. He'd shown her more emotion in the last few weeks since she'd returned from the Dome than in the many cycles he'd spent raising her.

"In other words," Finn bit out, "we should expect more of your secretive Luminary bullshit."

She expected his red skin to darken in anger, but it never did. He merely waited a few breaths and stated calmly, "Have you ever known me to be anything but methodical, *Dhala*?"

Now she felt her own anger. *What the hell is that supposed to mean?*

She didn't think too much on the why, but his refusal to share burned somewhere deep inside of her. The resentment coiled around her heart tightened. The room around her disappeared, leaving just Finn and Grim where they stood locked in a stare down.

She forced herself to breathe, willing her fists to unclench. He was right about one thing: if she truly wanted to avenge AJ and take down the Reliance, there was no room for emotion. If it wasn't useful in helping her accomplish her end goal, she had to get rid of it.

Just like she got rid of Conrad.

Staring Grim down in that moment, Finn realized something: the anger and resentment she felt toward her former mentor were useless. They were a hindrance more than anything in her bid for revenge; as useless to her as a stick in a sword fight.

She had to let it go.

Her shoulders relaxed infinitesimally, and she nodded.

"Okay," she told him calmly. "Tomorrow."

The word hung between them as the room around her came into focus once more. Everyone present—including the workers seated at the monitors—had stopped what they were doing to watch their interaction. Apparently, no one on Tuathan ever argued with the Luminary, because they all looked like they'd just seen a two-headed Goslan.

She knew Conrad and Iliana were watching her—she could feel their stares—but she refused to make eye contact. Instead, Finn squared her shoulders and walked out of the room, followed closely by Enyo and Aedan.

FIVE

By dinner that evening, time had begun to move differently for Finn. Being so far below the water's surface had already started to affect her in ways she couldn't have foreseen. Down here, there was no sun . . . no daytime or nighttime. They had nothing but the artificial lights dimming a few shades and a pleasant voice on an intercom to tell them dusk had arrived and dinner was now served.

She didn't know how things worked in the other sectors, but everyone in Tuathan's hub ate together. At least seventy-five people filled the metal chairs around a scattering of oblong tables. Several others carried metal trays through an assembly line where they were offered a selection of soups, baked goods, roasted meat, and vegetables by even more Tuathans wielding large serving spoons and ladles.

Several holoscreens mounted around the space showed images of the Inner Rings, as well as rotating live video feeds from several different planets.

Finn's gaze roved over all of the people filling the mess hall. She watched them sitting, eating, and having conversations with envy. It was all so clean and felt so *safe*. She couldn't remember the last time she'd had a meal without wondering where the door was and making sure her back was against a wall.

The loud hum of voices provided pleasantly familiar ambient noise. It felt like being back in the Dirty Molly on the Mud Pit, the safest yet craziest place she'd ever known. Lex, Sasha, Jax, and Axel chatted animatedly with a group of younger Tuathans. With the twins' bright periwinkle hair, Axel's large, Khaleerian frame, and Sasha's speedy movements, they were easiest to spot. Not far away, Zekiel, Isis, Carrow, and Tiri, filled another table. Having arrived late, Iliana and Madam Califax still stood in line for food. At one point, Finn caught sight of Shane's blond head and Conrad's dark dreads at the far end of the mess hall, but she didn't have a clear view.

Grim was nowhere to be found.

Finn set her tray on the table and planted her backside in a seat next to Aedan and Enyo. Unsurprisingly, the rest of the seats around them sat empty. She warily eyed the water on the other side of the hard-light projection surrounding them. Seeming to read her thoughts, Enyo bared her fangs and growled. "Why did the sanctuary have to be at the bottom of the sea?" she bit out.

Aedan smiled slightly—something he rarely did—and brought a spoonful of soup to his dark lips. "What? Sirians can't swim?"

Enyo rolled her tawny eyes in aggravation and shook her head. Her long, multihued hair swayed around her fur-covered shoulders. "We have no need to learn such things."

"Seems like there's a need now." Aedan's dark eyes were uncharacteristically playful as he teased the Sirian. Enyo was too annoyed to pick up on it and glared at the bald man.

"Are you telling me Solidarians know how to swim?" The sarcasm dripped from her low voice, but Aedan seemed content to play along. Finn had never seen the large man so carefree.

"I wouldn't know. I've never met any," he spoke around a mouthful of vegetables. "But I figure I can flail around enough to tread water."

"You have never met a Solidarian?" Enyo's mouth hung open in disbelief.

Aedan's fork scraped his plate as he took another bite.

"My mother was human," he shrugged his wide shoulders. "I never knew my father."

"Enough," Finn said quietly, finally wading into the conversation. "We've established that none of us know how to swim, so let's just move on and hope the Tuathans know what they're doing. We have more important things to talk about anyway."

Her two companions shared a look before giving Finn their attention.

"You appear to have . . . changed your mind about the Luminary," Enyo seemed to choose her words carefully.

Finn leaned in and lowered her voice.

"Grim is our best shot at taking down the Reliance once and for all. My feelings about him are irrelevant. He was right; he *is* the most methodical person I've ever known. He wouldn't try to take down the Reliance unless he was absolutely sure he had the means to do so."

"So, you trust him?" Aedan asked quietly.

"I didn't say that," Finn remarked. She motioned to the projections surrounding them. "But look around. The Tuathans are monitoring every Reliance feed as we speak. Their tech is *so* advanced, the Arcturians stole it for their own. Can you think of a better ally?"

Aedan set down his fork to address her. "You think the Tuathans will be enough to turn the odds in our favor?"

"It's not just the Tuathans. Grim has Reliance spies like Madam Califax and Mr. Green everywhere. We have the hybrids, and with Tiri on our side—"

Finn cut herself off before she could finish the sentence. She cursed herself for the slip. She had debated whether or not to tell her companions about Tiri's unique abilities and what they could mean for the galaxy. If the child could heal the soil once destroyed by the Arcturians, they would no longer need to depend on the Reliance for their air. But that kind of information was dangerous. She'd already learned that the hard way from Nova. She trusted Enyo and Aedan with her life, but Tiri was too important to take any unnecessary risks. Though she hated keeping something from them, she'd decided that some secrets were best kept that way.

"What about Tiri?" Enyo prompted.

They both watched her expectantly and Finn's palms began to sweat.

Before she could stutter out an answer, someone quietly cleared their throat behind them in a bid to gain their attention. The trio immediately ceased their conversation and turned in unison to find Iliana, Madam Califax, and the Chihiri and Saosin hybrids holding trays in their hands and looking more than a little uncomfortable.

The half-Saosin could pass for human with his leathery, talon-tipped wings still bound securely to his back with a harness. Finn's eyes moved over to the half-Chihiri. The iridescent scales covering her plumb-colored skin sparkled in the artificial light. Her dark eyes cast a disinterested glare at the table as she tossed her dark braids over a shoulder.

Iliana took a step forward and the hem of her silk dress brushed over Finn's boot.

"It seems you have room at your table." Finn's older sister motioned to the empty chairs. "May we sit with you?"

Though their interruption saved Finn from having to answer Enyo's question, the idea of trying to make small talk with her estranged sister, a Reliance senator's wife, and two of the hybrids she'd fought and nearly killed in the Dome hardly appealed to Finn. She began to shake her head and had just opened her mouth to tell Iliana to find another table, when Enyo jumped in before she could even take a breath.

"Yes, please sit down," Enyo offered eagerly. Apparently, the subject of Tiri was already long forgotten. The hybrid's yellow eyes remained glued to Iliana as she motioned with claw-tipped hands to the empty seat at her right.

What the hell?

Finn's eyes nearly bulged out of her head as she tried to silently communicate with Enyo. She spared her a cursory glance before returning her focus to Finn's sister. The half-Sirian even smiled—*smiled*—genuinely at the beautiful courtesan. Finn gave Enyo a look that promised pain, but she couldn't be bothered to notice.

The others took their seats at the table, with Madam Califax selecting the chair next to Finn, forcing her to either accept their presence or get up and leave. Finn sighed and shot another glare Enyo's way for good measure.

Enyo had yet to take her eyes off Iliana.

The courtesan's full red lips tilted in a smile as she whispered something to Enyo and returned her attention to the rest of the table. "Raven was just telling us how similar some of the dishes being served are to ones made on her planet."

"There are several from my planet as well," Mace said as he tore into a piece of crimson bread.

"Who is Raven?" Finn asked as she looked around the table in confusion.

"I am." Finn turned to the source of the slightly piqued voice and found the half-Chihiri scowling at her. "Which you would know if you ever bothered to ask."

Finn could've been imagining it, but she swore Raven's scales had darkened with her anger. The table went quiet. Even Aedan, who had previously been inhaling his meal, lowered the fork from his lips.

Finn knew she spoke the truth. She had never bothered to find out anything about the two hybrids rescued from the Dome. Her desire to take down the Reliance had given her tunnel vision, but she was learning the importance of strength in numbers. Even Grim knew he couldn't follow through with his plan—whatever that supersecret plan may be—alone.

As the Luminary, he had built a team of spies including humans, hybrids, and aliens to help him see it through. Finn wanted revenge and knew she was willing to kill the

Arcturians and their Reliance one by one with her bare hands if she had to, but it was far more important to her that she succeed . . . And her chances would be a lot better if she made nice with the locals. The Chihiri and Saosin hybrids could become valuable allies if she put in a little effort.

"You're right, I probably would," Finn tossed back casually. She kept her shoulders relaxed in indifference. Raven's scowl deepened at her calm demeanor. Obviously, she'd expected Finn to take the bait and fight back.

"I'm Mace," he raised his hand awkwardly and flashed a lopsided smile. Seeing it combined with the fall of his messy hair and round face, Finn realized he was much younger than she'd originally assumed, barely more than a kid.

Like AJ.

A pang of grief washed through her and she did her best not to show the agony she felt. His eager eyes reminded her so much of the boy she'd lost, it hurt to even look at him.

"Don't waste your breath, Mace. You saw what she did in the Dome." Raven's eyes rolled to Finn as she bit out, "She's cold-blooded."

Enyo's already stiff posture went rigid.

"What did you say?" she growled in a low voice.

The tension at the table ratcheted up several degrees and Finn felt it immediately.

If someone didn't do something soon, the tense scene would become a bloodbath. She sighed audibly as she realized she'd have to wade in. Before Finn could intervene, Madam Califax shifted in her seat. The plump woman folded her hands and rested them on her lap. They nearly disappeared within the piles of pink taffeta making up her skirt. Her nasal voice called out to the table.

"I believe the Tuathans prepare all of our planets' signature dishes. It's very inclusive of them, don't you think? It would be very rude of us to get so wrapped up in conversation we forgot to enjoy it."

The hard glint in her brown eyes contradicted her pleasantly mild tone. The rest of those seated around the table seemed too jarred by the clear reprimand from the starchy little woman to say anything else.

Madam Califax brought her folded hands up from her lap to clap twice before she said,

"Wonderful! Let's eat, shall we?"

The senator's wife picked up her fork with delicate precision and began taking small bites of what appeared to be some type of roasted meat. The others joined her not long after, as an awkward silence fell over the group.

Madam Califax shifted next to her again and Finn's nostrils flared slightly as a familiar scent wafted over to her. She turned to the woman with wide eyes.

"Your perfume . . ." she said quietly, as her gaze shifted to Iliana. "It smells like lillydung."

"Ah, yes." Madam Califax brought a hand up to her collarbone and smiled wistfully. "The lillydung plant is native to my home planet. Of course, this is made from synthetic lillydung . . . the real thing smells even better. My father was a farmer, you see, and he kept a secret stash of seeds at our home. He grew them there and each cycle the buds would blossom, and the smell would fill the entire house."

A farmer?

Just like Finn and Iliana's father.

Finn shot her older sister a raised eyebrow at the flood of new information. When she'd first started training Finn how to use her Teslan abilities, Iliana had stressed the importance of finding an anchor scent that held special meaning. Finn had chosen Conrad's uniquely scented hair wax. It couldn't be a coincidence that Iliana's anchor scent was the same plant that made up Madam Califax's perfume.

Iliana's face remained impassive, giving nothing away. Sighing in frustration, Finn returned her stare to the senator's wife, unable to fight her curiosity.

"How did you end up married to the senator?"

Madam Califax waved her hand dismissively.

"Oh, nothing too exciting, my dear. I trained to be a courtesan in my younger cycles; I imagine I would have done quite well." She appeared to be lost in memories for a moment as her eyes lost focus and she stared unseeing into the distance. After a moment she seemed to remember her audience and her body jolted slightly. "But when my husband sees something he likes, he takes it and well . . . the rest is history as they say."

"*You* trained to be a courtesan?" Finn fought to keep the shock out of her voice, but she wasn't sure she succeeded. Madam Califax smiled gently.

"Oh, yes. I was recruited at just ten cycles. Thankfully my instructions didn't go to waste." The little woman shot Iliana a private smile and Finn bristled. Her older sister's cheeks had turned the same unique red as her long hair.

"What do you mean 'didn't go to waste'?" Finn asked as her spine straightened.

Madam Califax waved a hand in Iliana's direction and her face softened with fondness.

"Fortunately, I had a wonderful student to pass my knowledge on to."

Iliana had been trained by Madam Califax?

Finn's gaze shot to her sister for confirmation, but Iliana was busy dutifully ignoring her. Finn forced her breathing to slow and tried to relax her posture as her face reassembled its features into a neutral expression. Why hadn't Iliana told her about the senator's wife?

Before the Dome, Finn would've been hurt to learn something so integral to the woman Iliana had become from someone other than her sister, but she could no longer afford to get upset by such trivial things. This was just one more missing piece in the puzzle of the life Iliana had led after they were separated, nothing more.

"And where does the senator think you are right now, Madam Califax?" Enyo interrupted quickly, sensing Finn and Iliana's disquiet.

"Oh, the imbecile thinks I'm galivanting in the Inner Rings doing some shopping for our next ball. Not very bright, that one."

With that statement hanging in the air, the group went back to uncomfortable silence as they finished their meal.

Later that night, Finn sat alone in her new quarters. Enyo occupied an identical room next to hers and Aedan slept directly across the hall. She figured eventually she'd end up in one of their rooms, but for now she needed some alone time.

Her head turned as she took in the walls around her. Each one had been painted a deep blue with gray trim. The lush bed was even larger than the one she'd had on *Independence* and the en suite bathroom was even more spacious. The motion-sensitive shower had multiple buttons and sensors she had no idea what to do with. A large oval window on the wall nearest to her bed provided a view of the layer of hard-light projections protecting them against the backdrop of the ocean's dark waters. A worn and cozy loveseat sat to the right of that. Various holopads littered the shelves above, providing a warm corner to settle in and relax.

Except she wasn't in the mood to relax.

Finn got up carefully and made her way over to the trunk at the foot of her bed. It had been filled with neatly folded shirts, pants, and socks in neutral colors before her arrival. Everything appeared to be clean and in good condition. She rummaged through the trunk, pushing her hand through the soft material, moving shirts and socks as she went. When her hand made it to the bottom of the trunk, she felt a smooth, wooden box and wrapped her fingers around it.

She made her way back over to the bed and got in carefully. She folded her legs, set down the box on the sheets before her, and took a deep breath. Finally, she opened the box and examined its contents.

The delicate silver chain of a necklace glinted and, in the light, the black and red streaks coloring the Khaleerian gemstone at its center looked even more striking.

Grim's necklace.

She'd swiped it off him weeks ago. He had to have noticed by now that it was gone—and probably who stole it—but the giant Khaleerian had yet to say anything.

The first time she held the necklace, she'd seen hazy images of a woman with wheat-colored hair and vivid-blue eyes holding a tiny, squirming baby wrapped in blankets. Of all the things she'd expected to see, the tender scene between mother and child certainly hadn't made the list. After, she'd put the necklace in a box and hidden it away. She didn't know why exactly, but she'd been too scared to try to siphon from the object again.

Finn couldn't explain it . . . something about the image of the beautiful woman in Grim's memories filled her with trepidation.

She reached out hesitantly and let her fingers hover a few inches above the gemstone. Even as the cold vise of fear wrapped itself around her heart, she forced her fingers down and wrapped them around the necklace.

It is dusk. Light from the three moons above her makes it easy to see her surroundings in the darkness. Finn is standing in a grassy clearing surrounded on all sides by trees the size of mountains. There are so many, they seem to form an impenetrable wall around her.

Movement to the left draws her attention and Finn turns to see Grim standing several feet away. He is just as big, but much younger than the Grim she knows now. His face lacks the lines formed from the countless cycles of a life spent in the Outer Rings and his eyes lack the hardness she is so used to seeing in them. The expression on his face is eager rather than guarded and Finn finds herself transfixed by the stark contrast from the man he is today.

His expression changes suddenly, and a wide smile breaks out across his face. Finn follows his gaze to the trees in the distance.

A woman with wheat-colored hair appears from behind one of their trunks and approaches. She appears to be human. As she crosses the clearing, her face and bright, blue eyes come into focus. She is the same woman Finn saw the first time she touched this locket. In that memory, she had been bathed in light . . . cradling a squirming bundle in her arms. Now, her hands hang at her sides.

She is beautiful—radiant even—beneath the moons' glow.

Something glints, drawing Finn's attention, and her gaze drops from the woman's face to see a silver chain around her neck. Dangling just below her collarbone is a Khaleerian gemstone.

Grim's necklace.

Finn's head shoots to the younger Grim where he stands next to her, waiting for the woman to get closer. The carefree smile still hangs on his red lips and, for the first time, Finn sees it reach his eyes. The wind kicks up, tossing the skirt of the woman's dress behind her and plastering the material to her lithe frame. She laughs in delight, but the sound is swallowed by the gust. Her hand comes up to her swollen belly and Finn finally notices the bump.

The breeze retreats as she closes the distance between them to stop directly in front of Grim. She is slender and taller than most women, but the top of her head still barely reaches Grim's shoulders. Her hand comes up to rest against his crimson cheek.

"Abaddon, my love," she whispers fondly.

Without thinking, Finn moves closer, until she is a mere foot from the couple's intimate embrace. Grim's large hand rises gently up to cup her belly in his palm.

"And how is Dhala *this evening?"*

Finn's heart beats a rapid rhythm in her chest at the familiar endearment.

"Stubborn, like her father." She smiles widely, but her eyes are tired. Grim sees it and wraps his arms around the woman. Her head rests against his chest and he rubs her back in soothing circles.

"She'll come when she's ready, love," he tells her in a soft whisper.

"I'm so afraid, Abaddon."

Why does she keep calling him that?

Grim pushes her back a few inches so he can bend to look her in the eyes. He holds her face delicately in his massive palms.

"Don't be," he whispers. *"I will not let anything happen to you or our daughter."* His fervent vow hangs between them for a moment. She nods her head slowly as a lone tear slides down her fair cheek.

Grim has a daughter? *Finn's mind reels and her head begins to spin.*

The woman pulls Grim's hands from her face and holds them tightly in her own. "They found a hybrid child today. He couldn't have been more than four cycles." *Her lips quiver slightly, and more tears begin to fall.* "They killed the parents . . . called the child's existence abominable. No one knows what happened to him."

Her hands release Grim's to fall to her belly as sobs begin to rock her.

Grim's voice deepens, and his eyes darken with anger. He pulls the woman back into his arms and rests his cheek against the top of her head.

"That will not happen to us. I will never let them hurt you or our child."

* * *

Insistent knocking at Finn's door pulled her from the memory. She instantly dropped the necklace back into the box and stared at it as though it had burned her.

Grim had never spoken of a wife or daughter. He had always told Finn he had no family other than Doc and the Dirty Molly.

Dhala. The expression bounced around her brain with all the delicacy of a Sirian drunk on dragon's breath. He'd used the word in its feminine form, the same way he did when referring to Finn.

A loud buzzing began to fill her ears and her heart pounded with adrenaline as she thought about everything she'd just seen and heard. The openness she'd glimpsed on the younger Grim's face baffled her. For the first time since she'd known him, she hadn't had to guess at what he was feeling . . . the love and adoration were there plain as day, shining through his eyes.

The man she'd just seen wasn't the same one she'd known for the majority of her life.

What happened to change him?

The volume of the knocking increased and Finn's head snapped to the door. She slammed the box shut and unfolded her legs. By the time her feet reached the door, the knocking had stopped.

Her hand came up and pressed the sensor to the left of the door's frame, and it opened immediately.

Finn found herself staring at Iliana's back.

Hearing the door open behind her, her sister turned around. She held her body stiff as her violet eyes met Finn's. Her teeth worried her full lower lip before her words tumbled out in an uncharacteristic rush.

"The Luminary introduced me to Madam Califax."

Her mind still filled with the overload of information Grim's memories had brought, Finn's shoulders sagged, and she cut her sister off.

"Iliana, not now—"

"No, Finn, I need you to know why I didn't tell you."

Finn sighed in defeat and rushed to move out of Iliana's way as her older sister pushed past her and into the room. Finn followed closely on her heels and pressed the sensor to shut the door behind them. She rubbed her temples in a bid to ward off an oncoming headache.

"Seriously, Iliana, I don't care," she said to her sister's back.

Iliana spun to face Finn and the long skirt of her dress twirled gracefully with the movement.

"I was a shell of a person when the Luminary brought me to Madam Califax. She made me feel safe . . . took the time to help me heal. She gave me the tools to survive and, in doing so, she brought me back to life."

"Is there a point to this delightful walk down memory lane?" Iliana ignored the sarcasm and fatigue in Finn's voice and took a deep, steadying breath. Her eyes filled with sadness and her lip quivered with emotion.

"You didn't have that, and it kills me."

Finn covered the lump rising in her throat and rolled her eyes.

"This isn't a competition to see who had it worse, Iliana." Her older sister's lips parted slightly, and she took a step forward, but Finn stayed her by holding a hand up, palm out. "And even if it was . . . I *did* have someone. I had Grim, remember?"

The man had raised her after all. She just had no idea who he really was. And what about his child? *Dhala*, he'd called her, the same endearment he used for Finn.

Iliana's brow furrowed in confusion.

"The way you talk about him I didn't think . . ."

The exhaustion finally replaced the adrenaline and Finn's shoulders sagged from the weight.

"Grim lied to me, but he also took me in and taught me everything I know . . . everything that has kept me alive all of these cycles." Finn thought about the countless nights she had spent curled up on the pile of blankets in Grim's office, listening to his deep voice read to her until she fell asleep. "I'm starting to realize things aren't as black and white as I thought they were."

Iliana let that statement sink in a moment. Her face softened and her posture relaxed slightly.

"You've changed, Finn." From her sister's tone, Finn couldn't tell if she was happy or distressed by that realization.

"I just have a new purpose now," she told Iliana.

"Revenge?" Iliana guessed, as fear crept into her expression.

Finn nodded in affirmation and hit the sensor to open the door. Iliana gave her one last look as she stepped out. Her eyes were sad, but the expression on her face became resolute. She turned to leave, but Finn couldn't let her go without saying something.

"I'm glad you had someone to keep you safe, Iliana," she whispered to her sister's back.

Her sister looked back over her shoulder briefly before whispering back,

"You too, Finn."

SIX

The next morning, the mess hall sat empty save for Shane Montgomery, Grim, Madam Califax, the Tuathan leader, Zekiel, and their small group of hybrids. Aside from Isis, Tiri, and her little friend, Carrow, all the key players were present.

After a surprisingly restful sleep, Finn had awakened to find Aedan and Enyo stretched out on the floor, one on each side of her bed. Aedan had been snoring soundly while Enyo slept with her face hidden beneath the veil of her heavy, multihued hair. Breakfast had come and gone in a rush of activity and jovial conversation.

Now, the highly anticipated meeting—at least 'highly anticipated' on Finn's part—with the Luminary was happening and she was anxious to get started. Her mind still swam with the onslaught of information she'd uncovered about Grim and Iliana the previous night, but she'd pushed those thoughts aside as best she could.

Today was about strategy, something Finn found herself more than eager to discuss.

Grim wore his usual attire of black pants and a black shirt. The short sleeves strained against the muscles of his red biceps and the boots on his feet added at least another inch to his already significant height. Shane and Conrad flanked him, while Zekiel rested against a wall several feet away.

Conrad's blue eyes had yet to look in Finn's direction. He'd forgone wraparounds today and his dreads were pulled away from his face and piled on top of his head. It only served to highlight the severity of his hard jaw and the dark expression clouding his features.

"We are here to discuss next steps," Grim stated casually as his dark eyes scanned the room. The light glinted off his shiny, black horns. "Our attack on the Dome has made us vulnerable. We were forced to reveal ourselves before we were ready." The room fell eerily quiet as everyone seemed to hold their breath waiting for Grim to speak again. Enyo and Aedan remained motionless on either side of Finn. "Now the Arcturians not only know they have an enemy . . . they know they have a formidable one. They will stop at nothing to find us and eradicate any inkling of resistance."

Murmuring from the corner drew their attention to the trio of newer hybrids they'd rescued from the Dome. Raven and Mace exchanged worried looks. Sasha raised her hand but began speaking before anyone had the chance to notice or respond.

"So, what does that mean?" the speedster asked nervously.

Grim kept his eyes on the group as he answered in a low voice.

"It means our plans have been expedited. Nothing more. As for next steps . . . all hybrids under my protection will begin training immediately. Many of you know the basics of combat, but I need competent fighters. This will require some guidance."

Shane's blond head snapped to Grim and his green eyes went wide with surprise.

"Training for *what*?"

The Khaleerian didn't even spare the captain a cursory glance as he growled, "War."

Finn shared a look with Enyo and Aedan. Enyo bared her fangs in a fearsome smile, while Aedan's eyes glittered with anticipation.

Finally.

"Umm," Sasha raised her hand again as she continued, "what if we don't want to go to war?"

Grim finally tore his eyes from the group long enough to glare at the Xandar hybrid.

"Then you don't belong here."

Sasha shut her mouth and folded her arms. Finn's eyes drifted to the rest of the room's occupants. Many of them exchanged worried glances. Iliana and Conrad's expressions remained neutral and impossible to read.

Shane looked furious as his handsome face reddened with anger.

"Since when has this been about going to war?" the captain hissed.

Grim stared at him for long seconds before answering.

"Since *this* began," he said, spreading his arms wide.

Shane's head moved back slightly in surprise, but Grim didn't acknowledge the captain's obvious distress. Instead, he turned to the Tuathan leader, Zekiel, where he stood apart from the group. His gray dreads had been pulled away from his lined face and he wore a tunic a few shades darker than his light-brown skin.

"How long before the weapon is ready?"

The Tuathan pulled away from his spot against the wall and joined them.

"Weeks at the most," Zekiel told him.

"We have no choice but to move forward with the plan," Grim continued. "Once the weapon is ready, we will take the fight to Arcturus."

Zekiel nodded in affirmation.

"Wait a minute," Shane growled as he closed the distance between himself and the giant Khaleerian. "What weapon?"

Finn watched the scene unfold with growing unease. Shane had always been the Luminary's most loyal follower, and by all appearances the most in the know compared to the rest of *Independence*'s crew. Now that Grim's intentions became clearer, it appeared as though the captain might be rethinking that loyalty. Shane's eyes narrowed to slits as he squared off with the giant Khaleerian.

"You have never once let us in on this plan of yours, and I've never asked . . . not once. We've willingly followed you blindly this entire time. *I* have followed you blindly. Now you're talking about war and weapons? I thought we were *rescuing* hybrids from the Reliance, not pressing them into service in your private army."

Grim leaned a hip against the table nearest to him and crossed his arms over his massive chest. He looked down his nose at the captain, seemingly unconcerned with this new display of defiance.

"And you think I should put my faith in you after what happened with the doxie?" he asked the captain casually. "How many times have I told you? Never take on passengers that I haven't personally vetted."

At the mention of Nova, the young doxie whom Finn had befriended back on the Mud Pit, Shane looked like he'd been struck, and Finn felt his pain in the pit of her belly. It mingled with the guilt that had already set up residence there, souring her from the inside.

Finn had put her faith in Nova and had chosen her to pilot their mission to Arcturus. The doxie had repaid her by betraying Finn and the others to the Reliance. Fortunately for them all, Nova was dead now, murdered by the very soldiers she'd turned Finn and AJ over to.

"That wasn't his fault," Finn told Grim quickly.

"Not just his, I agree," he said, as he held her stare, "It was also yours."

Finn sucked in a breath of surprise. Her throat burned with the desire to say something . . . anything.

There was nothing.

Several feet away, Conrad went rigid as the glow of his eyes brightened and shot toward Grim.

"And . . . mine," Grim continued quietly before the blue-eyed Conrad could speak. "The fault belongs to each of us. Now the Reliance knows everything Nova told them about us." Grim's gaze scanned the room once more—stopping briefly to examine the guilty expressions on Jax and Lex's faces—before his eyes landed on Finn. "I taught you better."

Her cheeks flushed with the heat of embarrassment and shame, but there was no defense for the mistake she'd made. Grim *had* taught her better.

"You're right," she said. Conrad turned to her and his eyes searched hers for a moment. She caught a glimpse of tenderness there—that she did her best to ignore—before it was gone. They both turned back to Grim as Finn continued. "It's safer for all of us if we don't know the plan. It would only take one of us saying something to the wrong person and everything we've all been working toward would be in vain." She looked at Shane and waited for him to meet her eyes. Only when his green gaze found hers did she finish in a soft voice. "And everyone who died so we could get this far . . . their death would be too."

Finn's brain conjured up the image of AJ's sightless eyes staring through the sky above the Dome and she flinched. Shane hung his head in sorrow and she knew his thoughts had also gone to the little brother he'd lost.

"You have no idea the lengths they will go to in order to stomp us out," Grim added. Finn barely noted the appreciation in the Khaleerian's expression as he watched her take a few gentle steps in the captain's direction. When she reached his side, she lowered her voice to a whispered plea only he could hear. "Please don't let his death be in vain, Shane."

She kept her focus on the captain for long moments until he regained his bearings and lifted his head. He avoided looking at her as he gave Grim an affirmative nod and the rest of the room let out a collective sigh of relief.

"Good," Grim leaned away from the table and stood to his full seven-foot height. "Training begins now."

* * *

Grim stood at the center of one of the sector's training rooms and waited patiently for the trainees to gather around him. The space was vast, about half the size of a freighter ship's cargo bay. His booted feet sank into the mats covering the floors and an array of impressive weaponry mounted to the walls behind him provided a menacing backdrop to the already formidable picture his massive body painted.

They formed a semi-circle around him, with many of them shifting on their feet nervously. Conrad and Iliana stood off to the side closest to Lex, Jax, and Axel. Meanwhile Raven, Mace, and Sasha huddled together in the center. Finn, Enyo, and Aedan kept their distance on the outskirts of the group and waited patiently for Grim to begin his instruction.

This, at least, was something familiar in the chaos of the last few weeks. She tried not to think too much about just how comforting it was to be standing here before him waiting for another training session to begin.

The noticeably absent Shane had disappeared after his confrontation with Grim. Though he had quieted his reservations about the training, it was clear he wanted no part in the process. Finn could hardly blame him. Out of a raw desperation to protect his little brother, the captain had fought hard against her decision to train AJ on *Independence*. It had taken a lot of persuasion on Finn's part, but eventually he'd given in.

And look how that turned out.

Now, AJ was dead, and all the talk of weapons and war had to feel like history repeating itself to the poor man.

"What now?" Mace whispered too loudly in Raven's direction. The Chihiri hybrid didn't respond, but kept cautious eyes on the massive Khaleerian before them.

Grim's head turned in their direction.

"Now we begin with a demonstration," his dark eyes moved to Finn as he motioned to the empty space next to him. "Finn will join me."

She will?

Every head spun in her direction and their unblinking gazes watched her with anticipation. Finn ignored them and took a calming breath. Having spent the better part of the last fifteen cycles training alongside the imposing Khaleerian, she knew exactly what he wanted.

She nodded slightly and forced her feet to move in his direction.

Once they stood a few feet apart facing each other, Sasha didn't even bother with the illusion of whispering as she called out to no one in particular, "This should be good."

Grim ignored her and her condescending tone in favor of keeping his eyes on Finn. He rolled his thick neck and stretched his wide shoulders. Seeing it, Finn's heart began to pound in her throat. Student and teacher faced off once again for the first time in a very long time. She had never allowed herself to admit it, but she'd missed this.

She'd missed *him*.

She fell into her fight stance automatically and waited for his imperceptible nod. When she finally got it, she flew into a blur of motion.

Finn blitzed to cover the distance between them and unloaded a barrage of kicks and punches on Grim. She focused the strikes on his knees while directing tight jabs at his midsection, attacking every exposed nerve cluster and organ that wasn't being defended.

Grim barely moved.

Shielding his most vital areas, he had only to simply shift slightly if Finn got around his guard. They continued this dance for several minutes, as Grim allowed Finn to showcase her agility. Her stamina had barely waned by the time a snide voice halted their movements.

"I thought you were showing us how to fight, not how to slowly get our asses kicked," Raven smirked as she shared a look with Sasha and Mace.

Grim's breathing barely changed, belying the incredible exertion of defending against Finn's repeated, unflinching attacks. The Khaleerian brought his feet together and stood to his full height as he turned to the group. Finn relaxed her stance immediately and followed Grim's line of sight to fall on Raven.

As she held the Luminary's eyes, Raven made a valiant effort of looking brave while staring down the red wall of muscle and unbridled strength.

"My turn then," the Khaleerian told Raven with his fangs bared in anticipation. His head swung back to Finn and waited for her nod. Finn gave it and immediately took a defensive stance. It only took two large steps for him to separate the distance between them. He swung a hard punch at her head so quickly that she didn't even see his shoulders telegraph the movement.

She ducked low at the last minute. The timing was so close she felt the heat of his fist as it sailed over the top of her head. Knees still bent and too close for an effective kick, her fist shot out to land several blows in quick succession to the Khaleerian's abdomen.

He barely flinched.

When fatigue stilled her seemingly endless attack, Grim took a step into her and his large biceps shot out to wrap around her upper body. He lifted until her feet left the ground and he held her in a painful bear hug. Struggling for air, she kicked her legs out in measured strikes and connected with his knees. When she hit bone, Grim grunted before throwing her with ease several feet away. She sailed to the ground like a rag doll and rolled.

With a speed that belied his size, the Khaleerian closed the distance between them. By the time she'd gained her feet, he stood directly in front of her. Before she could raise her guard, his fist shot out and connected with her midsection. The impact sent her flying bodily and she landed on a mat near the wall with a loud thud.

The display of might was more than impressive. From the corner of her eye, Finn saw the others observing them with rapt attention. Even Raven—who had folded her arms at her chest in a pose of pure obstinance—couldn't control the widening of her purple eyes as she watched Grim's powerful body move.

Once Finn could breathe again, she sat up. Grim was already towering above her and his big, red hands came down to grab her by the shoulders. Before his grip could tighten, she shifted quickly and dove down through his open legs. In a fluid motion, she gained her feet and ran at the wall a few inches to the left of the giant Khaleerian. Using her speed and momentum, she ran up the side and pushed off. She'd gained plenty of height and as she flew at him, she managed to clock Grim in the jaw with a powerful kick.

He stumbled back and shook his head. Smiling, his hand brushed his jaw before dropping and coming up with lightning speed to connect with her temple. Finn went down immediately.

He'd only used a tiny fraction of his impressive strength, but it still took her several long moments of forcing air into her lungs before the room stopped spinning. Wobbling, she shook off the impact and stood. Only when Grim had once again dropped his guard did she relax hers.

They both turned to their audience. While many of the others smiled and even applauded the demonstration—which included an excited "whoop" from Lex—Raven remained unmoving and continued to glare in their direction.

"What's the point of all this?" Raven groused as she motioned toward the mats. "We have *powers*. If I scream at the right pitch, I can explode your eardrums. The talons on Mace's wings are sharp enough to take *her* head off," Raven pointed a dark-purple hand at Finn and swung her braids over a shoulder. "And then there's Supersonic . . ." she finished, using Sasha's nickname from the Dome.

"You'd have to catch me to fight me," the speedy hybrid added with a smirk.

Grim stared at them for long minutes and said nothing. The young trio began to squirm under the silent scrutiny. Finally, the Khaleerian bared his fangs in a smile and opened his arms in a welcoming gesture.

"Finn?" he called to her.

After cycles by his side, she could easily read the intent in his black eyes.

They shared a look of understanding and Finn closed the distance between herself and Raven. When only a few feet separated them, she came to a stop and looked back to Grim. Realizing her intentions, Raven shook out her limbs, cracked her neck, and smiled brightly. Grim waited for both females to look at him before motioning with a large hand for them to begin.

The half-Chihiri immediately took in a breath, no doubt in preparation to unleash the eardrum-exploding shriek she'd been boasting. Before she could exhale, Finn snapped out a gloved hand and flicked Raven directly in the throat, dropping her to the ground. Raven clutched at her windpipe with bulging eyes as she gasped for breath. After a moment she managed a rattling wheeze.

Seeing his friend's distress, Mace jumped to attention. The boy let the harness drop from his chest and unfurled his massive wings, nearly knocking Sasha to the ground in the process. Thankfully, she darted out of the way faster than Finn's eyes could track. Mace tensed his body, preparing to fly to Raven's defense, but Grim appeared from nowhere, grabbed him by the base of his wings, and squeezed. The shock of pain and lack of blood flow to his appendages paralyzed him. He struggled frailly under Grim's smothering mass to no avail.

Sasha continued to flit around the room in a blur of movement, traversing the length of the training room in mere seconds. Grim maintained his hold on Mace's wings with one hand and tore a boot from the boy's foot with the other. The Khaleerian carefully took aim and threw the object into Sasha's path. In a flash of movement, she ran directly into the shoe's trajectory. The mass struck her in the stomach. The impact led to her tripping over her own feet and sent her flying to the ground in a heap.

When the dust settled, Finn caught Enyo's grin and Aedan's surprised look of approval. Conrad and Iliana's expressions were less easy to read, and Lex and Jax were openly giggling with delight. Axel appeared more nervous than anything as he stared at Grim in awe.

The Khaleerian glanced down at the captive Mace, then let his gaze travel to Raven, Sasha, and then the room as a whole.

"There is no doubt your powers are an asset, but an over-reliance on them is a weakness in and of itself. What happens when the enemy is prepared? What will you do when they render your abilities useless?" Grim released his hold on Mace and he fell fully to his hands and knees. Raven panted heavily as she glared up at them both while massaging her throat. "Fighting is about learning to work against your weaknesses while exploiting the weaknesses of your opponent. It is as much mental as it is physical. Beginning today, you will each learn fighting styles that complement your strengths. Conrad, Iliana, Enyo, Axel, and Aedan," Grim called out. "You will train with me, learning how to use your size and power to your advantage. Lex, Jax, Sasha, Mace, and Raven will train with Finn on the benefits of capitalizing on your speed and agility."

Wait, Grim wanted *her* to train the hybrids?

"Training with you is the only time I've ever really been happy."

AJ's cheeks had flushed with embarrassment as he'd made the admission to her after one of their sessions. A few days later he was dead.

Finn's eyes shot to her mentor, but he was busy helping Raven, Mace, and Sasha to their feet. Although somewhat begrudgingly, each member of the trio of fallen hybrids accepted the Khaleerian's help with little fanfare.

"How are we supposed to learn how to fight when I can barely walk after that boot fastball you just hit me with?" Sasha complained as she rubbed her abdomen and limped back over to the group.

"You will train harder than you ever have in your lives . . . and it *will* hurt." Grim made eye contact with Sasha and she gulped audibly. "However, we are fortunate enough to have an Aquariian healer in our midst. Each of you will visit with Isis in the evenings after our training sessions for healing."

Finn's mind whirled with the possibilities. What kind of toll would that amount of healing each day take on Isis? Even as she worried for the Aquariian, she couldn't deny the benefits of Grim's plans. Without the pain of sore muscles, broken bones, and bruises . . . the speed at which they learned and progressed would be unheard of.

"Split into your groups and begin," Grim ordered.

This time, no one uttered a single protest as they went to their respective sides of the room and began the hard work.

"I thought I told you to fix this?" Aedan glowered at Finn through a swollen eye and tenderly pushed a forkful of food between his split lips. His bald head had several small cuts above the brow bone and his dark knuckles were raw. "The Merlidian is out for blood now," he finished around a mouthful of vegetables.

He'd yet to visit Isis after their first day of training but was set to see her sometime after dinner. The Aquariian needed to take breaks between healings to recharge and avoid any lasting damage. While they still fought hard during sparring, this meant they had to exercise a modicum of restraint to keep from injuring each other too badly. Isis could handle the cuts, bruises, and broken bones, but regularly healing anything more than that would begin to take its toll on the Aquariian.

"Don't be such a baby," Finn teased half-heartedly. Guilt sat heavy in her stomach, making it difficult to enjoy the plate of delicious food in front of her.

During their instructions, Conrad and Aedan had been paired together for sparring. Seeing as how Conrad believed Finn had turned her affections toward the giant half-Solidarian, the fighting between the two men had turned vicious almost immediately. By the looks of it, Conrad had used the exercise as an excuse to purge some anger, landing punishing blow after punishing blow while Aedan did his best to defend against them.

Seeing as she'd intentionally fueled the misunderstanding between them rather than sort it out as Aedan had asked, she felt more than a little responsible for her friend's current bruised and battered state.

Despite the raw violence they'd displayed—both men were incredibly skilled, and Conrad's face had looked almost identical to Aedan's before his visit with the Aquariian—she knew both men had held back today. She only hoped they didn't kill each other by the end of the week.

Isis could only do so much.

Enyo plopped her tray on the table and took a seat next to Finn. Thankfully, the disruption gave Finn an excuse to ignore her guilt for the time being.

The Sirian hybrid took one look at Aedan and grinned around a mouthful of bread. "You look terrible."

Aedan dropped his utensils and scowled at them. After a moment, his eyes moved over the tables to find Isis standing near one of the mess hall's doorways. She waved him over with a slender, blue hand. "That's my cue." He lasered Finn with a hard stare as he pointed to her and said, "Fix. This."

Then he was gone.

Enyo bit into a large piece of meat hanging from the bone as she watched him go. "Fix what?" she mumbled through a mouthful.

Grimacing, Finn let her head drop into her hands and massaged her temples.

"You should've seen the look on her face when I dropped her."

Finn tilted her head slightly to see Raven beaming as she balanced two trays and eagerly boasted to Mace. The younger hybrids barely spared them a glance before planting themselves in the seats next to Enyo.

Enyo smiled around the bone she was currently gnawing. Dropping it to the plate with a thud, she leaned in closer to Raven and Mace. Her tawny eyes glittered with humor.

"She looked almost as surprised as she did when the Luminary took her down with your boot," she told Mace.

Raven let out a bark of laughter and slapped the boy on the back. The impact knocked the spoon from his hand. He smiled, even as his cheeks flushed with embarrassment.

"You should be taking this training seriously," Finn stopped massaging her temples long enough to chastise the group, "not turning it into a pissing contest."

"What's wrong with her?" Raven stage-whispered and motioned with her head in Finn's direction.

"She has something she needs to fix," Enyo stated matter-of-factly, before sucking the marrow from another bone.

Raven shared a confused look with Mace. Shrugging her shoulders, she picked up a three-layer piece of spongey cake and took a bite.

"Mmmm . . . Just like my sister used to make."

Her moan of pleasure set Finn's teeth on edge.

The two seemed completely at ease sitting together and chatting like old friends. The scene was a far cry from the thinly veiled animosity shadowing last night's meal.

The difference a day makes.

Raven and Mace resumed their animated chatter, only taking breaks to shovel food into their faces.

"Speaking of sisters," Enyo leaned close to Finn and whispered, "where is *yours*?"

Finn took in the eager expression on Enyo's face and rolled her eyes. Sighing, she dropped her head back into her hands and did her best not to kill everyone at the table.

SEVEN

The sun beats down on Grim as he waits patiently in the clearing, causing his red skin to glisten with sweat. His eyes search the tree line anxiously.

What planet are we on? *Finn wondered with some trepidation.*

Without the veil of darkness and mist, she is finally able to take in their surroundings fully. The vivid greens and blues of the grass and lush foliage are unlike anything she's ever seen. Flowers in every shade of the rainbow blossom around them, stinging Finn's eyes with their vibrancy. Not a single synthetic replacement with its characteristic artificial sheen could be seen anywhere. The closest thing she'd experienced to the raw beauty of this planet were the murals and drawings in Tiri's room on Independence. *Even the plant life on Cartan—the farming planet Finn had called home once upon a time— paled in comparison to what stood in front of her now.*

There is a slight rustle to the left and the human woman with wheat-colored hair emerges from behind a wall of bushes. In this memory, her abdomen is flat, and her angelic face is less full. Her blue eyes look worried.

"Abaddon!" she cries.

Grim turns and she runs into his embrace. Unshed tears pool in her eyes and she allows herself a moment of comfort before pulling away. She grabs Grim's forearms frantically.

"What is wrong, my love?" he asks in a gruff rumble.

"They're going to do it. They have plans to begin work immediately and with the alterations they've made to the Tuathans' tech, it won't take long."

Grim's confused eyes scan hers for a second.

"What are they going to do?" he asks carefully.

"They're taking it all away," she whispers as the tears begin to fall. "They're going to kill everything. All of the plants, each and every tree. Everything you see will be gone. And it's not just here . . . it'll be every planet they control save for a few left for farming."

"Farming planets?" Grim asks as his mind goes to work behind his dark eyes.

"God forbid they go without fresh produce," the woman scoffs. "The rest of the galaxy will be forced to rely on them for everything. Food . . . oxygen." She is forced to stop talking as a sob bubbles up in her chest. "This isn't why we came here."

Hearing the hiccup in her voice, Grim pulls her into his arms but he is far away, lost in thought.

A soft rapping at her door pulled Finn from the memory. She dropped Grim's necklace into the wooden box on her bed and waited a few seconds to be sure she wasn't imagining the disruption.

Another soft rap sounded.

Finn grabbed the box and returned it to its hiding spot at the bottom of the trunk near the foot of her bed and covered it with clothing. She wiped at her fatigued eyes and let out a deep sigh as she rose and made her way to the door.

Running her hand over the entry sensor, a louder, more forceful knock jarred her movements and made her jump. The door opened before her and she found herself staring at a wall made up of Grim and Iliana. The contrast between the Khaleerian's menacing appearance and Iliana's petite yet curvy frame—covered in delicate beige lace—made them an odd-looking pair to be sure. Iliana's long, red waves were piled high on her head and secured with pins made to look like lush blossoms in varying shades of yellow. Her violet eyes darted around nervously.

"You missed breakfast," she said in an uncharacteristic rush.

Finn glanced from her older sister to Grim. It felt jarring to see him now, so different than he appeared in his memories. Seeing the dichotomy between the two Grims only highlighted things about him she'd never noticed before.

She took in his giant frame and the hard lines of his face. It had been easy to miss given his confidence and efficiency. They distracted from the slight sag in his shoulders and the fatigue she'd never noticed lying behind his eyes, almost as though he carried some unspoken burden Finn didn't yet understand.

In the cycles since those memories from the necklace had taken place, his eyes had grown hard with a quiet determination and something else . . . something she couldn't quite place.

When their gazes met, she found her mentor's expression difficult to decipher. However, she could tell by the hard set of his jaw and the stiffness in his shoulders that something wasn't right.

Finn raised her brows. "I've missed meals before. That doesn't explain why you're both here looking like someone died."

As she said the words, she immediately regretted the casual jest. Registering the sarcasm coloring her tone, annoyance quickly replaced the concern in Iliana's eyes, but she said nothing.

"We're here to talk, *Dhala*." Grim brought his hand up to rest against the door frame and locked eyes with Finn.

She assembled her face into a neutral expression and thanked the Gods above she'd hidden his necklace before answering the door. They both watched her with silent expectation, and she sighed. They were two of the most stubborn people she'd ever known. If they wanted to talk, she wouldn't be able to put them off.

Though her stomach flipped with anxiety imagining whatever scenario had brought the unlikely duo to her door, she feigned mild annoyance and moved aside to wave them in.

"Have a seat," she told them as she motioned for them to the loveseat in the corner.

Iliana accepted the invitation and sat on the edge of the loveseat's worn, cream cushion with her legs crossed at the ankles and her hands folded neatly in her lap. Seeing as Grim's huge frame would likely break the loveseat in half, the large Khaleerian opted to lean against the wall with his arms folded across his wide chest.

Finn stood near her bed and mirrored Grim's stance.

"Well?" she prompted with more than a little annoyance.

Iliana glanced nervously at Grim and shifted slightly where she sat but remained silent. Just as Finn opened her mouth to snap at them, the Khaleerian unfolded from the wall.

"Starting tomorrow, Iliana is going to begin her own training with the hybrids."

Her gaze bounced between them as she tried to understand the heavy air filling the room at Grim's admission.

"Training for what?"

"Iliana has always maintained a level of control over her abilities that I have yet to see in any other." Iliana blushed slightly at the praise. "She can show the others how to tap into their full potential."

Finn pushed the compliment to the back of her mind, ignoring the sting in her chest it caused.

"Okay, that's great and everything, but did it really require an early morning trip to tell me? I could've just found out with everyone else."

"Well," Iliana said, wringing her hands with worry. "The idea got us thinking about you and your abilities."

"And?" Finn prompted when she didn't continue.

Seemingly tired of dancing around the topic, Grim brought his hands to his hips and held Finn's stare. "We're here to talk about what you did to Rock in the Dome."

At the mention of the hybrid who had taken AJ's life, the air left the room and Finn's lungs simultaneously. Her blood pounded in her ears as the gaping void of silence—save for the sound of her furious heartbeat—filled the space between them.

A switch had been flipped that day in the Dome, seeing AJ lying in a crumpled, bloody heap. She'd used her abilities on the Kreetian hybrid known simply as Rock, an obvious reference to his particularly stony appearance—and personality, prolonging his agony before putting him out of his misery. She could still remember the warmth of Rock's blood as she'd exploded his head with a hard-light shield and watched the pieces fly through the air like projectiles.

She released a ragged breath and forced a whisper through her lips. "I killed him. It's pretty self-explanatory."

Iliana's eyes closed briefly before opening again and focusing on her younger sister. "No, not that. We're here to talk about what happened before . . . when you touched him."

"And why would you be here to talk about that?"

Iliana uncrossed her ankles and stood. Her worried eyes scanned Finn carefully from top to toe. "Grim and I have a theory about what happened," she told her quickly. "You saw me use my abilities to force the Toad's henchman to relive his worst memories. You even asked me to teach you how I did it."

Finn remembered the ease with which her sister had merely brushed a hand against the behemoth's cheek and dropped him to the ground in a blubbering pile.

"Yeah, you practically turned his brain to mush in the process. Are you saying that I forced Rock to relive his worst memories?"

"No, what happened to him was different. I've never seen anything like it before." Iliana took a step closer and lowered her voice as she studied Finn. "I think you gave him *your* worst memories. You did, didn't you?"

She was right. In the moment, she hadn't just wanted Rock dead; she'd wanted him to *suffer* for killing AJ. She'd conjured up every horrible thing she'd ever seen or done—every lash

of the chancellor's whip, every scream, every drop of blood—
and channeled them into the touch of her skin against his.
Finn remembered the way Rock's eyes had glazed over, nearly
rolling back in his head, and the blood that had trickled from
his eyes like tears.

She nodded her head in affirmation, unable to find her
voice just yet.

"You and Iliana's abilities are similar but different," Grim
broke the silence to tell her something she already knew. "She
can siphon from people, whereas you can siphon from objects."

"Yeah, we've established I suck at siphoning from people.
But give me a teacup and watch out." Finn did her best to
cover the tremble in her own voice with sarcasm.

Iliana shared a look with Grim before speaking again.

"We think it's more than just a difference in how we siphon."

"When I gave you those Kyokushin books as a child, you
did not just siphon memories from them," Grim added. "It
was the same with the maps I gave you before jobs . . . as
though you had downloaded the information directly to your
brain until they became a part of you, like they were yours to
begin with. After a few sessions with those books, you fought
like you had been training in the style for cycles. And you
never forget the layout of a ship or building once you touch
its map. Not ever."

Grim spoke the truth. Even if she'd never once set foot
in the space, she could navigate it perfectly. And though he
was an excellent instructor, Finn had to admit she'd always
wondered if there was more to her fighting prowess than just
a competent teacher.

"What does this have to do with Rock?" Finn asked, as she
forced breath in and out of her lungs. She clenched her hands
into fists so he wouldn't see them shake.

"Your abilities, like those of all hybrids, are a genetic mutation," Grim stated matter-of-factly. "It would seem that *your*
mutation has taken on a unique form."

"And that form would be?" Finn's patience with the pair and their inability to get to the point had reached its limit.

"Finn," Iliana's words were quiet but measured as she said, "If you can download memories you siphon from objects, it is not outside the realm of possibility to assume you can upload those same memories into other people."

Finn's eyes shot to Grim. The Khaleerian leveled her with a stare full of meaning.

"I think you understand, the applications of such a power are limitless."

"When you touched Rock, you didn't just show him memories. You forced him to *live* them . . . all the pain . . . all the fear. He felt everything all at once, until his brain could take no more."

"The blood from his eyes," Finn murmured, lost in the memory of Rock's last moments.

"He was dead before you ever put that hard-light shield in his mouth," Grim finished the thought for her.

Finn's hands fell limply to her sides and began to shake uncontrollably. Even though she already wore gloves, she suddenly felt the need to add at least three more pairs and steel boxes for good measure. Knowing she truly did have the power to punish the Reliance filled her with anticipation, but the thought that she could hurt someone else in the process—someone like Tiri or Iliana—terrified her beyond measure.

Iliana's sharp gaze focused on her and she quickly closed the distance between them until she stood mere inches away. Finn retreated and all but fell when the backs of her thighs hit the bed behind her.

"Finn, it's okay," she whispered soothingly. "What you did to Rock was not the result of an accident or a lack of control. That day in the Dome, you used your abilities with focus and intent. You *wanted* to hurt him."

"Oh, well I guess there's nothing to worry about then," Finn shouted, as she threw her hands up in the air. "I only killed Rock because of my *murderous intent*. I'll just make sure to keep that in check while we *go to war*!"

Grim clucked his tongue at her hysterics and Finn's wide eyes shot to him.

"Despite the opinions you may hold about yourself, *Dhala*, you would never hurt your sister . . . or any of us for that matter. And even if you wanted to, like any hybrid, your abilities have limitations. You wouldn't remember this, but when we found you, you were in bad shape. Your eyes and ears were bleeding, and you were unconscious for an entire day. Killing Rock almost killed *you*. It took several healing sessions with Isis just to undo the damage you'd caused yourself."

"We want to understand your abilities more." Iliana reached out and grabbed Finn's gloved hand. Finn tried to pull away, but her older sister's grip tightened with surprising strength. "We can help you learn to use them . . . moderate them so you don't kill yourself in the process."

She stopped struggling against her sister's touch as the weight of everything she'd just revealed settled in. Then, something else occurred to her and she turned to Grim.

"This isn't just about helping *me* though, is it?"

Guilt flashed in his eyes for the briefest moment before he caught himself.

"*Dhala*—"

"Grim, this isn't about you and how much I may or may not hate you," she informed him matter-of-factly. The Khaleerian flinched but remained silent. "You want to make the Reliance pay just as much as I do, and you think these powers can help you. Tell me."

"There are some things I cannot share yet, *Dhala*."

Finn gritted her teeth at the Khaleerian endearment and rolled her eyes. She brushed a hand through her auburn waves in frustration.

"But you think I can help us win . . . don't you?"

"I do," he answered as he carefully guarded his expression.

On a short nod, Finn squared her shoulders and stepped away from her sister.

"Then, what are we waiting for?"

"Do you really think this will work?" Finn collapsed onto the bed and brought her legs up to cross them beneath her.

It was now well past lunch time and Grim had just departed, leaving only Finn and Iliana alone in her room. Aedan and Enyo had come to check on her hours ago, but the Khaleerian had turned them away at the door.

"I don't think," Iliana whispered, as she took a seat at the foot of the bed. "I *know*."

Finn's teeth worried her lower lip.

"If this works . . ." she trailed off.

"If this works, it will change *everything*," Iliana finished for her.

"No pressure," Finn muttered under her breath.

The courtesan moved a little closer.

"Try it on me," she offered quietly.

"What?" Finn shouted with no small amount of panic. "I can't do that. Grim isn't even here, shouldn't he be here?" she stalled in a rush.

"If this works, he won't mind."

She'd seen that determined sheen in Iliana's eyes before. It was a look she usually adopted right before she ignored Finn's wishes and did whatever she wanted anyway. Finn's mind scrambled for a way to put her sister off.

"'If he kept you from me then he will pay.'" Iliana's eyes narrowed as Finn quoted her words from several weeks ago back to her. "Isn't that what you said to me? I take it you've forgiven him for keeping us apart all these cycles?" she asked, referring to Grim.

"No." Iliana's answer was firm and emphatic. "But just like you, I can set aside my feelings when something I want is on the line."

Determination filled her voice and Finn did not doubt the veracity of her words.

"You want to take them down just as badly as I do, don't you?"

"Of course," she admitted quickly, "but that's not what I was referring to." Iliana's expression was unguarded in a way it rarely was. "What I want more than anything, Little One, is to keep you safe. You will see this through to the end even if it kills you. I know you well enough to know that. You want to punish the Reliance. I see how it has kept you going these past few weeks. I want to punish them too, but for me, it's only ever been about you, Finn." She moved even closer to Finn on the bed until mere inches separated them. "Everything I've ever done—becoming a courtesan, joining the Luminary's mission—all of it has been for you. To avenge the sister I lost."

"Iliana—" It was the only word she got out before her sister cut her off.

"I'll never get Kyra back; I know that too," she said referring to Finn's given name. "But I have *you*." Her eyes sparkled with fire. She reached a slender hand out until it was a hairsbreadth away from Finn's cheek and stopped in a contactless caress. "And I will fight to my last breath to keep you safe. I will not lose you again, Finn. So yes, I will work with Grim to see this through to the end. For you and for Kyra."

At the fervent vow, pieces of Finn she'd once thought irreparably broken began to knit themselves together. As was the case with any mend, they would never fit together seamlessly . . . but they would hold.

And maybe this time they'd be stronger.

The lower-caste seamstresses had a saying: *"The prettier the garment, the more likely to tear. The uglier the garment, the better to wear."*

They always lamented the poor stitching on Reliance-manufactured clothing and how easily it tore, referring to themselves as surgeons as they stitched sutures to hold together the ripped and dying frocks.

Finn had to clear her throat to cover the emotion fighting to escape her. Silently, she lifted her arms and pulled the gloves from her hands. She kept her eyes on Iliana as she reached out.

"Give me your hand."

EIGHT

Finn dodged a carefully aimed kick to the jaw and countered with a left jab. Iliana spun gracefully to the right just in time, narrowly avoiding impact. They separated to stand with their feet shoulder-width apart, one fist by the jaw and the other slightly outstretched, mirroring one another. The sisters burst into a riot of kicks and punches, each dodging, countering, and parrying the other's attacks so quickly that even Sasha had difficulty tracking their moves.

At first glance, the constant misses and hectic footwork appeared chaotic and sloppy, but it soon became apparent that they weren't connecting because they were executing the same moves simultaneously. The two were practically breathing in sync.

Finn broke away from Iliana and threw a roundhouse kick to the head that forced the courtesan to duck low and dive into a roll when the follow-up axe kick threatened to crack the crown of her skull. Before Iliana could re-engage, Finn was already in her face unleashing a barrage of lethal kicks that kept her off-balance and in retreat.

Despite appearances that the fight might be short-lived, a wry smile crept across Iliana's face and she dropped her hands to her waist in a move that anyone watching would consider the height of masochism. Though it looked like the courtesan had given up, Finn knew better. The fight wasn't over until Grim said it was. She threw a kick with so much snap that when Iliana dodged it, her braid flew up from the force. Next, she dodged Finn's sidekick that would have caved in her ribs, and the three jumping kicks that would've ended in a concussion had they actually landed.

Iliana leaned back, almost bending completely backward to avoid a kick meant to smear her nose across her face. She took a hopping step backward and shuffled her feet like an ancient-era boxer.

The rest of the fighters—with Grim at their center—stood in a semi-circle around the sparring duo. In her peripheral vision, Finn saw that most of them stared in Iliana's direction with shocked faces and mouths opened in stunned surprise.

Yesterday, Iliana had been the weakest link among them. It was hardly surprising given that her profession didn't exactly require the kind of skills necessary to be an accomplished combatant. But the courtesan exuded a natural grace in her movements and Finn knew that she'd eventually get the hang of it. Unfortunately, they didn't have that kind of time.

Certainly, no one in the room had expected her to become a competent fighter overnight, yet that was exactly what had happened.

Iliana feigned right with a telegraphed punch and Finn automatically moved with her to block it. To the shock and awe of everyone watching, the courtesan spun at the last second and landed a hard kick to Finn's midsection. The air left Finn's lungs in a rush and she stumbled back a few steps before righting herself.

Despite her fears, Finn had spent the afternoon with her older sister testing the limits of her newfound abilities.

"Think of your abilities as a faucet," Iliana had instructed. "When you siphon from another person, the memories stream from them to you. The only problem is your inability to control the flow."

Finn had smirked.

"Really boosting my confidence here."

Iliana had ignored Finn's attempt at humor.

"Rather than try to control it, I want you to focus on reversing it. Imagine yourself pushing the water back through the faucet."

She'd started with her memories from the books on Kyokushin, peppered with a few others, and finished with memories from her own experiences in combat. With her sister's instruction—and faucet metaphor—transferring the memories to Iliana (or "uploading" as she'd called it) had been a much easier process than any attempt Finn had ever made to siphon from another person.

When they'd finished, Iliana's eyes had widened with excitement, and she had studied her own hands as though seeing them clearly for the first time. "I felt what they felt . . . what *you* felt when you were fighting." Her wide eyes had risen to Finn's as she'd rubbed her wrist tenderly. "I felt the pain of every single blow like it was happening to me in real time."

Finn's brows had furrowed, and she'd taken a step forward, "Are you okay?"

"I'm fine," Iliana had rushed to reassure her. She'd pointed to her head as she'd marveled, "Everything is all here. My body remembers what it felt like to move the way you move. It's like I've been fighting for cycles." Suddenly, her mouth had grown tight, and her violet eyes had widened with worry. "How do *you* feel? Are you feeling faint?"

Finn had chuckled softly. "I'm great."

She hadn't been lying. Surprisingly, she'd felt hardly any fatigue uploading the memories into Iliana. The courtesan had still insisted her younger sister visit Isis just to be sure and Finn had begrudgingly agreed.

After, they'd met Grim in the training room and discussed the day's plan: they would demo the aftereffects of Finn's new ability for the rest of the hybrids. Grim had instructed them not to hold back.

Finn blocked another jab and countered with one of her own. This time, the blow connected hard with Iliana's nose before she could dodge it and the courtesan fell back against a wall. She brought her hands up to her face. When she pulled them away, her fingers were wet with the blood dripping from her nostrils.

"Enough," Grim called out and both sisters relaxed their stances.

Finn gave Iliana a once-over to make sure the courtesan's nose wasn't broken. When she saw that it wasn't, she met her sister's eyes and both women smiled.

"I bet you've been waiting a long time to punch me in the nose," Iliana whispered, her eyes sparkling with amusement.

"Longer than you know," Finn quipped back.

Isis waited patiently outside the training room and watched them through the large window. Finn motioned for her to come inside and the Aquariian headed straight for Iliana.

"I'm still not sure what I just saw," Lex called out. Her wide, amber eyes followed Iliana and Isis out of the room and only turned back when the door shut behind them. "Did someone switch the real Iliana out with a clone who can actually fight?"

"Clone or not," Jax's hands cupped his mouth as he yelled enthusiastically, "That. Was. Awesome!"

Sasha followed the pilots' lines of sight and tightened the dark ponytail at the base of her skull. When she'd finished, she looked back at Finn.

"No offense to your sister, but she kind of sucked yesterday. Now she fights like . . . well, *you*."

"Offense taken," Finn speared the girl with a glare. Sasha flinched and tried to cover it with an eye roll.

"Today, you have all been given an upper hand in your training," Grim stated quietly. The hybrids were forced to cease their animated chatter in order to hear him.

"How so?" Conrad's eyes narrowed into slits as he questioned the Khaleerian.

Before answering, Grim speared them all with a terrifying glower. "What I am about to say, does not leave this room.

If I find out any of you have shared this information—and I *will* find out—"

"What?" Raven scoffed as she shared an amused look with the others. "You'll kill us?"

"Yes." Grim growled the word and let it hang in the air between them. His dark eyes burned with the promise of retribution. "Without hesitation."

The smile faded from Raven's dark-purple face. She held the Khaleerian's gaze and gulped, withering under its force.

Finn bit her lip in an effort not to smile and caught Conrad studying her. After days of pretending she didn't exist, it seemed as though she'd done something to capture the blue-eyed hybrid's attention.

Lex grabbed the periwinkle poofs atop her head and began to jump up and down in vexation.

"Will you just tell us what's going on? The suspense is killing me."

Grim rolled his eyes at her theatrics and turned his attention to Finn.

"Shall we begin?"

The training room buzzed with energy.

They spread out in sparring pairs. Many of the males had removed their shirts while the females wore form-fitting pants and tanks. Their hair—all of various lengths and textures—had been braided. Each of them wore tape over their knuckles and around their wrists.

The sounds of bodies thudding together intermingled with their heavy breathing and the occasional instruction called out by Grim. Each of their faces showed how serious they took the training. Even the normally jovial twin pilots had traded banter for a grave sense of purpose that overrode their need to land a well-timed joke.

For the last two weeks, Finn had spent her days alternating between "uploading" the different fighting styles she'd gleaned from books and personal experience over the cycles and sparring with the others to ensure they properly honed the new skills. Iliana spent each morning with them, helping them tap into the potential of their abilities, but the afternoons belonged to Finn.

Every few days—like an assembly line—the hybrids would come to her one by one. They would close their eyes and with a brush of Finn's bare hand, those eyes would begin dancing behind their lids as they absorbed the memories she bestowed onto them. And every time she did, their muscle memory and instincts grew stronger and their skills sharpened.

For Grim's group of larger fighters, she focused on Judo and boxing, as well as other defensive blocking styles more suited to their immense strength. For Finn's group of smaller hybrids, it was Kyokushin with a few other offense-heavy styles peppered in.

Grim told them their resulting opposite styles— called *Beat the Weapon* for the smaller hybrids and *Trust the Shield* for the larger ones—formed two halves of the same whole.

The group's progress in such a short time was nothing short of remarkable.

She'd found that using her abilities so frequently and on so many, fatigued her in a way they never had before. However, each day she grew stronger, as though her abilities were a muscle she simply needed to flex until it strengthened. Up until now, she'd always felt like she had operated at the mercy of her abilities, even after she'd trained with Iliana and learned to master her unique skill of siphoning from objects. Despite the control she'd learned, there had always been a shadow of doubt looming over her when it came to touching others.

Not anymore.

Her hands no longer shook with trepidation when she removed her gloves and placed her bare palm on one of his arms. This new facet of her abilities gave her a laser-like focus she'd never had before. And with that focus came determination. Both gave her a sense of control she'd longed for but never been lucky enough to possess. When she touched them now, they only saw what she wanted them to see.

Of course, that focus and determination all but disappeared every time she had to touch Conrad. Uploading to him felt supremely awkward as they practiced avoiding each other's gaze, and Finn prayed her emotions didn't get the better of her. If they did, she might end up showing Conrad a memory she didn't want him to see or vice versa.

So far, she hadn't.

Finn focused on her opponent and tightened her guard. Lex bounced from one foot to the other, her dainty hands balled into tight fists level with her chin. Sweat glistened against her golden skin.

The pilot moved with a steadiness that belied her normally manic energy and her eyelids narrowed to slits in concentration.

She didn't give Finn a chance to make the first move and unloaded with a salvo of vicious strikes. Finn easily dodged them and rolled away from the flurry. The hybrid pulled her knee up like she planned to kick her opponent in the midsection and Finn dropped her guard low to defend. Halfway through the motion, Lex rotated her hip over and up, swinging into a roundhouse that just narrowly missed grazing Finn's temple.

"Nice!" Finn risked a moment to congratulate Lex, who followed up with another wild but ultimately predictable punch and kick combination.

After a few seconds of nearly identical dodging to Lex's charging burst, Finn took a step back and countered Lex clean on the chin with a single right cross. Spit sprayed from the pilot's mouth in an arc and her body spun around from the impact, before landing on the mats in a heap.

Finn closed the distance to stand over her as her dazed opponent began to sit up.

"What did you do wrong?" Finn asked her, as she offered the girl a gloved hand. She may have felt more confident in her abilities than ever before, but she still refused to be reckless with that confidence.

Lex took her outstretched hand and pulled herself to her feet as she released a puff of air. The twin periwinkle poofs on top of her head wobbled slightly with the movement. She brought a finger to her chin and popped her jaw, while simultaneously rolling her eyes as she pretended to think.

"I got punched in the head . . . *really* hard."

"If only sarcasm could keep you alive in the real world," Finn pointed out, bringing her fingers up to pinch the bridge of her nose in annoyance. "You surprised me with that kick, but instead of keeping me off-balance, you went back to the same attack pattern. Put simply, you got greedy. Then you got sloppy."

"Then I got punched," Lex pointed out matter-of-factly.

Argh! They are going to be the death of me. "Go get some water before I beat some sense into you."

"Hey, if it hasn't worked yet . . ." Lex trailed off as she tapped the reddened, already bruising skin at her chin where Finn's fist had connected. She smiled wide and blew Finn a kiss before turning away. Finn released a sigh of vexation from somewhere deep in her soul and watched the pilot skip to the back of the room.

Eat, sleep, fight. Eat, sleep, fight.

They never strayed from the routine, with many of the crew displaying a focus and a discipline she hadn't thought them capable of. Every day held more of the same, yet each of them devoured their training with a voracious appetite that rivaled that of a Khaleerian. Inevitably, as groups were wont to do when they spend every waking moment together, the young hybrids had begun to form a bond that ranged from grudging respect to outright friendship.

They'd been so consumed with their training, Finn barely had time to think—let alone question—Grim further about his plans for "war" and the "secret weapon" he'd mentioned their first day on Tuathan.

A thought flashed briefly in Finn's mind and, as had happened often over the last two weeks, a wave of guilt swiftly followed. She hadn't seen the captain once in the last two weeks. He had kept to himself ever since she'd begged him to go along with the training.

A sharp grunt of pain sounded to Finn's right and she turned, pushing Shane and her guilt to the background to focus on the sparring duo nearest her.

Jax rushed in, swarming Mace with a wall of kicks and punches. The winged hybrid avoided most of the strikes while holding a high guard, and spun quickly to take the hits he couldn't defend on the distal side of his leathery wings. With his usual degree of cockiness, Jax grinned at Mace's retreat and relaxed his guard infinitesimally.

Mace's head turned slightly and noted the subtle change in his opponent's stance. Without hesitation, the boy flew into action—literally—and used his wings to propel his compact body forward as his feet left the ground. He tackled Jax in a blur of movement. The two went to the ground hard and rolled to a stop with Mace on top. He then used his forearm to put pressure on Jax's throat. He waited for his opponent to tap on it before letting him up, as a wide grin broke out on his face.

"Hey, no fair. I thought we weren't using our abilities today," Jax whined. Several of the lavender spikes of his hair were damp with sweat and hung in his eyes. Some days, they sparred no-holds-barred, using their abilities to gain the upper hand. Other times, they fought without them, using only their skill to win.

"You're just mad I wiped the floor with your ass." The boy's bright smile never wavered, and his dark eyes danced with humor and pride as he helped the pilot to his feet.

"Well, *duh*. My ass is far too pretty to be wiping floors," Jax grumbled and brushed his hands against his pants. His

amber eyes shot to Finn and went wide with mock indignation as he pointed to Mace. "Did you see that? He cheated!"

Finn let out a short laugh and brought her hands to her hips.

"I saw you relax your guard." Jax rolled his eyes at the
subtle reprimand, but she ignored his theatrics and turned
her gaze to Mace. "Good job, kid."

The instant the words drifted from her lips, Finn froze,
and her chest squeezed with pain. Oblivious to her distress,
Mace beamed with pride at the praise, and his sun-kissed
skin reddened with embarrassment . . . making him look so
much like AJ, the accompanying grief punched a fist-sized
hole into the center of Finn's heart.

She expelled an awkward cough and moved in the opposite direction, trying to shake off the painful reminder. She
retreated with the slowest gait she could manage, not wanting to look like she was running away. Her feet came to a
stop as she passed by Iliana and Enyo where they sparred a
few feet away.

Enyo stalked the mat, moving back and forth while keeping eye contact with Iliana. The courtesan maintained a
tight "Steel Dam" high guard and watched the feline hybrid's
pacing over her own taped wrists. Enyo gave Iliana a lopsided smile, revealing a row of sharp fangs.

Finn remembered the first night she'd met the half-Sirian.
She remembered the way Enyo had sprinted into a dive and
slashed a Reliance soldier's throat without blinking . . . before
Finn herself had even managed to blink. The soldier had been
dead before he'd had a chance to scream.

Fortunately, Enyo kept her claws sheathed during training.

"Your guard is too rigid," she called through her smile.
"Makes you open to sweeps."

After a beat, Enyo's yellow eyes gleamed. Demonstrating
the validity of her words, she dropped her weight slightly and
kicked a lean, furred leg out. With graceful calculation, she
hooked it behind Iliana's knees. Given that the courtesan's

peripheral vision was obscured by her hands, she had to scramble backward. Enyo easily flipped the beautiful redhead ass over teakettle.

Iliana landed roughly but made no noise other than a sharp grunt on impact. She rose slowly, her indigo eyes intent as she kept a steady gaze on Enyo, who bounced on her toes with her fanged mouth tipped in a half-grin.

She was toying with the courtesan.

Despite Iliana's impressive progress, she still proved no match for the ferocious hybrid and they both knew it. Though Enyo obviously had a crush on Finn's older sister, her feelings had not interfered with their training. A true *N'Goza* would never take it easy on anyone. To Enyo and her people, such an act would be considered a clear—and unforgivable—sign of disrespect. Given the way Enyo's eyes lit up with unmasked desire every time Iliana walked into the room, it was clear the furred hybrid would rather eat her own hand than disrespect Finn's sister.

Iliana got back into her ready stance, adjusting her position to the more mobile "rampage" stance. Shifting her weight forward with both fists in front of her, Iliana's eyes lit with determination, while Enyo's danced with amusement . . . and just a touch of respect.

"Too aggressive," Enyo explained, her grin expanding as she eyed the courtesan with a predatory gaze. "Now there is no way for you to defend against a more forceful opponent." She shot forward and launched a barrage of punches that battered Iliana's arms and forced her to retreat or else fall beneath the torrent of blows. "This is not a dance; you have to *feel* the moves."

Iliana flexed her sore arms and shook them out while contemplating her next step. After a moment, she settled into the balanced "jailbreak" stance, distributing her weight with a slightly heavy rear leg.

Enyo regarded her for a moment with a degree of mirth.

"Much better. You are more suited for—"

While she was mid-sentence, Iliana hopped forward and thrust her knee toward Enyo's stomach. When the half-Sirian moved to defend it, Iliana jerked her leg back and shifted the power from the kick into a right straight punch that drilled Enyo directly between the eyes, bloodying her nose.

"You're talking too much," Iliana rolled her shoulders as she egged the female on.

Finn's chest swelled with pride and she bit her lip to keep from grinning outright.

"So I am," Enyo said in a husky voice. She wiped at her nose with the back of her tufted fist, which only served to smear blood across her face. Her eyes heated and her lids went half-mast as she looked Iliana up and down slowly, pausing briefly to linger on her curves.

She surged forward, covering several meters before Iliana could prepare. As soon as the female was in striking distance, Iliana retreated three measured steps, then changed angles. Her sudden display of competent footwork took Enyo by surprise, and before she could re-engage, Iliana unleashed a barrage of rapid-fire punches to the side of her face. Instead of falling, Enyo turned it into a roll and returned to her feet a couple meters away.

The two exchanged and parried bone-crushing strikes, nearly ending the fight with a single blow multiple times . . . had any of them landed.

Enyo spun and threw a punch, but Iliana anticipated it. She shoved her shoulder into Enyo's armpit and grabbed her by the wrist, before heaving the larger hybrid bodily to the mat. Finally, she added her own body weight to the force that slammed Enyo onto her back. Iliana straddled the female and waited for Enyo's swimming vision to focus on her.

"If you ever toy with me again, I'll do worse than this," she hissed.

Enyo's bloody lips spread into a macabre grin. With a shift of her hips, she rolled. Taking Iliana by surprise, she kept going until the courtesan lay beneath her in the same position she'd held Enyo in mere seconds ago. Straddling Finn's sister, Enyo leaned down slowly until their noses almost touched. She ran a finger down Iliana's cheek tenderly and whispered, "I am counting on it, *Weywun*."

Had Finn not stood so close, she might have missed the whispered promise. She didn't know the meaning of the Sirian word, but the way Enyo had said it—her voice dripping with promise—Finn wasn't sure she *wanted* to know. Iliana's cheeks and exposed collarbone flushed a pretty shade of pink, and her tongue came out to swipe nervously at her lower lip. Enyo's eyes flared hungrily as she tracked the movement. As the courtesan continued to stare up at the female holding her down, Iliana's breathing increased, pushing her chest into Enyo's with every exhale. Several seconds passed, yet neither woman moved.

Flushing with secondhand embarrassment at the women's obvious attraction to each other, Finn hastily pursed her lips to whistle at the duo, signaling an end to the fight—or whatever this had become. Before she had a chance to inhale, a loud roar turned their attention. Finn spun to see Grim and Axel in a heated standoff. Axel's normally tan skin had darkened to a deep and angry crimson, and his already significant mass had expanded to at least twice its usual size. Now, the mild-mannered half-Khaleerian stood horn-to-horn with Grim . . . and he looked spitting mad.

They had all learned the hard way that—like all Khaleerians (with the exception of Grim)—Axel's abilities and his anger went hand in hand; one feeding the other in an endless cycle of rage and bedlam.

Over the last few weeks, Grim had worked with Axel individually, teaching him to control the intense anger that caused the switch from gentle giant to red-skinned berserker. Eventually, he would learn to capitalize on his Khaleerian strength without losing that careful control, the same way

Grim had. For the most part, Axel managed to keep the beast leashed during his sparring sessions.

Something had changed today though, and that careful control had snapped.

Grim dodged a punch that would have caved in his head, then another intended to pulverize his windpipe.

"Find your control, Axel. Your strength does not just come from your size and muscles; it lies in your restraint. *Focus*," Grim coached, while he kept moving to avoid the hybrid's fury.

Axel's only response was a guttural bellow that rent the air as he attempted to batter Grim with his massive strength. Grim anticipated the rush and grabbed the young fighter's horns. He then turned to the side before digging his heels into the mat. Using both arms, he wrenched Axel's neck so hard a loud pop sounded, signaling a tendon had torn itself loose.

Axel practically frothed at the mouth as he fought through the pain and struggled against Grim's hold. Without mercy, Grim lifted him and slammed the male face-first into the mat with so much force, Finn could feel it through the floor.

"Stay down, boy." Grim relaxed his hold slightly so as not to further injure the younger Axel.

Axel ignored the growled order and surged upward, throwing Grim off like a cloak with a loud roar of fury. The huge Khaleerian landed unceremoniously, but quickly returned to his feet, his eyes never leaving Axel's. He held out a hand, palm down, and slowly approached the male as one would an injured animal.

"You are too lost in your rage to be effective. Stand down. I do not wish to injure you further."

Spittle gathered at the corners of Axel's mouth as he panted through bared fangs, too lost in his berserker rage to see reason. In response to Grim's calm tone, he pounded both fists against his chest and yelled unintelligibly.

"If you will not learn control today, you will learn pain," Grim warned. He moved his right foot to the rear and bent his knees. When he raised both hands, palms out, he stood in the defensive "bullfighter" stance—one specifically created for taking on the Khaleerian berserker fighting style.

Without hesitation, Axel launched forward with the speed of a vicious predator and lowered his head in an attempt to run Grim through. The Khaleerian barely acknowledged the young male's horns, and instead grabbed one with his right hand. Using his left knee, he lifted Axel into the air and yanked down hard, slamming him onto his back.

Grim returned to his stance just in time for Axel to scramble to his feet and throw a wild overhead punch with enough power to end the large Khaleerian's life. Instead of meeting it head-on as many would have expected, her former mentor swept his rear leg in a backward arc, causing Axel to fly past him.

Barely deterred, the hybrid came back immediately, swinging his arms in deadly arcs. Each one came closer and closer to connecting.

Having separated from Iliana, Enyo hustled to Finn's side and moved toward the two giants as though she meant to interfere. Finn stayed her with a hand to her furred forearm and a slight shake of her head.

She turned to the rest of the crew watching the fight with varying degrees of horrified expressions and added, "Everyone stay back."

Grim threw a sharp three-punch combination that flattened Axel's nose and shattered the bones around one eye. Even still, he remained standing.

"I will need to apologize to Isis after this," Grim grumbled before adopting "red rain," a formless set of techniques used to maximize damage in close quarters.

As soon as Axel was within arm's reach, several things happened at once. Grim threw a vicious knee that further shattered the broken bones in Axel's face. The Khaleerian then followed up with a wall of punches. Each one snapped Axel's head back with so much force, the flesh on Grim's knuckles blew apart.

As Axel's hands came up to guard his ruined face, Grim grabbed one arm and lifted him above his head. He dropped him onto one shoulder, dislocating it. Axel howled in pain, which only served to fuel his unbridled rage. When the young male spun to strike with his uninjured arm, Grim grabbed it by the wrist and threw his legs over Axel's face and chest, effectively trapping his arm. Axel snapped his fangs and continued to buck and grab at Grim. In response, the Khaleerian wrapped his legs around the appendage and arched his back, hyperextending and breaking the arm at the elbow.

The hybrid's ferocious roar echoed around them as he ripped free from Grim's hold. Axel's breath came ragged and hoarse as he regarded the Khaleerian with rage-filled eyes.

"Last chance," Grim panted from the exertion of keeping the young male at bay. "Stand do—"

He wasn't given a chance to finish. Axel leapt forward and once again bared his fangs, this time in an attempt to tear out Grim's throat.

He shouldn't have bothered.

Grim intercepted the charge, but instead of attacking him high, he grabbed Axel by the ankle and jerked his leg upward. Once Axel was airborne, Grim dug his fingers into Axel's hip and twisted his hands in two different directions.

He howled in agony, but Grim didn't stop until he heard the bones in Axel's femur, patella, and shin splinter and shatter. Finn's stomach turned at the sound and she winced as Axel screamed in pain and fell to the mat in a motionless heap.

As he lay there, the rest of Axel's bones began to snap and pop as they shifted inside his body and he returned to his normal size and color.

"Continue with your training," Grim growled as he lifted the pale, young man. His eyes shot to Jax. "You come with me." Jax rushed to obey. Before they reached the door, Grim called to Isis where she stood in a corner and watched the hybrids with equal parts concern and interest. "Isis, meet us in my quarters in fifteen."

As soon as the door closed behind Grim, Jax, and Axel, the room erupted into movement as the fighters resumed their sparring. Despite their worry for their friend and the extreme levels of violence they'd just witnessed, each one had learned it wise not to argue with Grim. Now, not even the boldest of them dared to question the Luminary's orders.

Finn switched directions and made her way over to Isis.

Isis's silver eyes focused on her as she neared. As they registered her approach and the undoubtedly shell-shocked expression on her face, the tall, blue female forced a weak smile. Finn snagged a nearby towel and doused it in ice-cold water from one of several buckets against the wall.

Cool droplets ran down her heated skin as she wiped her face with the cold cloth and settled it around the back of her neck. She tightened the end of the braid hanging over her shoulder and attempted to return the Aquariian's kind smile.

"Enjoying the show?"

The smile fell from Isis's face and her lips twisted in disgust she didn't try to hide. "'Enjoying' is not the word I would use. But I understand the necessity behind Grim's instructions."

Finn followed her stare over to Raven and Sasha where the two sparred several feet away. Raven threw a haymaker that Sasha easily slipped. Even at unpowered speeds, the speedster proved too fast. Undeterred, Raven followed her movements and launched a five-punch combination. Sasha continued to dodge them until Raven changed things up with a hard kick to the midsection that finally connected. Her momentum was cut short as she doubled over from the impact. Sucking in a breath, Sasha tried to straighten up to defend. Raven continued to pepper the girl with potshots, then used clever footwork to dance away from Sasha's telegraphed power punches that never landed.

With every whiff, her eyes narrowed further in frustration.

After almost getting clipped with a hook to the temple, Raven dodged left just as a gleam took over Sasha's eyes and she launched herself with frenzied superspeed at the half-Chihiri. Surprised, Raven struggled to defend against Sasha's remarkable velocity. The hesitation cost the dark-purple fighter and she was just a few seconds too slow. The bone of Sasha's shoulder connected with the girl's face with a sickening *crunch*. Blood gushed from Raven's wide nose and she doubled over in pain.

Isis flinched at the sound and a grimace shadowed her symmetrical features.

"Dammit, Sasha!" Raven's muffled yell stopped Sasha's celebrations. "You used your powers!"

Sasha grinned and shrugged her shoulders before resuming her celebration.

"I take it you're not looking forward to healing that later?" Finn prodded in a casual tone. She wouldn't ask outright, but she needed to know how Isis was holding up. Healing them day in and day out had to be taking its toll on the woman.

Isis shifted her silver gaze back to her and Finn took a moment to study the woman's face. Some of the iridescence had left her blue complexion and the area under her eyes looked to be a few shades darker than the rest.

From fatigue?

Folding her slender hands in front of her, Isis returned her stare to the sparring duos a few feet away. Lex had run a towel over to Raven and she and Sasha stood shoulder to shoulder as they helped to press the material to her face and stem the flow of blood.

"You don't need to worry about me, Finn."

Either she hadn't been subtle enough in her questioning or the Aquariian was even more astute than she'd been giving her credit for.

"How *are* you feeling, though?" Finn pushed. "Healing all of us so regularly has to be exhausting."

Isis's lips tilted in a small smile and she shrugged her shoulders. "It is what my people do."

"Yeah, I know . . . ebbs and flows with nature," Finn repeated Isis's words back to her, "You're still not answering the question."

The female's smile widened. "I appreciate your concern, Finn, but I am well. The Reliance drones on this planet have several blind spots, thanks to the Tuathans. Tiri and I tend to gardens in each of them. I have everything I need to keep my strength up."

Long moments passed as she studied the Aquariian, looking for some hint of deception. She found none. Finn decided to let the matter drop and the two fell into a casual silence as they watched them. They stayed that way, with only the sounds of the occasional grunt or thud of flesh connecting with flesh between them, until Isis finally broke it.

"You've done well with them."

"I feel cheap taking the credit," Finn quipped as stared at her gloved hands. "My abilities did most of the work."

"You have a way of bringing people together, Finn. You always have. Those people have become a true team over the last two weeks. That you *can* take credit for."

Her whispered praise brought a blush to Finn's cheeks.

Fortunately, she was saved from having to answer when the room went quiet. The skin on Finn's arms buzzed with awareness as she turned to see that all the bodies in the room had stilled.

All the bodies save for two.

The frozen hybrids' gazes were focused on the far side of the room where the low hum of violence filled the air. She was used to them sparring hard with everything they had—Gods knew they kept Isis working overtime because of it—but they never fought each other with the intent to commit grievous bodily harm.

The same could not be said for the duo sparring across the mats.

Aedan and Conrad fought like their lives depended on the outcome of their match and they intended to do as much damage as they could to one another in the process.

Conrad flexed his hands repeatedly. His eyes blazed as he stared at Aedan across the mat. Without warning, he launched himself at Aedan with astonishing speed. Aedan evaded the flying high knee aimed at his chin and the subsequent winging hooks, causing them to miss their mark by mere centimeters. He continued to defend, taking the stinging rain of Conrad's wild punches on his arms, but didn't respond with any type of offense.

Conrad huffed in frustration before re-committing to the onslaught, and another fusillade of attacks hammered anything that Aedan's high guard didn't manage to defend.

"I don't suppose you know what that's about?" Isis's sharp gaze assessed Finn with a knowing stare and broke her focus on the fight. Only then did she realize her mouth had been hanging open.

"Not the slightest."

Had her voice not quivered, she felt sure the Aquariian would've believed her. Instead, the female's silver eyes hardened, and she clicked her tongue with disappointment.

"I'm needed in Grim's quarters. You'd better put a stop to that before they hurt themselves," she motioned to the two locked in a fierce battle, "in a way I can't heal."

Before Finn could respond, the Aquariian turned and exited the room with long, graceful strides. With a will of their own, Finn's eyes returned to the mat.

Conrad landed a punch, followed by a sneaky elbow throw that opened a wide gash over Aedan's left eye. The injury sprayed blood immediately. Aedan retreated to assess the damage, but Conrad was already all over him, and a relentless barrage of malicious intent followed. Still retreating, Aedan tried to blink his bloody eye clear. Conrad took advantage of the distraction and unloaded a series of vicious punches and elbows to the other's blind side, landing a hard straight that had Aedan stumbling backward.

"Enough!" Aedan growled. "Whatever you think is going on between me and Finn, you're wrong." Conrad's chest heaved with exertion, but he was too far gone into his rage to hear anything Aedan said. Aedan's face was a grisly mess of blood and bruises, and as Conrad took a step back to catch his breath, Aedan advanced.

Approaching him, Aedan held his hand to the cut above his eye. When he'd almost reached striking range, he flicked his hand forward. Flying droplets of his dark blood landed in Conrad's eyes, turning the blue to red, and partially blinding him.

"Do you think you can intimidate me?" He launched a knee at Conrad's unprotected midsection and connected with the hard flesh of his abdomen. "I was raised in the Dome. It's going to take a lot more than a lovelorn *boy* to cow me." At the clear insult, Conrad's jaw clenched. He wiped at his eyes, attempting to clear them. Aedan swung a short hook to Conrad's abdomen, barely missing his liver, pushing the air from Conrad's lungs in a rush. All the while, he kept up his dialogue. "I would kill you where you stand if I didn't think it would upset Finn."

Conrad stumbled backward, but Aedan wouldn't let him reset. As soon as Conrad attempted to create space, Aedan filled it. Rather than throw a barrage of strikes as Finn would have done in the same situation, Aedan stalked Conrad and sniped him with precision punches. Each one was thrown with the clear intent to frustrate and damage simultaneously.

Within seconds, Conrad's lips were split, one eye had swelled shut, and his nose was clearly broken. He breathed deeply from his mouth. Taking advantage of his opponent's condition, Aedan paused a moment to sear the flesh above his eye shut with the heat generated from his hands.

"I didn't want this," he told Conrad, "But I don't leave fights unfinished and I'm tired of letting you use me as a punching bag just because you're too stupid to put two and two together."

Aedan cocked his arm back to deliver a finishing blow.

It never connected.

Aedan's arm froze and hung midair, inches from Conrad's face. Aedan stared at his immobile fist in confusion. Bringing his other hand up to grab his immobile forearm, he attempted to propel it into motion, but the appendage refused to budge. Finally, his puzzled gaze flew to Conrad's. His eyes radiated an azure glow of warning. The half-Merlidian narrowed his eyes in concentration—his hybrid abilities on full display— and Aedan was flung back by the unseen force.

"You talk too much," Conrad told the half-Solidarian.

The air around them crackled with energy. The hair of Finn's arms stood on end.

Released from Conrad's hold, Aedan's eyes focused in, an equal mix of fury and determination. As he straightened, smoke began to waft up from the dark skin of his arms and tiny licks of flames began to form at his fingertips.

All at once, Finn's muscles unlocked, and she sprinted over to the pair. She knew they'd never hear her whistle, as focused as they were on killing each other. Before he could unleash the flames building in his hands, Conrad double-jabbed Aedan in the chin and he fell back against the wall. The bald hybrid brought his hand—now engulfed in flames—up to his mouth and spit blood. His black eyes looked as though they too would begin to shoot fire, though Finn didn't believe such a thing was possible even with his abilities. He prepared to push away from the wall and launch himself at Conrad.

Finn dove between them.

"Stop!"

She held an arm out to Aedan's chest, careful to avoid the blaze. She kept him back with minimal pressure and his hands began to cool, dousing the flames. Her other arm shot out at Conrad as she stared down the glow of his angry eyes. The large man had already moved to strike another blow, but paused mid-punch when he saw her. His giant fist stopped mere inches from her face, before dropping to his side.

Aedan pushed her away gently and straightened from the wall. Steam wafted up from his arms and he looked to be a breath away from lighting the whole place on fire. Both men's large, sinewy muscles flexed with aggression and their chests heaved with each heavy breath. Conrad swiped at a dread that had fallen loose during their struggle and leveled Finn with a glare that should have turned her to stone.

"Since when do you get a say on when the fight ends? Last I checked that was the Luminary's job," Conrad growled, breathing heavily. His words were slightly muffled by his swelling lower lip.

"Grim isn't here, which is probably why you both felt so comfortable trying to kill each other when you *should* be preparing for what lies ahead." Finn let that sink in as her eyes scanned the room. "You're not here for fun and," she returned her furious glare to Aedan and Conrad, pausing her examination at each of their bloody injuries as she looked them both over, "you're *definitely* not here to live out some barbaric pissing contest over who has the bigger bulge in their pants."

"Yeah, we all know I'd win that contest anyway!"

Jax had cupped his hands at his mouth to yell. Some of the tension leaked from the room as a few of the others laughed at his jest.

Finn bit her cheek so hard she tasted blood. She counted to five as she waited for the blaze of anger to fade and took a deep breath. "We're done for today. Hit the showers and

get some dinner," she ordered. As they began to file out, Finn
returned her attention to Conrad and Aedan and lowered her
voice. "*This*," she motioned between them, "doesn't happen
again. Get me?"

Conrad gritted teeth his teeth and shot a humorless
smile at Aedan.

"Afraid I might hurt your lover boy?"

"Time's up, Finn," Aedan growled.

She knew what he meant. Honest to the Gods, she hadn't
meant for the lie to go on this long or lead to such violent
consequences, but now that it had, there was no way in hell
she planned on setting the record straight here and now.

Aedan must have read as much in her eyes. His expression
became thunderous, and she withered under the heat of it.
She pleaded with her eyes, silently begging for just a little
more time. Seeing it, some of the aggression leaked from his
body, replaced by resigned frustration. His wide shoulders
sagged slightly.

Finn offered him a barely perceptible nod, as her eyes
screamed their gratitude. When she could no longer take it,
her guilty stare flitted away from his and she moved from her
position between them. Conrad's eyes stared between them,
their glow intensifying.

"Those kids need someone to look up to," she muttered,
soldiering on with her lecture. "I don't know what Grim has
planned for the Reliance, but whatever it is *will* get ugly . . . for
them and for us. What you two pulled today can't happen again."

No one spoke for long moments. The awkward silence
rolled over her in waves, leaving discomfort in its wake. Both
men still squared off, their stances dripping with aggression
and their eyes shining with the promise of violence. Finally,
when Finn felt sure she could take no more, Aedan nodded
once in affirmation. Then he rolled his eyes and stomped
away. It was clear his patience had run short, and she'd begun
to test the limits of his loyalty.

As Aedan was one of two people Finn actually relied on these days, the realization that she may have pushed him too far stung.

Sighing, Finn decided she would find the time to set the record straight with Conrad. Maybe he'd be angry enough about the lie, he'd forget he ever liked her and leave her alone as she'd originally intended. Yes, she'd find the time . . . it just wouldn't be today.

Conrad shifted slightly, reminding her of his presence. When she looked back up at him, the bright glow of his eyes held hers. The anger she glimpsed in them was palpable. She could see nothing in them of the affection that had once shone so brightly there each time their gazes had connected. The glow slowly dimmed, apathy sliding into place behind them and replacing the anger. He looked her over once more with a detached stare, before he too turned and stomped away without a word.

Fighting back the urge to shiver, Finn threw a curtain over her thoughts and forced herself to focus on something mundane. *Shower. Eat. Sleep.*

She was so lost in the thought, that she almost didn't notice Conrad stopping abruptly a few feet from the door. He took an abrupt step back as it opened to reveal Zekiel. The Tuathan's long, silvery dreads swayed with his steps as he rushed inside.

Finn noted the concerned expression shadowing his features and tensed. His amber eyes took in Conrad, then the empty room, before finally falling on Finn.

"Where's Grim?"

The urgency in his tone spurred Finn forward and her gut churned with dread. She made it to them in short seconds, never taking her eyes off Zekiel.

"What's happened?"

"Grim," the Tuathan leader repeated impatiently. "Where is he?"

"In his quarters," Conrad answered.

"Go and get him. Meet us in the control room." When Conrad didn't immediately move to follow orders, Zekiel yelled, "Now!"

Finn jumped in surprise at the authority in the normally docile man's tone. Rather than reacting with annoyance as most would do when spoken to in such a way, Conrad moved with lightning speed to rush out of the room and follow Zekiel's command.

Something bad has happened. Something really *bad.*

Zekiel glanced over at her and made an impatient gesture with his hands for her to get moving.

"Come with me."

NINE

The copper tang of fear coated her tongue and throat as Finn stood near a console in the control room and forced shallow breaths in and out of her lungs. She watched in silence as all of them—with the addition of Grim, Shane, and Isis—joined her and Zekiel in the control room. The captain had picked a hell of a time to make a reappearance. Her eyes took him in from top to toe, and she couldn't help but notice the extreme differences in his appearance since the last time she'd seen him.

The hollows of his cheekbones seemed more defined, and his clothes hung a little looser, as though he'd lost weight. A week's growth of dark-blond stubble covered his chin and his vibrant, green eyes looked dull, with little life behind them.

From behind him, Iliana's panicked indigo gaze found Finn and the courtesan rushed around him to her side. Enyo and Aedan followed closely on her heels.

"What's going on?" Enyo whispered under her breath.

"I don't know," Finn whispered back.

Grim made his way over to Zekiel and towered over the Tuathan leader when he reached his side. The Khaleerian's dark eyes shone with fury—at what she had no idea.

"Tell me," he ordered.

The fish markings on Zekiel's cheek began to glow. He pushed a few buttons on a round pad he held in his hand and the images on the holoscreens floating above them changed until they all showed the same thing. Finn's breath lodged itself in her throat as she took in the familiar muck-covered streets of the Mud Pit.

"Things have been quiet in the Outer Rings lately . . . too quiet. We've been watching closely, had our ears to the ground. There was nothing . . . until today." The muscles in the Tuathan leader's face twitched slightly. The glow of his markings shone brighter, and his amber stare focused on the screen in front of him. The images changed to reveal dozens of pods taking off into the sky, spraying mud and grime in their wake. "The soldiers began evacuating the Mud Pit this morning."

"What do you mean, *evacuating*?" Grim growled. His dark eyes scanned the screens and his large, red hands balled into fists.

"Just a few groups at a time, not enough to draw attention . . . until now." Zekiel motioned with his head to the countless pods readying to break atmosphere. "That was the last of them. There is no longer any Reliance presence on planet. Only the Mudders remain," he said, referring to the Mud Pit's lower-caste residents.

The screens switched again and flashed back to images of the Mud Pit's streets. Many of the lower-caste population—from peddler to doxie—braved the caustic rain to watch the pods disappear from sight. Their bewilderment was clear even through the screens.

"Why would they do this?" Iliana asked.

"Yeah, and why are *we* here?" Raven jerked her thumb between herself and the hybrids nearest her—Lex and Sasha—and her eyes widened. In any other situation, her obvious puzzlement would have been comical. Many of the other hybrids mirrored her confusion as they looked at one another uneasily.

"Sir!" One of the Tuathans seated behind a console at the back of the room waved an arm in the air to gain Zekiel's attention. "Sir, they're shutting off the oxygen!"

The room exploded into a cacophony of shouts and commotion as the Tuathan's fingers began to press keys rapidly and several others spoke into the comms at their ears in hushed voices. Dimly, Finn heard someone release an agonized yell, followed by the sound of fists slamming against the walls. Hands grasped at her, shaking Finn's shoulder, but she barely felt it. She couldn't tear her eyes from the screens.

They're shutting off the oxygen.

She heard a desperate cry and recognized Iliana's voice.

"Do something!"

"Dear Gods," Shane whispered.

"There is nothing we can do." Zekiel's voice was ragged with emotion. "I'm so sorry."

They can't do this. They can't just kill an entire planet.

Even as she thought the words, Finn knew they weren't true. The Arcturians had already proven they could do whatever they wanted; this was just another horrifying example.

"I can't watch," Raven moaned.

Several of the others echoed her sentiment and fled the control room in a rush.

Still, Finn didn't look away.

The people of the Mud Pit began to realize something wasn't right. Their movements became sluggish, their breathing labored.

Hot tears carved a pathway down Finn's cheeks as she watched them fall to their knees one by one.

None of the screens showed images from inside the Dirty Molly but she knew Doc would be there, like he always was, pouring drinks and keeping the mood light with one of his ridiculous stories. The reptilian alien never failed to elicit a laugh once he really got going. She could imagine him waggling his nose in a way that would cause his glasses to teeter on his nose.

Doc.

The last time she'd seen him, he'd been pouring her a shot of the bar's finest dragon's breath as a special treat for her birthday.

Her chest ached so fiercely, she bent over in anguish.

"I can turn it off," one of the seated Tuathans offered.

"No!" Finn's scream split through the air and echoed around them. She felt Iliana, Enyo, and Aedan closing in behind her, lending her strength with their presence. "We have to see," she babbled, her voice high with her rising panic. "Someone has to bear witness."

"Leave it on." Grim's order left little room to be disobeyed. The screens remained on.

She couldn't put it into words they would understand, but these were her people and they were dying.

Finn tore her eyes from the horrifying images for just a split second to lock eyes with Grim. This was their home . . . the place that had brought them together. Anyone who didn't know better would have looked at the set of Grim's jaw and carefully masked features and assumed he felt nothing for the Mudders' suffering. But Finn did know better. She recognized the clench of his fists—so hard, the dark-red skin of his hands lightened to a pale pink—and the emotion behind the dark depths of his irises he tried to hide from her.

He gave her a short nod as if to say, *I am with you*, Dhala. She returned her gaze to the screens before the new wave of racking sobs could tear itself free from her chest.

Panic began to set in among the Mudders as more and more of them fell. Many scratched desperately at their own throats, willing to tear them out if it might grant them one more breath of precious oxygen. Eventually, their movements stilled. A rogue sob finally tore its way free, and she felt a warm hand wrap itself around hers and squeeze. Finn latched onto her sister's fingers and held on tight.

They watched until the very last one stopped moving.

"This was a message," Grim growled. His dark eyes scanned the room, menace firing from their dark depths. The Khaleerian's entire body vibrated with rage.

Finn's own shock had begun to wear off and started turning to a fiery anger.

An uncomfortable silence surrounded the group. The rest of the hybrids had rejoined them in the control room with the addition of Jax, a now-healed Axel, and a pale-looking Madam Califax. The genteel little woman looked ill, giving her a ghostly visage that stood stark against the backdrop of red fur she wore draped around her from neck to ankles.

"You're right," Zekiel told Grim. "There have been no reports of the death toll on the Mud Pit. This was meant to punish you and the disobedients . . . quietly."

Punishment?

The destruction of an entire planet's populace was hardly comparable to the spanking of an errant child. Yet, that was exactly how the Reliance most likely viewed their actions today. After all, none of them would miss a few million lower-caste Mudders.

"This was retaliation for the Dome." Grim took a step forward and outstretched his arms as he addressed the room. "The Reliance has just shown us exactly how they intend to fight in this war . . . *dirty.*"

"Hardly surprising," Lex muttered under her breath. The female's amber eyes shone with an intense anger out of character for her normally jocular disposition.

"Enough! We're all just standing around when we should be out there drawing blood!" Raven's braids swayed with her angry movements as she yelled.

Enyo grunted her agreement. The feline woman hadn't spoken since they'd been called to the control room, but her body thrummed with a violence that rivaled that of Grim and Finn's. Conrad stood next to Aedan at Finn's right, surprising her with his willingness to be in such close proximity to the one he'd been treating as his mortal enemy. Conrad's azure eyes glowed with emotion as he folded his muscled arms over his chest.

"How exactly are we supposed to fight back?" Finn asked. "They can kill an entire planet in minutes. What's to stop them from doing it again?"

Grim turned to her. His eyes lingered on Finn a moment before he spoke. "Regardless of how you may feel, you will not let it make you foolish. This changes nothing but our timeline. The Arcturians will be expecting our emotions to get the better of us. They'll be waiting for us to seek retribution, most likely with an arsenal at their backs ready to strike us down."

"We have to do something!" Mace pushed.

Grim's hard gaze left Finn to address the winged hybrid.

"We will. Half of you will leave tonight with Jax and Lex. You will take *Independence* and collect our allies."

"What allies?" Finn's voice sounded rough from the motions choking her.

Madam Califax hugged her own arms as though fighting off a chill. "There are many others like me throughout the Union. We need to get them here on Tuathan where they'll be safe."

"Some of our identities have already been compromised." Grim exchanged a look between Finn, Iliana, Conrad, and Shane. Ever since the Dome, the Reliance had been looking for the five "dangerous disobedients." Fortunately, the rest of them had yet to be identified. "We will need volunteers to accompany the twins."

"So, who wants to join our merry band of rescuers?" Jax asked with a grin. The humor didn't quite reach his eyes, however.

Aedan immediately stepped forward. Heat radiated from him. "I'll go."

Grim looked him up and down, nodding in approval.

"What are you doing?" Finn hissed at him in a low voice.

Aedan's dark eyes flitted between Finn and Conrad with meaning.

"I could use a change of scenery."

He was leaving because of her. Guilt wrapped itself around Finn like a familiar, worn blanket. Enyo's eyes flickered, showing just a hint of surprise at Aedan's choice, but she said nothing. The three of them were supposed to be a package deal . . . together until the end. She knew Enyo would remain on Tuathan with her, no matter how badly she wanted to help with the rescue. But Finn's selfishness had pushed Aedan too far.

"I'm sorry," she whispered to Aedan.

"It's for the best," he muttered gently. "They're going to need muscle to accomplish their goal." Suddenly his handsome face broke into a wide grin, revealing straight, white teeth. "And I've got plenty of those."

She recognized that he was letting her know all was forgiven, further solidifying her belief that he was a much kinder man than his menacing presence allowed people to see.

She forgot their audience and flinched when she looked away from Aedan to find Conrad watching their whispered conversation intently. His mind worked behind his glowing gaze, studying her as though she were a puzzle he couldn't quite put together. Her skin grew hot under the scrutiny. Discomfort made her retreat, and she broke eye contact with the hybrid immediately.

Axel was the next to volunteer, but Grim immediately shook his head in denial.

"You are not ready," he told the young half-Khaleerian, his tone softening.

"Please," Axel begged. "I need to do this." His skin had already begun to darken a few shades and his muscles bulged slightly more than they had before.

Grim raised his brows and looked Axel up and down with meaning.

"You would rescue them just to let your lack of control get them killed?"

The Khaleerian's gentle tone offset the harshness of his words slightly, but Axel still winced and hung his head in defeat. After a moment, he took a step back, obvious disappointment clouding his features, ending the argument. Raven and Mace were the next to volunteer and earn Grim's approval. In a move that shocked Finn, Madam Califax also threw her figurative feathered hat in the ring.

Next, it was Shane's turn to step forward.

"*Independence* doesn't leave without me on it." His firm tone and the stubborn set of his stubbled jaw left little room for argument. Grim immediately shook his head.

"The Reliance knows you are working against them now. Your presence would put everyone else at risk." Grim motioned to the twins and the other volunteers. "Would you forfeit their lives for pride?"

Shane's green eyes spit fire but he shut his mouth.

"The rest of us will remain here and prepare the weapon." Grim turned to Zekiel as he bit out a harsh, "Your timeline just moved up."

"But we're nowhere near ready," Shane stepped forward to interrupt. "Not to mention all the hybrids out there we haven't gotten to yet."

"We have what we need." Grim's hard tone brokered little room for argument. Several of the room's inhabitants sucked in a shocked breath as his words settled.

"What we *need*?" Shane whispered. His eyes widened with incredulous disbelief. "What the hell is that supposed to mean?" The captain's blond brows furrowed as realization began to dawn. "Are you saying that all this time we've been rescuing hybrids, we've really been recruiting them to fight *your* war?"

Silence.

No one even dared to breathe as the two squared off. Shane looked angrier than she'd ever seen him. The top of his head barely reached the Khaleerian's chin, but he refused to back down or be cowed. The captain's square jaw tilted slightly as he stared defiantly up at Grim.

"And what about this weapon? There are innocent people out there in the Inner Rings . . . good people who don't agree with the Reliance. Think about the collateral damage."

"They just killed an entire planet and all you can think about is your rich buddies?" Raven sneered.

"I have little empathy for those who disagree, yet reap the benefits of those they claim to abhor," Grim interrupted, reclaiming Shane's attention. "Our enemy is ruthless . . . or have you not been paying attention? If we want to win, we must be willing to fight just as dirty."

"If we play by their rules, we're no better than them. There must be another way. And what about me? I'm upper caste . . . I was born into it. Am I expendable to you? Is she?" he asked, pointing at Madam Califax.

Grim's eyes flitted over to the woman briefly before returning to Shane.

"Yes."

To Madam Califax's credit, she didn't even blink at Grim's casual agreement. Perhaps she already knew as much and didn't care. Shane sputtered in astonishment when Grim refused to elaborate. The captain's irate gaze flashed to Finn before returning to the Khaleerian.

"Finn was spot-on, and I didn't believe her . . . refused to believe her. But this is just about winning for you, isn't it? Nothing and no one else matter, as long as *you* beat the Reliance, isn't that right?"

Grim's apathetic gaze hardened.

"You have been a trusted ally, Shane, but if you no longer have the stomach to do what needs to be done, you are free to go anytime you wish." The Khaleerian leaned down and bared his fangs inches from the captain's face. "Just bear in mind, if you try to warn anyone of what we intend to do, it will be your last act in this galaxy."

Shane's mouth dropped open, and he moved back as though he had been violently pushed. His eyes flashed around the room in expectation. Was he waiting for someone to step in and set the Luminary straight? No one moved. Finally, Shane's gaze fell to Iliana.

"You're with me right, Iliana?"

Iliana's indigo eyes saddened, but the rest of her face remained carefully blank. She regarded him casually, as though the captain had just inquired about the weather. She said nothing for a long time. Shane's shoulders began to droop with every passing second. They straightened slightly with hope when the courtesan finally spoke, only to fall once more when her words reached him.

"If we stop now, nothing will change. We will always be hunted, as will our children and every generation that follows, until they wipe us out completely."

The truth of what she'd said settled somewhere deep within Finn. Until now, her end goals had been short-sighted and—if she were being totally honest—a little selfish . . . everything she'd ever accused Grim of. She'd gotten lost in her desire to *punish* the Reliance for everything they'd done . . . For AJ. *For Sophie.*

Watching the three of them locked in a staring contest, none of them relenting, Finn finally understood Grim's apparent lack of caring and his determination. This fight was no longer about them and their desire to see the Reliance fall . . . it was about the future of every hybrid, as well as those who had yet to be born.

Sasha broke the continued silence by stepping forward with immense haste and blurting, "I never signed up for this."

Finn's tight grip on her emotions slipped. The rage she'd carefully kept simmering finally boiled over.

"No, you just signed up for rescue and safety from the people you tried to kill," she spat.

Sasha's brown eyes widened with indignation and just a touch of wariness. "I never tried to kill you."

"Well, you certainly didn't help," Aedan added with a harsh growl as he took Finn's back.

Sasha looked between them and her wide eyes narrowed to angry slits. "It's not my fault AJ is dead."

Finn's hands itched with the urge to commit violence. Dimly, she heard a ringing in her ears and watched somewhat detachedly while her body took control and lunged for Sasha.

"I told you not to say his name!"

Sasha darted away in a blur of movement so fast, it looked like she had teleported across the room. One second, she was within striking distance, and the next she wasn't. Finn ignored the people screaming her name and grabbed a small knife from the sheath at her ankle. She palmed it and took aim, launching the blade at Sasha just as she came to an abrupt stop several feet away. It sunk into the meat of her thigh with a sickening squelch and Sasha fell to the ground with a pained cry before she even had time to flinch.

"Gods, Finn." Shane looked at her with a horrified gaze. His eyes drifted over her in disbelief as though she'd just sprouted horns and spit fire. "Was that necessary?"

"The blade went through the fat of the girl's thigh," Grim defended, struggling to hide the pride shining through his dark eyes. A fang came out to bite his crimson lip and hide the grin fighting to spread there. "Isis will have no trouble healing it."

"I don't have fat!" Sasha screamed between moans of pain.

Enyo spun to face Finn. She pounded her shoulder with a congratulatory punch that left Finn's arm stinging and chuckled outright. Aedan leaned down and squeezed her other shoulder.

"Good form," he whispered. "Next time, aim higher."

TEN

"Are you sure you want to do this?"

Finn stared up into Aedan's dark eyes and hoped he couldn't see the desperation in hers. Both his and Enyo's friendship had been like a balm to her battered soul these last few weeks. The idea of separating from either of them filled her with dread.

She and the rest of *Independence*'s ragtag crew—as well as Zekiel and a few of the Tuathans—had gathered in the docking bay to see their companions off. She had no idea where their mission would take them or how long it would be before they returned.

If they return.

Finn shook off the unwanted thought and refocused her attention on Aedan.

"Finn, I'm not leaving because of you, so you can let yourself off the hook," he told her gently, before motioning toward the younger hybrids preparing to board *Independence*. "They need me."

He spoke the truth. Aedan had proven himself to be a vicious warrior through and through. They'd all be safer with him on board.

"Why would you leave because of Finn? I thought you two were *close*." Enyo's lips twitched and her yellow eyes narrowed in mock confusion as she joined the pair.

Finn had since filled her furred friend in on the situation with Conrad and Aedan, only to have Enyo laugh hysterically for a full five minutes before unloading a barrage of constant ribbing and mockery.

Finn rolled her eyes to Enyo and feigned indignation.

"Mention it one more time and I'm telling my sister you have mange."

The female's eyes darkened with fury, but she clamped her mouth shut at Finn's threat. Ignoring her, Finn turned back to Aedan.

"Keep them safe," she told him in a low voice. Aedan's eyes flashed, filling with pain, and she realized her mistake immediately. She'd asked him the same thing in the Dome . . . the day AJ died. "I mean," she rushed to correct herself, "I know you'll take care of them—"

"I will," he interrupted her. He spoke the words like a vow, one she knew he intended to keep. "Take care of each other," he ordered them sternly, looking each in the eyes, before turning and making his way to *Independence*.

He didn't look back.

In the distance, Raven, Mace, Jax, and Lex chatted animatedly and said their goodbyes to the Tuathans. Hugs and complicated handshakes were exchanged. After a moment, Jax looked up. His amber eyes searched the bay until they landed on Axel and he immediately excused himself to approach him.

Axel stood far away from the others, looking despondent. His wary eyes tracked the pilot's approach, but Jax didn't seem to notice, never losing the spring in his step. He strode right up to the giant hybrid, grabbed his horned head, and pulled the male down for a passionate kiss. Axel stiffened in shock for a moment, before he, for all of his massive muscularity, all but melted into the pilot. After a moment of letting Jax take the lead, he reached down and lifted the half-Tuathan slightly to deepen the kiss and gain better access. Finn was pretty sure she saw tongues.

Lex whooped loudly, calling everyone's attention to her brother and his passionate lip-lock with the half-Khaleerian. Several of the others joined in with catcalls and applause.

When the pair finally pulled away, Jax was smiling lascivi-
ously and waving his hands in an attempt to egg their audience. Axel's skin reddened for a reason that had nothing to do
with his Khaleerian heritage. The pilot whispered something
to him and Axel nodded as a smile spread across his face.

Suddenly, the horned giant lifted Jax into his arms like
a bride and carried him to the ship, while the pilot waved
to every person they passed. Some of the tension left the
room as the others watched them go, laughing and cheering.
Finally, they crossed the distance to the ship in what was
quickly becoming one of the most dramatic goodbyes Finn
had ever witnessed.

Her heart ached as, one by one, the other hybrids began to
board *Independence* and disappear from view.

"They will be fine, *N'Goza*. You've trained them well,"
Enyo assured her, seeming to sense Finn's worry.

Finn spoke without turning, eyes locked on the depart-
ing ship. "I don't exactly have the best track record when it
comes to friends."

Sophie and AJ were dead. Conrad hated her and Tiri
barely looked in her direction the few times she'd seen the
girl. Granted, it had been all her fault for pushing them away
but still . . .

"You have me and that is all you need," the half-Sirian
declared. Finn smiled at Enyo's certainty. Her tawny brows
furrowed, daring Finn to contradict her. She didn't.

Shane and Sasha entered the bay then, carrying a few bags
filled with their belongings. Their arrival received much less
fanfare than the rest of the group. Both had agreed to hitch a
ride with *Independence* as far as Gliese, where they would be
dropped off. Neither had said what they planned to do after
that. Given the seriousness of Grim's threat and the ease with
which they all knew he would carry it through should they
disobey him, she knew whatever the duo ended up doing, it
wouldn't be warning the Reliance.

Shane reached Conrad where he stood near the ship. She had assumed he would join his brother in leaving Tuathan. For whatever reason, he had decided to stay. Finn tried not to think about the ache that had settled in her chest and refused to be rubbed away when she'd believed he was going, or the relief that had filled her when she realized he wasn't.

The pair bent their heads together in discussion for long moments, before finally grasping each other's hands. Conrad pulled Shane into a masculine embrace, one arm around his back, while the other held his hand. As Sasha passed them, she avoided Finn's eyes. She made her way to the ship with hurried steps and climbed inside without so much as a "see you later."

When Shane pulled away from Conrad, he surprised Finn by heading in her direction. Conrad followed a few feet behind, giving them space while also remaining close. When the captain reached her, his greens eyes flashed to Enyo.

"I need a minute with her."

Enyo ignored Shane and looked to Finn, refusing to be dismissed by anyone other than her friend. Finn gave her a nod, suddenly wearier than she'd been in days.

"It's fine," she said.

Enyo's eyes narrowed to slits in a silent warning to behave, before she turned and took off in the opposite direction. Out of the corner of her eye, Finn saw the furred hybrid making a beeline for Iliana. Shane waited until she was out of earshot and turned back to Finn.

"I figured of all people, I owed you a goodbye," the captain told her.

His green eyes regarded her with fondness, and she couldn't help but think of all the times they had instead eyed her with varying degrees of vexation and disbelief. Their relationship had always been a rocky one, since the day she'd hitched a ride on his ship and turned his life upside down.

"Why, because I've made your life a living hell?"

Shane flashed a megawatt smile that—she noted with surprise—reached his eyes, reminding Finn how handsome the
captain could be when his features weren't weighed down by
exhaustion and grief.

"Something like that."

They stood in awkward silence for a moment before Finn
broke it to ask, "What will you do?"

"I don't know." The captain's head dipped to avoid her
gaze. He wasn't quite quick enough though, and Finn noted
the tears pooling there. "I only ever wanted to keep AJ safe;
that's why I joined the Luminary in the first place. My whole
life has always been about him. Now that he's gone," the
captain cleared his throat to cover the break in his voice, "I
just can't seem to force myself to see it through."

At the mention of AJ, Finn felt a wave of fresh anguish
come over her. Her hands fisted at her sides, but the rest of
her remained immobile.

"Shane—"

At the sound of his name, his gaze came back up to meet
hers. "This plan of Grim's . . . I just can't be a part of it. I
want to help the hybrids, I really do. But after everything
that's happened . . . all the death. Somehow it feels like defil-
ing his memory."

Some might consider his decision cowardly, but she knew it
wasn't cowardice that had led the captain's path to diverge from
hers. She also knew how hard this had to be for him. He hadn't
been the same since AJ's death, and she understood his pain in a
way many of the others couldn't. Whereas Finn had channeled
her grief into revenge, Shane had chosen a different course.

"I understand, Shane. *He* would too." Some wordless fear
kept her from saying AJ's name aloud, as though the mere
act might cripple her with grief and a sense of failure that she
hadn't protected him.

"He wouldn't have wanted you to punish yourself, you
know?" Finn's breath caught in her. By unspoken agreement,

this was a subject they typically avoided. Shane's eyes softened as he took in her discomfort. "I always worried about him so much. The way he was . . . so angry all the time. Until you," he whispered softly.

Finn's heart began to pound furiously and she felt her eyes tearing up. "Shane—"

"You *saw* him, Finn. You saw him in a way no one else could—not even me—and you made him so damned happy."

One of the tears gathering at the corner of his eye fell, tracing a pathway down his stubbled cheek. She tried to stop him from speaking, but she couldn't get the word out—found herself choking on it. The captain bit out a hoarse laugh. "I think I was jealous of you. I'd never seen him like that . . . so happy and carefree. I couldn't believe I'd busted my ass for *cycles* just for the hint of a smile, and you came in and changed everything in a matter of weeks. I was a jerk when I should have been thanking you."

His laughter died, leaving his lips tilted in a sad smile. "I think the only thing that's kept me from falling apart these last few weeks is the knowledge that before he died, he was happy. I honestly didn't know if he'd ever get there, but *you* gave it to him. You got him there. I need you to believe that."

Finn clenched her fists until her knuckles cracked, but still, it didn't stop the tears from falling. She expelled a shallow breath, releasing the meteor-sized lump that had lodged in her throat. She didn't deserve this. She hadn't earned this man's kindness, but she soaked it up all the same. Had it been anyone else, she could've resisted. She could've swatted away their words like gnats. But not with Shane.

"I don't—I can't," she stumbled over her words. The captain finally took pity on her. He brought a hand up to squeeze her shoulder.

"Take care of yourself, Finn."

He didn't wait for a response. Turning, Shane walked away. As he passed Conrad, he tagged his brother behind the head and pulled him close until their foreheads touched. Releasing him, Shane climbed the ramp and disappeared inside *Independence*.

All the while Finn struggled to gain control over her emotions. She swiped at the wetness on her cheeks and forced air through her lungs. She had managed a few inhales and exhales by the time Conrad reached her side.

"I swear to the Gods," she told him in a menacing tone without looking up, "If you came over here just to be a dick, I'm going to kick you in yours. Hard."

When he didn't respond to her threat, she finally allowed her head to swing in his direction. He'd parked his large frame mere feet away. Her eyes moved over his dark complexion, marveling at the way it shone against the harsh glow of artificial lights. They drifted up past the markings covering the muscles of his arms and chest and stopped on his handsome face. His full lips turned down in a frown, but his eyes told a different story. They softened slightly when he noticed the remnants of her tears.

Conrad held his hands up in supplication.

"I just came to check on you. I know this must be hard for you." He motioned to the ship preparing to depart. "Are you okay?"

Finn nearly choked on a humorless laugh.

"Hard," she repeated in a low voice dripping with sarcasm. "You're going to have to be more specific. Are you referring to the culling of an entire planet we just watched or the fact that our home is taking off without us in it?"

It felt strange to refer to the ship—the place that had served as the site for so much upheaval and trauma in her life—as "home," but as she watched the doors close and the engines fire up, she realized that was exactly what it had become.

Home.

Though it was just a ship, and an outdated one at that, she realized that she would miss *Independence* just as fiercely as she would the people inside it. She took in the reflection of the artificial lights bouncing off the glossy, rust-colored plating of the ship.

Her eyes scanned down the aggressive modified scoop of the bow, a common addition to Dogwood '88 class ships. It made potential pirates think twice about trying to boost their wares. She memorized everything she could see—from stern to bow and the stubby rear nacelles that never seemed to serve a purpose.

Conrad shifted at her side, drawing her attention. Recognizing what she'd just given away, she clamped her mouth shut. He had a way of disarming her, getting her to reveal things she wasn't even ready to admit to herself.

Conrad tilted his head slightly, and his eyes narrowed in confusion. She blinked as she looked up at him, wondering what could've caused his sudden bewilderment. She studied him for a moment, looking for some trace of sadness at seeing the ship leave with his adopted brother on it. Aside from the confusion coloring his features, he appeared more at ease than she'd seen him in weeks.

"Wait, why aren't you going with Shane?" she asked him. "I thought you two were a package deal. Shouldn't you at least *pretend* to be sad?"

He brushed off her question as though he hadn't heard it.

"Actually, I was talking about the Solidarian." His gaze flitted back to the ship before returning to hers. "I know you must be upset to see him go, especially after everything that's happened." He explained his motives slowly, as though she were a toddler who had barely learned to grasp the English language.

"Oh, right," Finn mumbled. For a moment, Shane's emotional speech had thrown her off so much, she'd completely forgotten.

I think the only thing that's kept me from falling apart these last few weeks is the knowledge that before he died, he was happy. I honestly didn't know if he'd ever get there, but you gave it to him. You got him there. Whatever happens next, I need you to believe that.

Why couldn't Shane just say goodbye like everyone else? She would've gladly accepted a slap on the back and a jerk of the chin, rather than the emotional knife to the heart he'd given her.

"Finn?" Conrad's whisper jolted Finn out of her thoughts. She met his gaze and the compassion she glimpsed there tore at her. The urge to accept any comfort he was willing to give nearly undid her, overwhelming her desire to keep him at a distance.

With a level of restraint she hadn't known she possessed, Finn cleared her throat and crossed her arms at her chest. She forced her face to reassemble its features into an apathetic expression and glared at Conrad.

"Are you just going to stand there or what?"

Instead of watching his jaw clench in anger and his face shut down as she'd expected them to, his eyes sparkled, and his lips twitched slightly as though he were fighting laughter. She certainly hadn't expected that reaction. She couldn't remember the last time she'd seen him so jovial. And how could he look so amused when he'd just said goodbye to the only family he had left?

"That depends, are my future children safe?"

His words were so unexpected, it took a full minute for them to sink in. He glanced down meaningfully, and she followed the direction of his gaze until . . .

Too late, she realized what he'd meant and hurried to look away, all the while cursing herself for her earlier threat. Both of her traitorous cheeks flushed with the heat of embarrassment, and she knew Conrad had noticed when he coughed quietly to cover a chuckle.

Jerk.

Refusing to be deterred, Finn straightened her shoulders and rallied.

"I think I can restrain myself." She feigned nonchalance and examined the gloves on her hands as though they fascinated her. "Besides, I'd hate to deprive you of the experience of a bunch of little Conrad's following you around and annoying you for the rest of your life."

His smile widened to a devastating grin, the dimple on his cheek making a rare appearance. Her heart pounded in her chest.

"Who says they'd be annoying?"

"They'd be yours, Conrad. How could they possibly be anything else?"

Conrad chuckled and Finn realized her error. He thought they were flirting.

"Fair enough, *Hellion*."

She could've sworn her heart had stopped beating. The moment he used the endearment, it brushed against her skin like a caress. He hadn't called her by that nickname in weeks. In fact, he'd stopped using it altogether after she'd returned from the Dome. The loss had stung, but she'd known it was for the best.

Today, something had changed, she just didn't know what.

The glow in his eyes had dimmed somewhat. Now, they glittered with uncharacteristic mischief as he leaned down closer, closer, and closer still, until his face stopped a few inches from hers. Finn was too shocked by the boldness to move away.

"What the hell are you doing, Conrad?" She meant to yell, but instead, the words came out as a harsh whisper.

His eyes held hers for long seconds before he smiled and said, "I'm changing tactics."

What the hell did that mean?

Before she could ask, he pulled away suddenly and shot her one last, long look. Her uneasiness grew until it became a torrent of anxiety slamming against the walls of her chest. Every muscle in her body locked tight, freezing her on the spot, when all she wanted to do was run. He reached up an index finger and tapped her nose like she was the cutest thing he'd ever seen.

Finn saw red.

Before she had the chance to unlock her frozen limbs and make good on her threat to kick him in the family jewels, he walked away to join the Tuathans at the other side of the bay, leaving her alone with her swirling thoughts.

Finn's gaze traveled around Iliana's room as she folded her legs beneath her on the emerald-green, shell-shaped velvet chaise. The sisters had just finished another training session wherein Finn continued to work on the different facets of her ability to upload memories into others. Now that she knew such an ability could be weaponized, she needed to work on control. More specifically, she needed to be able to use her abilities without causing internal bleeding and coma . . . either to herself or the recipient.

Finn's eyes scanned the space with curiosity. Whereas her own room looked utilitarian and held only the basics, Iliana had made herself at home on Tuathan by adding her own personal flourish to the space, as well as some very expensive furniture.

Artwork in various shades of pink dotted the walls in golden frames. Said walls had been painted a dusty rose, perfectly accented by rose gold wall sconces and geometrically shaped decor. Silk sheets in a deep berry hue covered her bed and fresh flowers—not synthetic—perched on her bedside table in a rose gold vase.

The room looked like pure decadence.

Finn studied Iliana where she sat across from her in a similarly shaped chair the same shade as the chaise.

"Were you always this gauche or is this a courtesan thing?"

Her sister smiled behind the paisley teacup perched in her hand and took a sip. She had her legs crossed at the knee, pulling the creamy satin material of her skirt taut against her shins. Her wavy red hair had been immaculately styled in a tight chignon at the back of her neck. The style might have looked severe on anyone else, but it complimented Iliana's slender neck—draped in diamonds—and her soft, dewy skin expertly highlighted by makeup.

She looked beautiful . . . and stiff.

Did she ever let loose and relax?

"You forget, I've been coming to Tuathan for many cycles." Her indigo eyes took in the room around them with pride. "This is the one place I've been able to cultivate for myself. I quite like what I've done with it."

Finn took in the space a second time, looking a bit deeper than she had before. Once she looked past the expensive furniture and accoutrement, she noticed things she hadn't before. Though supremely feminine, the dreamy decor lacked the overt sexuality of her room on *Independence*, with its wood furniture, red silks, and flickering candles and incense. Next to the vase and flowers, her bedside table housed twin bookends in the shape of bird's wings. Between them, Finn noted several worn, leather books, including a copy of *The Adventures of Tom Sawyer* detailing the escapades of the less interesting—in her opinion—friend of Finn's namesake.

Had Grim given them to her?

The more she looked around, the more signs she recognized of the sister she'd known in her childhood; the princess who loved pretty things. Finn turned back to her sister. Despite her rigid posture, which had to be ingrained from cycles worth of training, Iliana seemed more at ease than Finn had ever seen her.

"It's nice, Li."

Iliana raised her delicate brows at the modified nickname and a slow smile began to spread across her face. The smile faded slightly as she leaned forward and lowered her voice. "I think we've discussed the room decor enough for today. There's another topic I'm more interested in."

Finn mirrored her movement and leaned forward as well, cracking a smile as she did. "There's no one else in the room. I don't think you need to whisper."

Iliana rolled her eyes and carefully set the teacup and saucer on a nearby table. Returning to her normal volume she said, "What happened between you, Aedan, and Conrad?" She feigned nonchalance by brushing imaginary crumbs from her lap before adding, "I've heard things, but I'd rather get the story from you than listen to gossip."

Finn sat back against the chaise with a little too much force and rolled her eyes. Since when did people start caring so much about the goings on in her life? *Probably around the same time those two tried to kill each other over a lie you told*, she mused darkly.

She could tell from the curious light in her gaze that Iliana's thoughts had followed a similar path. She'd been there, after all, the day Finn had been forced to break up the murderous hybrids. Still, they were supposed to be preparing for a war for the Gods' sake. Shouldn't people be focusing on that instead?

Finn's stomach churned every time someone mentioned Conrad's name. She'd spent the last seventy-two hours studiously avoiding him. It was bad enough trying to process everything that had happened in the last few days and deal with the swarm of accompanying emotions, but now she also had to contend with Conrad "switching tactics."

Whatever that *means.*

She noticed Iliana's eyes held the same determined glimmer Finn had glimpsed there countless times and she knew her sister wouldn't give up until she'd pulled the truth from her.

Time for a subject change.

Finn had the perfect one in mind.

"Actually, I'd rather discuss you and Enyo. Does the fur get in the way or does it enhance the experience?"

Her sister choked on the tea she'd been sipping, and the delicate cup clattered against its saucer when she set it down a bit too forcefully. She'd meant for the joke to take the courtesan by surprise and turn her attention from prying, but she hadn't expected such a visible reaction, or the rare blush that rose to Iliana's cheeks at the mention of Enyo.

Finn took in her sister's visible discomfort and shot the courtesan a rueful smile.

"You're a *courtesan*; isn't talking about this kind of stuff an occupational hazard?"

Iliana gave Finn a healthy dose of side-eye and straightened the necklace at her throat.

"I'm choosing to ignore the way you just said *courtesan* like it was a dirty word."

The muscles around Finn's mouth relaxed and her grin turned sheepish.

"Sorry. I just meant that I've never seen you so flustered."

Iliana pinched the bridge of her nose and breathed deeply; the definition of haughty indignance. She closed her eyes and then opened them to stare at Finn. The embarrassment seemed to leave her in a rush. As though an unseen switch had been flipped, the color faded from her cheeks and her features reassembled into the careful courtesan mask she usually wore to hide her emotions.

Interesting.

"I'm not flustered; I just don't want to discuss this with my sister. It's uncouth."

Sensing an opportunity, Finn rushed to agree.

"You're right, we should probably avoid the subject and anything else like it in the future."

"Agreed," the courtesan sniffed.

Finn waited in silence for her sister to clue into the fact she'd just been tricked. Realization finally seemed to dawn on the courtesan, and she frowned. She pointed a red-tipped finger at Finn in accusation.

"That was your plan all along, wasn't it?"

Finn's smile widened to a grin and she chuckled in victory.

"It's not my fault you can't spot a trap a mile away."

Feeling proud of herself, Finn bent over to snatch Iliana's teacup. As she took a large gulp, she just barely managed to hold back a wince from the bitter taste. Iliana watched her, the sparkle in her eyes contradicting her fierce frown.

"Fine, I won't question you about Conrad or Aedan. Happy?"

Placing the teacup back on the table, Finn shot Iliana a wink.

"Deliriously so."

Her sister feigned an eye roll and snatched the teacup from Finn's hand.

"Anything else we can't talk about?" the courtesan asked in a casual tone.

"I think that covers it . . . for now."

The sisters sat in companionable silence for several minutes. As they did, Finn's mind began to drift, and she found herself thinking of Grim. A few hours after the hybrids had departed on their rescue mission with *Independence*, Grim had announced he would also be leaving. Unlike the hybrids, however, he promised them all he would only be gone a few days. She'd tried to question him further, but he'd refused to elaborate. Interestingly, Isis and Tiri had stopped showing up for meals around the same time, making it easy to connect their absence with Grim's.

Where had they gone?

Even after everything that had happened, the Khaleerian still had so many secrets. So many, she wondered if she'd ever uncover them all in her lifetime.

"You seem like you have something on your mind."

Startled from her thoughts, Finn swiveled her head toward Iliana. In a matter of seconds, she made the decision to share some of what she'd gleaned from Grim's past. Maybe her sister could fill in some of the missing pieces.

"Did you know Grim was married?"

Iliana's mouth dropped open in surprise.

"What?"

"Grim had a wife," Finn told her. She didn't know why, but it didn't feel right to mention the baby. As confusion crept into Iliana's eyes, Finn rushed to explain. "I took his necklace. I've been siphoning from it."

Iliana seemed genuinely puzzled by the admission.

"Why?"

"He's spent cycles plotting against the Reliance. He found the other hybrids . . . he found *us*, and he's been guiding our lives for as long as we can remember. Aren't you even the least bit curious why?"

"Of course. I just didn't realize you were." She watched her sister's mind work behind her indigo gaze. "The two of you were very close, weren't you?"

Finn didn't bother answering the question. "It doesn't matter anyway. I've been siphoning for weeks and I've barely gotten anywhere." She glanced down at her traitorous hands, safely covered by gloves. "It's like my abilities are on the fritz."

"Maybe it's not your abilities. Maybe it's you." Iliana's softly uttered statement took her by surprise. When she lifted her head, her eyes sought out her sister's. Iliana held out a hand in entreaty and rushed to continue. "I just mean . . . what if you're blocking yourself? Perhaps you're not ready to see whatever memories lie in that necklace."

Her mind raced. She'd never heard of such a thing, but then again, she still knew very little about hybrids and their abilities. *Could Iliana be right?*

"Is that even possible?"

"Finn, you can siphon memories by touching objects and can upload the information into other people. I think it's safe to assume the notion of possible and impossible no longer applies." When she made no move to respond, Iliana studied her face for a moment. Whatever she read in Finn's expression had her reaching for her little sister's hand and offering a comforting squeeze. "You just need to keep trying," she whispered.

A soft knock at the door startled both sisters and their heads swung in the direction of the sound. Iliana stood and smoothed the wrinkles in her satin skirt before making her way over to the door's sensor. It opened to reveal Isis patiently waiting outside.

"Welcome back," Iliana smiled warmly.

The Aquariian looked tired, and the strained smile she offered the courtesan fooled no one.

"I wish I could stay and visit, but I'm actually here to collect Finn."

At the sound of her name, Finn immediately stood and moved over to the pair.

"Is everything all right?" she asked, a sinking feeling of dread chilling her bones. She didn't think she could handle any more bad news in such a short time span.

Isis looked at her, her eyes were unreadable.

"Grim needs you."

ELEVEN

Finn focused on deep breathing and eyed the billowing train of Isis's purple robes as she followed the slender Aquariian down the halls of the Tuathan safe haven. Her relief over their safe return had been marred somewhat by her sense of unease. She could only come up with one reason for this summons: Grim had finally noticed his necklace had gone missing and he'd assumed—correctly—that Finn had it.

Isis's feet glided across the floor as she continued to silently lead Finn down the hall past the quarters and through another to stop in front of one of the empty training rooms Finn had yet to explore. The thick glass of the window outside had been covered by black, matte rubber, shielding the goings on inside from view.

Finn tilted her head to gaze up into the Aquariian's iridescent blue face. The healer's silver eyes projected sadness, and the pinched corners of her mouth betrayed the tension and fatigue she attempted to hide.

"Go ahead. Grim is waiting for you inside."

The first thing Finn's eyes landed on when she entered the training room was the lack of mats. Instead, the floors were covered by yards of white plastic. Under the low lighting, the barren space held a menacing glow that sent Finn's stomach to churning.

"What the hell . . ." she trailed off on a whisper.

"We are over here, *Dhala*."

We?

Grim stepped out of the darkness, the dim light highlighting the crimson of his skin. He wiped at his hands with a cloth, leaving a trail of red staining the material. *Blood?* Upon closer inspection of his knuckles, she noticed a few of them had split. Given the toughness of his skin, he would've had to hit something *hard*—repeatedly—to incur that kind of damage.

"Increase brightness," the Khaleerian commanded.

In response, the artificial lights above them brightened several degrees. With the added visibility their glow provided, she could see that the pupils of Grim's dark eyes had dilated, and his breath came faster and heavier than usual. The first could've been a result of the lights changing, whereas the last indicated exertion. Several dark splotches stained his black, sleeveless shirt. Given the amount of spatter, she knew his arms and face probably also bore stains, but the color blended into his complexion seamlessly, making it impossible to know for sure. Heart beating quickly, Finn did a quick scan of his body for more injuries that might explain the condition of his clothes. She found none.

The blood belonged to someone else.

"What happened?" she asked, unable to keep the concern out of her voice.

Rather than answer, the Khaleerian's eyes drifted to the center of the room. She followed his line of sight and found a chair . . . with someone in it. The mysterious figure had been tied to the seat with expertly knotted rope and their head—obscured by a cloth hood—hung limply, chin to chest. They appeared to be of average height and build—and barefoot, she noted—but the rest was indiscernible. However, judging from the shape of his body, he appeared to be male. She could tell from the expensive silk of their shirt that the captive belonged to the Reliance's upper class. As she continued her examination, she noted a distinctive marking on the individual's chest where his shirt had opened to reveal bare skin.

Ice filled Finn's veins as she recognized the symbol.

The scales of justice covered the length of his chest. Only Reliance government officials bore that mark. Finn was well-acquainted with the mark, as she'd seen it every day during her captivity and torture at the chancellor's hands.

She'd been so lost in the sight of the prisoner, she jumped when Grim next spoke.

"Isis just healed the damage I inflicted." His bloodthirsty eyes speared the unmoving captive with unabashed hatred. Though he spoke quietly, his voice reverberated with hatred. His body thrummed with it. His muscles bulged and he appeared to be close to erupting. "He should be awake soon," he gritted through his fangs.

"Who is he?"

Rather than answer, Grim's angry strides thudded against the floor, wrinkling the plastic coverings as he made his way over to the prisoner. The man flinched slightly at his approach and Finn realized the prisoner was already conscious. The Khaleerian pulled the sack free and the man's head came up slightly, revealing his face.

The ice in Finn's veins shattered.

Dark eyes dripping with malice held hers as the man's thin lips twisted in a sneer.

The chancellor . . . An unending nightmare made flesh.

"I thought—I thought I killed you," she said, as she took in his familiar features and slick, dark hair—the result of a dye job, no doubt. The shock of seeing him alive nearly brought her to her knees, but thankfully she'd managed to sound nonchalant, if not a little bored.

How did he survive Viper's poison?

The entire right side of his face where'd she'd cut his cheek with a poison-tipped dagger was now a mess of scarred flesh. The veins in his face were raised and black. A layer of milky white film covered his unseeing right eye.

Just like Sophie's.

The chancellor had always been a vain man. Seeing the grotesque and permanent destruction she'd inflicted, some of the fury at seeing him alive dissipated. He would no longer be able to look at his reflection without thinking of her . . . and Sophie. Satisfaction began to overwhelm her rage as she realized he would now have to live through the same pain he'd inflicted on Finn's one and only friend.

"Cyclops is a good look for you," she said casually. She turned to Grim and added, "I'm thinking a monocle would really tie the whole thing together, though."

Some of the wrath shadowing Grim's face dissipated, as pride washed over the Khaleerian's harsh features. He smiled, his chest shaking with the hint of a chuckle.

She turned back to their audience to find the chancellor's uninjured left eye had narrowed and his sneer became a hateful glare. She continued to hold his stare, unwavering, and watched with satisfaction as apprehension began to seep into his eye. His pride wouldn't allow him to show such transparency for long and she watched as he covered it with an angry bellow.

"Bitch!" He practically foamed at the mouth as he fought against his restraints to get at her.

Grim leaned down and punched the man's stomach so hard, his chair flew back several feet with him still tied to it. Both hit the floor with a crash. The Khaleerian stalked over to where he struggled on the floor, gasping for air, and righted him and his chair. She couldn't begin to imagine the internal damage that one punch must have caused.

Poor Isis.

"Let us try that again," he suggested to the chancellor. The man continued to glare weakly as struggled to breathe, but said nothing. "Good," Grim purred. He gave the chancellor one last long look filled with the promise of pain and motioned for Finn to follow him to the other side of the room.

She trailed after the Khaleerian, stopping when he did, as soon as they were out of earshot.

"I am proud of you, *Dhala*," he told her quietly.

Finn motioned to the walking nightmare tied to the chair. "What is this?"

"I left for the Inner Rings three days ago to find him. The chancellor has information we need, and *you* need to learn how to recreate what you did to Rock in the Dome without killing your target." The Khaleerian glanced back at the chancellor and growled. "Two birds, one stone."

Finn reminded herself to keep her voice down. Holding Grim's gaze, her brow furrowed in confusion and disbelief.

"You want me to torture the information out of him?"

"Using your abilities," he corrected.

"Wouldn't it just be easier to have Iliana siphon the information from him?"

"*For him.*"

Grim's low whisper dripped with malice.

"What if I can't control it? I could kill him."

"Yes," he agreed.

Finn sighed and rolled her eyes.

"If I kill him, we don't get the information we need."

"If you kill him, I will dispose of his body and go to sleep tonight with a smile on my face." When she simply continued to stare at him in disbelief, he continued.

"There are others we can question."

He seemed unconcerned with the possibility. His answer came so swiftly . . . so *casually*, she had to blink away the surprise. He made no effort to hide his clear hatred for the man—hatred that stretched deeper than just his animosity toward the Reliance. Hatred on her behalf.

Remembering what he'd said about Isis healing the damage he'd inflicted, Finn's eyes widened.

"You said Isis had to heal him," her eyes scanned his knuckles and stopped on the cuts she found there. Cuts he obviously hadn't bothered to ask Isis to heal. "What did you do to him?"

Grim clenched his fists. His answer came to her low and menacing, confirming what she'd already guessed. "Not nearly enough."

She'd never seen Grim so close to losing control. He knew what she'd endured at the chancellor's hands and he'd shed his careful, methodical hold on his anger for the chance to mete out punishment on her behalf. Better still, he was giving her the chance to do the same. A strange sense of warmth began to spread through her. For the first time in a long time, Finn's anger at Grim receded. Yes, he had deceived her—an unpardonable sin—but Finn felt herself moving beyond it, because before he deceived her, he had saved her and had protected her and had brought her back from the darkest of places, a place that the man in the chair had sent her. And siphoning from Grim's neckless had given her a new knowledge and understanding of Grim's own pain and what drove him. And even if a part of that had been using her and her sister and keeping them apart, she knew in this moment that she forgave him. And while she still had much to say to him, most of it not nice, at this moment, she could only say, "Thank you, Grim."

Grim grinned. "Are you ready to get started?"

"Tell me where we are!" As soon as they returned to his side of the room, the chancellor's angry demands began. His eyes—filled with lingering pain from the force of Grim's punch—lasered in on Finn as he bared his teeth in fury. "As soon as I get free, and I *will* get free, I am going to burn this place to the ground."

Finn and Grim exchanged amused glances. The man's outburst only served to highlight his desperation. Seeing their humor rather than the fear he'd hoped to illicit, the chancellor's eyes narrowed to slits and he clamped his mouth shut. He winced and favored his right side, indicating at least one broken rib. Looking at him now—helpless and at their mercy—she struggled to remember why she'd been so afraid of him in the first place.

Grim bent down until he stood nose to nose with the chancellor.

"Now, I know for a fact that you are familiar with this process, but just in case you need a refresher, I am going to ask you some questions. If you do not answer to my satisfaction, I will give Finn the opportunity to *motivate* you."

The chancellor's eyes flared at her approach, and his mouth dropped open slightly when he noticed she'd removed her gloves. A cold smile curled Finn's lips as she stared down at him.

"You seem nervous. I thought you would be excited to see my *gifts* up close . . . considering all the work you put into honing them."

The warm licks of Finn's anger began to spread like wildfire as she recalled his words back in the Dome. *That* torture *as you call it, only made you stronger . . . pushed your abilities to the forefront.*

The way he'd spoken with such conviction, as though he'd done her a favor by locking her up and subjecting her to torture, she knew the bastard believed it too. She regarded the man seated before her with unveiled disgust and waited.

Grim stood to his full height and glowered down at the chancellor.

"Where are the Arcturians?"

Finn kept her features neutral and fought the urge to swing her surprised gaze in the Khaleerian's direction. She'd always assumed his plan involved the forefathers in some way, considering the Reliance and the Arcturians were a package deal. She just hadn't expected the interrogation to begin with *that* question. What did Grim have planned for the golden aliens? Fortunately, she managed to keep her attention focused on the chancellor. His expression carefully blank, their prisoner examined them both with a disinterested stare.

"I don't know what you're talking about."

"Let me refresh your memory. You and your Reliance friends removed them from Arcturus a week ago. Where did you take them?"

"It should hardly matter to you, considering you'll be dead soon." His dark eyes found Finn's and his lips twisted in another sneer. "You were dead the moment you brought me here."

Rather than display anger or frustration at the chancellor's words, Grim shot him a satisfied smile.

"I was hoping you would say something like that. Last chance, where are the Arcturians?"

Though his eyes sparked with renewed fear as he glanced between them, the chancellor remained silent.

Grim's smile widened to a grin.

"Finn," the Khaleerian said, motioning her forward with relish. "Your turn."

Without hesitation, Finn moved forward and latched onto the chancellor's forearm with her bare hand. Distantly, she heard his muffled shout of alarm, but it was difficult to make out. The loud buzz of his memories threatened to overtake her.

You can do this, she told herself. She gritted her teeth with resolve and panted from the exertion. Though her heart raced, Finn shut out the buzzing and forced herself to take a deep breath, focusing on her sister's words, *Think of your abilities as a faucet. When you siphon from another person, the memories stream from them to you. Rather than try to control it, I want you to focus on reversing it. Imagine yourself pushing the water back through the faucet.*

Erecting a giant mental wall, Finn blocked the chancellor's memories, fighting for entry, and instead imagined a stream. She concentrated on her own memories of her time as the chancellor's captive. Each moment of fear and agony stacked on top of each other, melding into one giant, pulsating wave of energy in her mind. Afraid to release it all at once and kill him on her first try—as she'd done with Rock—Finn pulled back, slowing the flow from a steady stream to a gentle trickle. She focused on Sophie's face, twisted in fear as her lifeless eyes stared upward, unseeing.

Inhaling deeply and using every ounce of strength she possessed, Finn pushed the current outward, directing it into the man seated before her. As the electric tingle of energy passing from her hand to his arm increased, his gaze fixated on some faraway point in the distance.

Suddenly, his face twisted in horror, as though he were in the throes of the most terrifying nightmare. And technically, he was, only it was Finn's nightmare and not his. The man's ensuing agonized screams tore through the training room. He struggled against his bonds in a desperate attempt to scratch his own eyes out. His body thrashed about with his writhing, nearly sending the chair toppling to the ground again.

As Grim steadied him with a hand to the back of the chair, the chancellor's eyes grew even wider. The veins on his neck bulged as the memories Finn fed him sent his blood pressure skyrocketing and fear filled him. His chest heaved with harsh, jagged breaths and blood began to dribble from his ears and the corner of his good eye.

Finn maintained contact as long as she dared, releasing him at the first sign of blood. Her desire to finish him proved strong and she took several steps backward so as not to derail Grim's interrogation by murdering his captive. The Khaleerian might go to bed that night with a smile on his face should the chancellor die, but when it came down to it, neither one of them wanted to be delayed in getting the information they needed.

She also had her own health to think of. Uploading regularly to the fighters during training had increased her stamina somewhat, but torturing the chancellor required even more focus and energy. She'd already begun to feel a little light-headed—whether from the shock of seeing the chancellor alive or the exertion from using her abilities, she couldn't be sure—and she didn't want to end up unconscious and recovering for days as she had been after the Dome.

"You look a little pale, Alistair," Grim noted calmly. "Are you feeling all right?"

The chancellor released a gargled breath in response, followed by a low moan.

She hadn't often heard him referred to by name, just his title. It sounded even more pretentious coming from Grim's lips.

"Would you like to answer my question now?" Grim asked in a mocking tone. Once again, he bent low and got in the chancellor's face. The prisoner's head lolled to the side as he struggled to focus on the giant Khaleerian before him. "For the sake of honesty, I should tell you . . . I am hoping you say no."

Rather than answer, or simply unable to, the chancellor vomited on the Khaleerian's boots and passed out.

Finn double-tapped the heavy, vinyl bag hanging from the ceiling and followed up with a roundhouse kick that sent it swinging. She'd forgone gloves in favor of tape around her knuckles and wrists. As the bag swung back in her direction, Finn unleashed another jab and kick combination, sending it flying all over again. All the while, she focused on her burning muscles and the sweat beading on her warm skin.

After Grim had secured a clean pair of boots, they'd waited for the chancellor to wake. As soon as he did, they'd begun the process all over again. Several times, Finn had worried she'd killed the man. By the end of their second round of questioning, the strain had taken its toll on Finn. Her muscles became weak, and her brain swam with wave after wave of dizziness. Add that to the increasing nausea and she'd begun to fear Grim might need another pair of boots.

The chancellor had yet to answer any of their questions. Though she refused to complain, it seemed Grim was still as strangely attuned to her wellbeing as he'd always been and seemed to know how far he could push without damaging her. Not long after, he'd called in Isis for a round of healing—both for Finn and the chancellor—and they'd been dismissed for the day. The Khaleerian didn't seem surprised by the chancellor's endurance, but Finn had thought for sure the man would've cracked by now.

Finn adjusted her stance and launched another barrage of punches at the bag in front of her. Despite her hatred for the chancellor, she hadn't expected to enjoy his torture as much as she had.

With every touch of her skin against his, she'd regained a little of the power he'd stolen from her. She'd reveled in his pain—this man she held responsible for so much misery in her life—and anticipated the next day with relish.

All along, she told herself she did it for AJ and Sophie, but as she panted and prepared for her next strike, Finn finally admitted the truth. She'd done it for herself—for the innocent child she'd been and the damaged woman she'd become.

Lost to her dark thoughts and feeling more energetic after Isis's healing than she had in days, Finn kicked the bag so hard it tore, sending grains of sand cascading in rivulets to the floor.

"Please tell me it's not my face you're picturing on that bag." Panting, Finn whirled and came face to face with Conrad. He stood in the doorway, a smile on his face, and chest bulging against yet another black tank top. His blue eyes trailed over her body, still glistening with sweat, and came to rest on her face. "I see you're working through something. Does this have anything to do with why you've been avoiding me the last few days, Hellion?"

"Stop calling me that," she snapped as she ripped the tape from her knuckles and threw it to the ground.

At her outburst, Conrad's grin brightened, and his dimple made an appearance. The big man's tone became gratingly cheerful.

"I will, as soon as you stop acting like one." He glanced down at the growing mound of sand on the mat. "So, who's got you on the warpath this time?"

Finn tapped her chin and squinted up at him.

"Well, let's see. It could be the big lunk who can't take a hint." When Conrad didn't rise to take the bait, Finn rolled her shoulders and stretched the sore muscles there, hoping to outwait him. When he still hadn't spoken several minutes later, she rolled her eyes and sighed. "It's the chancellor, okay? He's the face on the bag. Or maybe I'm the face on the bag," she rambled. "It's been a confusing day."

The events of the day had left her feeling vulnerable and she cursed herself for her honesty almost as soon as the words left her lips. Conrad's dazzling grin immediately faded, and his eyes filled with concern. Each emotion showed plain as day on his face. It was the first time in weeks he'd allowed them to be so transparent and Finn found herself transfixed by the sudden change in him.

I'm changing tactics.

His baffling statement from their last encounter echoed in her head and her pulse quickened with alarm. She couldn't help but stare as his features softened and he took a step toward her, closing the gap between their bodies. His eyes held hers with such tenderness, she nearly collapsed against him. How long had it been since he'd looked at her with anything other than apathy or disinterest?

She hadn't realized how much she'd missed their closeness or how deeply she'd mourned the loss of their casual banter and affection.

She hadn't allowed herself.

Conrad brought a gloved hand to her chin.

"The chancellor is dead, Finn. You've already slayed that dragon."

She was so shocked by the casual touch, she forgot to move away. He pinched her chin gently between his thumb and index finger before lifting them to trace her cheek with the latter. As his words finally sank in, the casual intimacy of his caress jarred her enough to pull away slightly.

"No, I didn't. He's tied to a chair in the training room next door," she told him. Now that she'd gained a little distance, the much saner part of her brain had come back online. Her brow furrowed in annoyance and she crossed her arms at her chest. "Although he probably would be dead if you hadn't stopped me before I could finish the job."

She'd been so close to ending the monster from her child-hood for good that day in the Dome, until Conrad had grabbed her and given the man a chance to escape. Though she couldn't really muster up much anger over his actions anymore. If it hadn't been for Conrad, she never would've had the chance to make the chancellor suffer.

At her words, Conrad froze on the spot. His hand dropped away and his eyes glittered dangerously as he whispered, "What did you just say?"

Finn struggled to keep up with Conrad's mercurial mood changes. Her eyes drifted over his clenched jaw and suddenly murderous expression. Realizing too late what she'd done, she just barely stopped herself from slapping a palm against her forehead.

"Of course, Grim didn't tell you." She felt like an idiot for blurting it out so casually. He would want as few people in the know as possible. Finn took a step into his space and lev-eled him with a glare meant to intimidate. "If you tell anyone, I will cut out your tongue and feed it to you at dinner."

Conrad showed no reaction to her macabre threat. In fact, he acted as though she hadn't even spoken.

"What did you just say?" he repeated the question. His voice was deceptively calm, but the sudden glow in his eyes coupled with his rigid body language told a different story.

"The part about cutting out your tongue or the part about the chancellor being alive?" she hedged.

"Finn," he growled in warning.

"He's alive," she muttered.

"In the next room," he repeated woodenly, "tied to a chair."

"Yes," she breathed.

As she watched, frozen by fascination, the bright glow of his eyes went from dangerous to downright terrifying. Without uttering a single word, Conrad turned and began stomping in the opposite direction toward the door. After watching his retreat for several feet, Finn finally came unfrozen and yelled to him, "Where the hell are you going?"

He paused mid-step and turned, giving her a perplexed look that suggested she'd just lost her mind . . . or become suddenly and incredibly stupid. All traces of the affable hybrid from a few minutes ago had disappeared. The glow of his eyes trapped her as he spoke around clenched teeth.

"I'm going to kill him."

"What? Why? Grim and I just spent the last two hours torturing him for information. If you kill him and waste my time . . . ," she struggled to find a threat worthy of such a misdeed but came up short.

Swatting away her attempt at intimidation like an errant insect, Conrad walked back over to her, his voice deceptively quiet.

"You tortured him?" Finn rolled her eyes at the murmured question in an attempt to cover the sudden pain in her chest. His disappointment weighed on her. She should've prepared herself for his judgment. After all, this type of reaction was the exact reason she'd resolved to push him away in the first place. She found herself so busy fanning the flames of indignation and preparing several defenses for her actions, she almost missed the low whisper that left his lips next. "Please tell me you made it hurt."

She realized she was holding her breath and forced air into her lungs. Silence hung between them for long moments. Suddenly feeling disarmed by the unexpected question, she straightened her spine and crossed her arms at her chest.

"Doesn't torture go against your noble sensibilities?" she managed to choke out the soft whisper.

This time it was Conrad who rolled his eyes. The action had her blinking in surprise.

"I'm not Shane, Finn." He sighed and ran a frustrated hand over his dreads. His rigid posture deflated somewhat as he exhaled, but the anger in his glowing gaze remained. "If you would've listened to me just once these last few weeks instead of pushing me away, you would know that."

Finn bristled at the accusation.

"Maybe I didn't feel like seeing the pity in your eyes or listening to you try to let me off the hook for *killing* people," she defended under her breath.

"Saying you didn't have a choice is not letting you off the hook; it's just the truth!" Conrad barked, not missing a beat. He brought his fingers to his temple and closed his eyes for a moment in silent vexation. When he opened them next, their glowing depths burned with intensity. "If you don't think I would've done the exact same thing in your position . . . that I wouldn't march into that room right now," he pointed in the direction of the training room next door, "and slit that bastard's throat for what he did to you, then you really don't know me as well as you think you do."

She opened her mouth to argue but, as was becoming Conrad's frustrating habit, he'd made a valid point. Her mouth silently opened and closed, floundering for a response.

"I can see you're finally *hearing* me," he murmured. The glow in his eyes dimmed slightly, a sign he was calming down. "You know, it would've been nice to have this conversation weeks ago. You could've saved us all the time and spared your boyfriend the broken bones and bloody noses."

Boyfriend. The word sounded silly coming from him. Almost as silly as the idea of using it to describe the giant before her. Focusing on that last bit, she finally decided to come clean.

"Aedan . . . isn't my boyfriend," she admitted in a low murmur. "He never was."

He surprised her by nodding immediately.

"I know that now. And if I hadn't been so blinded by jealously and an impending war, I would've figured it out a lot sooner." As his eyes scanned her face, his features softened somewhat, and his voice lowered a decibel. "You're a shit liar, Hellion."

She stared up at him for long moments, letting his words sink in and fill up the hollow places in her chest.

"You really don't care that I killed those people, do you? Or about the torture?" Disbelief warred with hope as the truth settled deep within her.

"Of course, I care." When she bristled slightly, he brought his gloved hands up and rushed to continue. "I care about *you* and how all of it has been affecting *you*." He scrubbed one hand down his face, and she finally noticed the lines of fatigue around his eyes. "But honestly, the only thing I can think about right now is the fact that there is a man next door who hurt you in ways I can't even begin to imagine. And I'm standing here explaining things to you that should be obvious, when all I really want to do is go in there and rip his head clean off his shoulders!"

By the time he'd finished, his voice had become an angry growl and his eyes had narrowed with murderous intent. Conversely, Finn felt as though a great weight had been lifted from her and she suddenly felt the urge to laugh. Instead, she smiled, feeling the action transforming her face. Seeing it, Conrad's head jerked back in surprise.

Slowly, the anger leaked from his expression and warmth filled his eyes. He looked at her with such intense caring that she began to blush. So much about their future still hung in the air, uncertain. As focused as she'd been on revenge, Finn hadn't expected to live through whatever lay ahead. They were going to war after all. But perhaps they could let themselves enjoy whatever time they had left.

"So, what you're saying," she moved into his space and placed her hands on his chest. His blue eyes flared in response and his pupils dilated. "Is you need a *distraction*."

"A . . . distraction sounds like exactly what I need," he whispered hoarsely.

The tension leaked from his frame as his hands wrapped around her waist and pulled her against him. Finn fought the urge to melt into the hard wall of muscle. Instead, she gazed up at him and smiled at him playfully. His eyes drank in the sight of her mirth. His head dipped and his mouth came so close to hers, his warm breath caressed her face.

Before they could connect, Finn spun out of his hold and backed up several feet. She disregarded the confusion coloring his expression and assumed a battle-ready stance. His eyes narrowed on her fists at her chin and his mouth set in a hard line as he took in her wide stance and bent legs.

"What are you doing?"

"Getting ready to spar," she bit the inside of her cheek to keep from laughing at his bafflement. "You said you needed a distraction."

Ever so slowly, realization began to dawn. Some of the confusion left his face, replaced by a teasing smile and a gleam in his vivid-blue eyes.

"Riiiight." Conrad mirrored her stance, widening his legs to shoulder-width apart and shaking out his fists before bringing them up to his chin. "I'm not going easy on you," he warned.

Finn's eyes sparkled as she fought a rising grin. Rather than answer, she threw her leg back and launched it forward between his legs. Demonstrating just how well he knew her

Conrad threw his hips back and brought his arms down to defend his manhood. Too late, he realized her kick was a feint . . . a distraction.

Finn reversed her telegraphed knee to throw a right cross aimed at Conrad's hard jaw. He tilted his head and ducked, causing her fist to graze his face. His stubble scratched her knuckles. He brought his fingers up to rub the spot where she'd nearly connected and grinned.

"Cute," his eyes heated as he spoke. "However, you're forgetting something."

Finn rolled her neck and bounced on the balls of her feet.

"Oh yeah? What?"

Suddenly, she was ripped off her feet by an unseen force and sent careening backward until her back slammed high against the wall, her feet several feet above the mats below.

The blinding light of Conrad's glowing eyes washed over her. "That."

Conrad held Finn in place with his mind. With a devilish grin tugging at his lips, he walked toward her like a stalking predator. He dragged her down the wall until her eyes were level with his, her feet still over a foot from the floor. Using his abilities, he brought her arms high over her head.

Conrad leaned in close until their noses almost touched and pressed his hands against the wall on either side of Finn. The heat of his gaze took her breath away. "Any other tricks you wanted to try out while I have you here?" he asked on a sultry whisper.

The longer Finn watched him, the heavier her breathing became. She knew he could feel it. She tilted her chin slightly and leaned closer until her lips grazed his ear. She felt him shudder against her and smiled. Her nose grazed his cheek as she whispered through gritted teeth.

"Please let my hand go."

The request—rather than command he most likely expected—caused him to pull his head away slightly and lock eyes with her. Whatever he saw in hers caused his blue eyes to flare and heat even further. She felt his abilities fading from her right hand and wiggled it loose with minimal effort.

She held his gaze as she brought her palm down from the wall and caressed his cheek. His eyes closed at the contact and he sighed, cutting off the glow illuminating her face. Seeing as he could no longer see her, Finn felt safe smiling.

She focused on one very specific memory: one of the many she had of her time training under Grim's tutelage. This particular memory, though, included a spar between her and her mentor in which Finn had grown a bit too overconfident, resulting in the Khaleerian delivering an uppercut to her chin so hard that she still felt the phantom pain to this day. Cradling Conrad's face in her hand, she pushed the memory from her skin to his.

The hybrid's dark eyelids popped open an instant before he flew backward. He landed on the mat with a grunt. The rest of his power still holding her in place released, and she dropped to the ground, using her right hand and the opposite knee to brace her fall.

Conrad sat up with a start and his hand came up to massage his jaw. His baffled gaze fell on her as she stood, and his eyes narrowed. Finn held her hands up and backed away in mock surrender.

"Hey, you started it," she told him, fighting back a grin. Realizing what she'd done, his eyes widened in surprise, only to be swiftly followed by a slight twitch of his lips. With graceful fluidity, Conrad took to his feet and shook out his fists. He rolled his neck, his dreds swinging as he did. Finn caught sight of the tattoos that ran up from beneath his shirt to his neck. *Gods, he was beautiful.*

Eyes shining with pride, he adopted a standard midrange stance and motioned for Finn to make the next move. A thrill shot down her spine. She thumbed her nose and dropped her hands low. Bouncing on the balls of her feet, she began to close the distance between them. As soon as she was in range, Finn pelted Conrad with a fusillade of lightning-fast punches that he struggled to defend against.

Whether by a lack of focus or an abundance of over-confidence, Finn slowed down for the briefest of moments. Taking advantage, Conrad grabbed her by the forearm and barreled into her, pushing her backward as he continued to advance.

This time when her back slammed against the wall, his gloved hands held her wrists in place. With a will of their own, Finn's legs came up to wrap around his hips. They both breathed heavily, the frantic exhalations bouncing between them and leaving Finn dizzy. Conrad's unique scent surrounded her, making it difficult to think clearly.

"Just to say," she boasted somewhat dazedly on a whisper, "you seem thoroughly distracted."

He smiled, but his eyes held a far deeper hunger in their depths. Dipping his head closer until only a breath separated his lips from hers, he whispered hoarsely, "I'm getting there."

He had only to lean forward a centimeter and their lips would finally touch. Instead, he tilted his head an inch to the right and kissed a gentle trail from the corner of her mouth to the side of her neck, just below her ear, sending a delicious shiver through her. On instinct, her legs tightened their hold around his hips.

"Missed you," he murmured against her skin.

"Conrad." His name came out like a desperate plea from her.

His hand released one of her wrists to grasp the hair behind her head and she immediately brought hers down to brace against his shoulder, clutching him close in case he misunderstood and decided to let her go. The fingers tangling in her hair tightened in response. It was the only warning he gave before closing the gap between them and crushing his lips against hers.

Thank the Gods.

Her tongue swept out to trace the seam of his lips and he groaned. Their lips crashed against each other like waves on the shore, and for several moments the heat built between them, becoming an inferno. Before she lost herself completely, Finn forced herself to separate from him and gulp in several breaths of air. She moaned as she pressed her forehead to his cheek, before muttering, "If we're going to do this, it has to stay casual."

Conrad looked down and used a finger to nudge her chin upward. He looked into her eyes and then kissed her hard one more time, before breaking away and resting his forehead on hers. She could feel his heart beating as he held her close.

"Whatever you say, Hellion," he growled, the rumble reverberating throughout her entire being. His head descended, deepening the kiss once more as he pressed his flesh against hers with increased urgency. Lights flashed behind her eyes and heat flooded her. If any of his memories pressed against her mind for entry, she barely felt them . . . she could only feel his strong body pressed against hers.

Conrad continued to kiss her like she held all the oxygen in the world and he was drowning. She met his frenzied passion with equal fervor, holding her own as she crushed her mouth to his.

Just casual, she told herself, fervently clinging to the lie the same way her limbs clung to his.

It was the last coherent thought she had before everything else faded away, as she gave herself over to him.

TWELVE

ater that night, Finn tiptoed down the hallway, clutching her boots to her chest. Conrad's quarters were only a few doors down, but the return walk back to her room felt like miles. When she'd left him—looking sexy and rumpled with the sheet covering his waist and his muscled chest and markings on full display—his eyes had narrowed in confusion, before frosting over with anger as he swiped a hand through his loose dreads.

"Where the hell do you think you're going?" he'd asked in a raspy grumble.

"Back to my room," she'd said as she'd hastily finished dressing. "I told you, this is just casual . . . that means no sleepovers," her eyes had hardened with resolve as she'd stared down at the blue-eyed Conrad. "And no *cuddling.*"

For whatever reason, her determination had seemed to delight him and some of the tension had left his expression as a wry grin had taken its place. Finally, after a few beats of silence, he'd raised his eyebrows suggestively and whispered, "Cuddling wasn't exactly what I had in mind."

Even as her stomach had flipped with anticipation and her resolve had begun to falter, Finn had forced herself to back away. She'd left Conrad to his mirth, which only seemed to increase as she'd practically run from the room to put some distance between them.

Finn closed the distance to her door and juggled her boots, freeing a hand to wave it in front of the sensor. As it opened before her, she hesitated, the temptation to turn around and run back to Conrad's room nearly overwhelming her. Gods, they'd only been apart for mere minutes . . . She felt like a meteorhead itching for her next fix.

Movement behind her drew Finn's attention, and she turned to see Enyo shuffling out of Iliana's room, her disheveled, multihued hair shielding her downcast head. The half-Sirian's pants appeared to have been hastily pulled up and left unbuttoned. Her shirt had been put on backward and the short tufts of hair covering her body appeared to be even more unruly than usual.

What the hell?

"Enyo?"

The female's head snapped up. Her yellow eyes scanned the hallway before coming to rest on Finn. She examined her friend's wild, unkempt hair, swollen lips, and the boots clutched to her chest. Like clockwork, Finn felt a blush of embarrassment rise in her cheeks.

Time to deflect.

"What are you doing?" she asked a little too loudly. Finn ran her fingers through her hair in an attempt to tame the wild, auburn waves.

"Getting food from the kitchens." Enyo measured her words carefully.

Finn's eyes flitted between the courtesan's door and Enyo.

"For my sister?" she prodded. When she failed to walk through the door to her cabin, it closed in front of her. Finn ignored it and kept her attention on Enyo.

"Yes."

Frustrated with Enyo's purposely short answers, Finn released a sigh of vexation.

"Why are you getting food for my sister?"

"She's hungry."

Stubborn ass.

"Okay, new question . . . Why is your shirt on backward?"

Enyo sniffed the air, glancing between Finn, her bootless feet, and Conrad's door.

"Because we were doing the same thing you and Conrad were obviously just doing." Her lips curved, revealing fangs. She shrugged her shoulders casually and turned her nose up in the air as her eyes lit up with humor. "Only we were probably doing it much better. My ears are *still* ringing," she admitted dryly.

Finn groaned and dropped her boots to the floor so she could use her hands to cover her ears.

"Gods, Enyo. Too much information."

"You asked," she pointed out logically.

"Well, I take it back. I don't need the image of my best friend and my sister going at it burned into my brain, thank you very much."

Enyo stilled.

"Best friend?"

Finn rolled her eyes and bent down to snag her boots.

"Like you didn't know," she scoffed.

Enyo came unstuck. She puffed her chest up in a show of supreme satisfaction.

"Of course I know I am the best of all your friends," she waved a hand casually. "I am just happy to hear you finally admit it."

Finn covered a chuckle with a cough and eyed Enyo up and down.

"So, I take it I won't be seeing you the rest of the night?"

"Unlike your man, I actually have stamina," she purred in answer.

"Shouldn't have asked," Finn groaned and waved the other away. The movement caused the door to open before her once again and she sped through in a hasty escape.

Throwing her boots on the ground, Finn plopped down and sat cross-legged on her bed. Her mind drifted to the afternoon's events. As she pictured Conrad's face, flush with passion, every molecule of her skin buzzed with renewed energy and awareness. With Aedan gone, and Enyo preoccupied and missing in action, Finn found herself alone and wired without an outlet.

Despite her desire to maintain at least a semblance of distance, the temptation to find her way right back to Conrad's room and lose herself once again in his dizzying touch rapidly spread like an infection. Though he had seemed to agree when she'd shared her request to keep things casual, she had a sneaking suspicion the big man had merely pacified her for the time being. She knew better than to think he'd give in that easily. Given his stubborn nature, he was probably just buying time until he could convince her otherwise. And based on the way Finn was feeling right now, the big man might have a better chance at success than he even realized.

Which was precisely why Finn remained glued to her spot on the bed.

With the chancellor so close, she could practically smell the evil wafting from him in waves and the impending threat of war; she couldn't afford to have her mind clouded any further. There was simply too much at stake.

She could only think of one acceptable distraction.

Finn pushed forward and stretched across the mattress on her stomach until her chest hit the foot of the bed. Her dark auburn waves hung over the edge as she brought her hands down to sift through the opened trunk there. When she found the wooden box, she snatched it up and once again pulled herself into a sitting position with it on her lap. Opening the lid, she snagged Grim's necklace from where it rested inside and began to remove her gloves.

Iliana had suggested that Finn's problems siphoning from the necklace could be a result of a mental block—one of her own creation. If Iliana's theory could be believed, Finn was standing in her own way, keeping herself from the answers she'd been so desperately seeking. She certainly didn't *feel* like she'd been blocking herself, but it wasn't out of the realm of possibility. Her brain had a habit of erecting invisible walls to keep herself safe. She figured there couldn't be any harm in at least continuing to try.

At this point, she had nothing to lose.

Finn brought her bare hand down and grasped the necklace in her fingers. Her skin buzzed with the onslaught of memories dancing at her fingertips. She welcomed them, allowing the imaginary faucet to run at full flow.

The room around her faded away, transporting her to familiar surroundings, as a memory began to take shape in her mind.

Grim stands in his office and stares down at a shadowed corner of the room. The blaze burning in the fireplace on the opposite wall casts a glow over the Khaleerian's features and highlights the glossy sheen of his dark horns.

Bending down to a squat, Grim makes himself as small as possible and extends a large, red hand toward the shadows.

"Do not be afraid," he says gently. "I will not hurt you."

In response, an agonized, feral cry fills the room as a small figure darts out on all fours into the light. A fall of dark, matted hair flies around the child's pale face. The dark mass is too saturated with dirt to see the pretty auburn color lying beneath. Torn, muddy material drapes her frail body like a sack. She is so thin, it is a wonder she has remained upright. Running on pure adrenaline, the girl lunges for the Khaleerian's outstretched hand, snapping her teeth violently.

Grim pulls his fingers back in time to avoid the child's snapping jaws but remains kneeling. After missing her target, the girl flinches and crawls backward, as though waiting for the large male to strike. When he doesn't, her wide, indigo eyes scan his broad shoulders and huge muscles. The savage light in them retreats slightly, replaced by confusion.

Seeming to catch herself, her gaze narrows once more, and she lets loose a wild shriek. She pounds her hands on the floor in warning, her little chest rising and falling rapidly with her fearful breath. In her mind, Finn locks onto the protruding bones of the little girl's sternum and she winces. Grim moves forward slightly, keeping his hand out in a conciliatory gesture.

The child snarls and screeches, halting the Khaleerian's approach.

"Everything is all right, little one," he soothes with seemingly unending patience. Recognition lights the girl's indigo eyes, and her rabid movements cease. Spots of blood color her exposed wrists where the scabs there have yet to fully heal. She seems uncertain as she watches the Khaleerian. "You are safe, Dhala."

Ever so slowly, Grim reaches behind himself and snags a crusty piece of bread from the plate resting on his desk. Still squatting, the Khaleerian approaches the child with painstakingly unhurried movements. She growls and snaps at his approach, but her eyes watch the morsel in the advancing male's hand with unmasked hunger.

Grim extends the offering and the child immediately snatches it from his grasp, before scurrying back to put distance between them. Her head descends and she tears into the bread with frenzied movements, causing crumbs to fly in all directions.

Keeping his eyes on the child, Grim reaches back around and snags a large trench coat from the chair behind his desk. He approaches the girl again with slow, deliberate movements. To give her time to adjust to his nearness, he pauses each time she growls around mouthfuls of bread. When he is close enough, he flicks out a wrist and wraps the trench coat around the child's tiny frame. She jerks in response but doesn't move away.

Keeping his hand outstretched, Grim moves away from the child. When he reaches his desk, the large Khaleerian finally stands to his full height and takes a seat in the extra-large, cushioned seat behind it. The child continues to watch him from the corner of her indigo eyes as she tears into the bread.

As though he's forgotten the girl's presence, Grim ignores her and pulls a book from the top of a large pile at the far end of his desk. The fancy scribble on the spine reads Grimm's Fairy Tales. *Leaning back in his chair as though he doesn't have a care in the worlds, Grim opens the first page and begins reading.*

With his attention elsewhere, the girl studies him openly. She shoves the last bite of bread in her mouth and crawls backward until her spine hits the wall, never taking her gaze from the Khaleerian. Grim's gruff voice continues reading, the sound combining with the crackle of logs on the fire. Heat from the fireplace fills the space, lulling the girl as her eyelids become heavy. She blinks slowly, helpless to fight her obvious fatigue as the food in her belly couples with the cozy heat of the fire and Grim's low rumble.

The child pulls the coat tighter around her shoulders and her eyes drift closed. Within minutes she is sound asleep in the corner. Once he is sure she is sleeping, Grim closes the book and sets it down. He watches the girl for long minutes. The reflection of the fire's embers sparkles within the depths of his fathomless gaze.

Finn moves away from her younger self and approaches the Khaleerian, studying his face. As he watches the girl, a myriad of emotions plays across his normally unreadable expression: sadness, anger, affection, resolution. Finn finds herself transfixed.

A quiet rap turns his attention in the direction of the door as a stoic mask falls over his features. The person on the other side doesn't wait for permission and the door opens to reveal Doc on the other side. Finn's chest squeezes at the sight of her old friend. His reptilian gaze falls on the child sleeping soundly in the corner and softens. His eyes move to Grim.

"*I came to check on you both,*" he whispers, so as not to disturb the sleeping girl. "*I see you survived.*"

"*Barely,*" Grim returns with genuine amusement. "*I almost lost a finger.*"

Doc chuckles softly. As he scans the child's face—peaceful in slumber—his eyes widen in surprise.

"*Gods, she is young. I couldn't tell what with all that snapping and spitting . . . not to mention the dirt.*" Doc's smile widens to a warm grin, taking the bite out of his words. Despite the deep rumble of their voices, the girl remains dead to the worlds, snoring softly. "*Shall I call someone to collect her?*"

"*No!*" Grim's protest comes swiftly . . . too swiftly and a bit too loudly. Doc's brows arch in surprise and the little girl in the corner shifts slightly and groans. They hold their breath until the sound of her snores once again carries over to them.

"*Very, well,*" Doc says carefully. "*I'll just go and fetch some pillows and blankets from the boarding house next door.*"

Grim nods his appreciation and the reptilian alien takes his leave. When the Khaleerian's eyes fall on the child, they fill with emotion—more than she's ever seen from him. He sags back into his chair and rests his head in his hands as though no longer able to hold up the weight.

Suddenly, the scene changes. When Grim's office comes into focus this time, he is still seated in his chair, but his clothes are different. A book rests poised in his hand as he reads aloud in a low murmur.

He checks to see that the child resting atop a pile of blankets in the corner is sleeping. Her fall of dark-red hair obscures her face but from the slow rise and fall of her chest, she appears to be out. Grim pauses his narration and sets the book down to pull something from his desk. Once he has it, he slips it around his neck.

Wait a second.

Finn has seen this memory before, the first time she ever touched the Khaleerian's necklace. Finn turns toward the open doorway, knowing from her previous experience in this memory that Doc would be walking through it any minute. Sure enough, the reptilian alien appeared.

"I assumed you would have sent her away to her sister by now." Doc wipes his hands on the apron he wore behind the bar and levels Grim with serious eyes. His bespectacled gaze is thoughtful. "You've never kept any of the others this long."

Grim finally tears his stare from the sleeping girl and gives the bartender his full attention.

"Is there a question in there somewhere, Doc?"

The alien smiles imperceptibly and adjusts the glasses where they perch on his short, scaled nose.

"Just wondering what makes this one different."

"She reminds me of someone," Grim says in a low, pained whisper.

"Will you be keeping her then?" Doc doesn't seem to be too upset by the possibility, simply curious.

"She's not a pet, Doc," Grim growls in annoyance. Doc merely continues to stare deep into the Khaleerian's eyes knowingly. Grim expels a frustrated breath of defeat. "Would it be so crazy if I did?"

"Yes," Doc answers immediately.

This is where the memory had ended last time. Finn braced herself to either be hurtled back to her room—still without answers—or be thrown into another memory.

Neither happened.

The room around her and its occupants remain in focus. Doc watches Grim for long moments and the Khaleerian seems to itch under the scrutiny.

"I've known you a long time, my friend," the bartender says quietly.

"And?" Grim mutters through clenched fangs.

"Things have been different since the little one arrived. You have been different."

"Make your point, Doc, I have work to do and so do you," Grim growls, clearly losing what little patience he has left. Or perhaps he just doesn't like the turn the conversation has taken. Either way, the Khaleerian looks fit to be tied.

His ire barely fazes the bartender.

"My point is, just because it would be crazy doesn't mean you shouldn't do it."

Finn snapped into awareness, letting her eyes drift over the familiar walls of her room as her mind reeled from the memory she'd just witnessed. Hearing the rest of the conversation painted everything in a slightly different context.

Seeing the memory of their first meeting—seeing herself so feral and broken—had been a shock to Finn. She'd forgotten how bad things had been for her struggling to survive on the streets of the Mud Pit . . . before Grim had come into her life. Perhaps she'd just blocked the unpleasantness out.

Her mind raced as she quickly analyzed everything she'd just seen. Most of it was information she already had, except for that last memory. Suddenly, Finn remembered something Grim said and froze.

"She reminds me of someone."

Who did she remind him of? Could that be the reason he'd taken her in?

Grim had always maintained he needed her to serve a "greater purpose," but the conversation between him and Doc alluded to something else . . . something deeper.

Finn threw the necklace into the box and slammed the lid down, nearly cracking the wood with the force. A wave of unease washed over her. The sensation spread from the center of her stomach—now churning with nausea—to the tips of her fingers, leaving numbness in its wake. She tried to tamp it down, tried to tap into the blanket of cold dispassion she'd clung to these last few weeks, but the intensity of her emotions refused to be banished.

The desire to rush down the hall and seek solace in Conrad's arms returned tenfold.

Instead, Finn pulled back the covers and got into bed. With a shaky voice, she commanded the room's lights off. Once darkness shrouded her, she forced her eyes closed and tried to shut off her thoughts.

She prayed with everything she had that sleep would claim her.

It never did.

THIRTEEN

"**W**here are the Arcturians being kept, Alistair?"
Grim's voice sounded bored as he continued relentlessly to question the chancellor for information. Last night's session with his necklace had done nothing for Finn but stir up emotions she'd rather keep buried. She still had so many unanswered questions for the Khaleerian. Questions she would always be too afraid to ask.

The urge to scratch at her dry, fatigued eyes nagged at her, but she didn't want to draw attention to the fact she hadn't slept. When she'd opened her eyes that morning, she'd been as on edge as she'd been the night before when she forced herself into bed. Nothing had changed but the time. Her emotions were a live wire too dangerous to touch.

Dimly, she heard Grim's voice pressing against the onslaught of her distracted thoughts and forced herself to focus on the interrogation before her.

She looked up to find the chancellor studying her with a hyper focus that belied the pain in his glazed eyes. Her skin began to crawl under his examination, and she forced her spine to straighten, while reassembling her features into a disinterested expression.

"Finn," Grim called to her. She kept her gaze on the chancellor, barely hearing the Khaleerian as he spoke to her. Something about the prisoner's expression alarmed her and she found herself unable to look away. As she watched, his thin lips twisted in a satisfied smile. "Finn!" Grim repeated, louder this time.

She finally tore her gaze from the man and gave Grim her attention. The Khaleerian examined her for a moment, before motioning her forward with impatient hands to get started on their captive. She followed the unspoken order without hesitation, closing the distance between herself and the captive and placing a bare hand against his forearm.

Effortlessly, she pushed away the din of his encroaching memories and reversed the flow. She focused on one memory in particular of an exceptionally gruesome session of torture at the chancellor's hands; one of the first of many lashings she'd earned from his whip.

Staring into the man's eyes, hoping he could see the unmasked hatred shining brightly from hers, she poured the pain and emotions into him. Training with her sister and practicing on the chancellor had fine-tuned her abilities. As a result, the prisoner clenched his teeth so hard she heard one crack and his face paled with agony at her touch, but he remained conscious.

His body went limp when she released him, and his head fell forward as he took large, gulping breaths. Grim nodded his approval and spoke to the back of the prisoner's head.

"Where are the Arcturians being held, Alistair?"

The chancellor shook his head slightly and looked up. He gave Grim a cursory glance before focusing his attention on Finn.

"Has he told you who he really is?" His eyes flitted back to the Khaleerian and narrowed. "I wasn't sure at first; everyone just assumed you'd killed yourself centuries ago."

Centuries? She knew some races lived a long time, centuries even, but if such a thing were true of Khaleerians, wouldn't there be more of them running around the Outer Rings?

"Shut up," Grim growled in warning.

"He doesn't need to tell me who he is; I already know," she half-lied. From the memories she'd siphoned from his necklace, she knew his real name at the very least.

She felt Grim tense at her side. It took everything she had not to turn around and look at him to gauge his reaction.

The chancellor's eyes flashed between them. His smile remained firmly in place.

"Then you're willingly allowing yourself to be used?" He tsked in disappointment and Finn bristled. "You had the potential to be so much more than a pawn. If only you had remained under my tutelage . . ." he trailed off.

Finn's mouth opened in disbelief at the man's audacity, even as his words poked at the back of her mind. She did her best to swat them away and glared down at the chancellor.

"It is difficult to use someone when they share your goals," Grim whispered, reclaiming the prisoner's attention.

Finn let her gaze drift up to study the Khaleerian. His pupils had dilated in anger, the edges bleeding into his irises. He held his massive hands in clenched fists at his sides and his skin looked darker than usual. The chancellor also examined the Khaleerian's furious stance and arched a brow. His smug smile widened.

"Perhaps you're not as emotionless as you seem," he motioned toward Finn with his head. "It seems you've found yourself a replacement daughter."

Grim stiffened a moment before he moved with astounding speed. He punched the chancellor in the face so hard, he—and the chair he was tied to—went crashing to the floor. The prisoner spit blood and several teeth along with it. As she stared, frozen from the chancellor's words and Grim's violent reaction, the Khaleerian prowled over to him and righted the captive with more force than necessary.

All the while, the chancellor's words bounced around Finn's head with dizzying force. *It seems you've found yourself a replacement daughter.*

She thought about Grim's words to Doc in the past. *She reminds me of someone.*

Was it possible he saw traces of his mysterious daughter whenever he looked at Finn? Is that why he'd kept her?

Stepping back, Grim turned to Finn and motioned with his horned head to the chancellor.

"Again," he ordered. When Finn didn't immediately move to follow his order he yelled, "Again!"

She rushed to the prisoner, her hand already lifted and poised to strike. Before she could touch him, the chancellor lifted his head and speared her with hate-filled eyes. His lips twisted in disgust.

"You were always such a desperate little orphan . . . so eager to please . . . latching on to anyone you could. First me and now *him*," he snapped his remaining teeth at Grim.

An inferno of fury washing away the traces of doubt and unease filled Finn. Her lip curled and her voice dropped dangerously low.

"I *never* wanted to please you. I plotted your death more times than I could count."

"Oh, really? Wasn't it you who cowered for cycles while I beat your little friend within an inch of her life? What was her name? Sophie?"

White spots began to blur her vision and her mouth went dry. Her hands began to shake from the force of her desire to wrap them around his neck and squeeze.

"Finn," Grim came up behind her and bent close to her ear. "Disengage," he ordered.

She barely heard him. Every noise had been drowned out by the blood rushing through her veins and the buzzing in her ears that signaled she was close to snapping. The chancellor waited for her to look at him before launching in again, relentless in his bid to tear through her.

"You mean nothing to him," he hissed. "You're nothing but a sad *substitute*."

Everything went quiet as a low hum filled Finn's head. She finally gave in to her desire and brought her hand up to the chancellor's neck. She squeezed, watching in delight as his eyes began to bulge from his head. Faintly, she heard Grim yell. Finn ignored everything but the monster before her and pushed every black memory, every single moment of pain into his body. Blood began to trickle from his eyes, and she squeezed harder.

It was the last thing she did before everything around her went dark.

Finn awoke to a pounding headache. She opened her eyes and saw blue skin. Isis hovered over her, her silver eyes downcast and filled with worry. As the room came into focus, Finn felt the pressure of the female's hands against her chest, warmth spreading where the Aquariian's slender fingers had touched her.

"She's awake," Isis said, with a hint of relief tinging her voice.

A shadow fell over them both as Grim bent over the pair. His dark eyes studied Finn's face, relief flooding his features.

"How do you feel?" he asked carefully.

Finn finally remembered how she ended up unconscious on the floor.

I snapped . . . completely lost control.

She sat up so fast her head swam, and she nearly clocked Isis in the nose. Thankfully, the Aquariian moved out of her trajectory in time and placed a steadying hand on Finn's shoulder.

"The chancellor," she whispered hoarsely, "where is he?"

"He's alive," Isis assured her, before looking away and quickly adding, "barely." Her silver eyes flitted to Grim as she moved to stand. "We need to get him to the medical ward now. I've done enough to keep him breathing but I'm too weak to fully heal him. Without medical attention, he will die."

Grim held her gaze unflinchingly. "Good." The single word was muttered without feeling.

Isis sighed and waved her hands in agitation. It was the most upset she'd ever seen the tranquil female.

"You know our efforts are useless without the Arcturians. We need to find them *now*. We do not have time to secure another captive. Surely you can look past your own feelings to see that."

Grim's jaw set in a mulish line and his mind went to work behind his dark eyes. "What do you suggest?"

"Allow me to care for him in the med ward," Isis replied instantly. "Iliana can siphon what we need from him there."

Finn fought the urge to punch the ground in anger. She had failed. Once again, she'd been unable to control the torrent of emotions stirred up by the chancellor, and she'd snapped. Her guilty gaze flitted to the prisoner's prone body and then drifted up to Grim. He felt her stare and looked down at her with dark, unreadable eyes. Still holding Finn's stare, he addressed Isis, "Go and get Zekiel and the others to help you. We will need to post guards outside the ward. I don't want anyone going in or out I haven't approved. I will have Iliana brought to him immediately."

Finn's throat closed up with her shame, and the urge to cry became increasingly difficult to ignore. Instead of giving in to the compulsion, she fixated on a tiny spot of gray marring the otherwise pristine walls. She sat in silence as Isis sped from the room. The minutes passed by so slowly, they felt like hours. Still, she remained silent. Her eyes never left the tiny spot on the wall. As if sensing her disquiet, the Khaleerian said nothing.

After a few minutes, Isis returned with help. Finn refused to tear her eyes from the wall, as they dragged the chancellor away.

A deafening stillness settled over the room. Alone with Grim now, neither one of them seemed willing to break the silence. Finn allowed her eyes to drift away from the spot on the wall and seek out her mentor. She found him looking at her, as though he'd been waiting for her. Sighing, she finally allowed herself to speak, ignoring the ragged edge to her voice.

"Was he telling the truth?"

Grim's expression went carefully blank. "About what?"

His purposely obtuse response poked at the emotions stirring up inside of her. She lost the loose hold she had on her anger and exploded. Finn came to her feet, ignoring the wave of dizziness that hit her, and glared at the Khaleerian.

"I've been siphoning from your necklace, *Abaddon*." Grim went so still, he looked like he'd stopped breathing. Finn continued, undeterred. "I know you had a wife before all of this started." Her voice dropped to a whisper. "I know you had a daughter."

"I do not deny it." His voice was soft, dangerous.

Finn threw her arms out in vexation. "Well, was the chancellor telling the truth? Am I just some crappy substitute for some kid you had centuries ago?"

Grim winced slightly and his eyes darkened with emotion. "If you are asking me that question, you have not learned as much as you think you have from that necklace."

"And since when do Khaleerians live for *centuries?*" she asked as her eyes scanned his body. "How old *are* you?"

"Finn—"

"Just tell me!"

"I am two hundred and sixty cycles."

Finn's jaw almost hit the floor. She knew of no alien races capable of living such an absurdly long time. Grim had to have surpassed his life span a few times over.

"How?" she managed to whisper.

"A special mixture of pure meteor extract. It took me many cycles to perfect, but once I got the formula right . . . I can live indefinitely so long as I take it daily."

"So, you can't be killed?"

"Death from natural causes does not affect me."

"And unnatural causes?" she pushed.

"I am still vulnerable to injuries and even death, but the Aquariian healers have always helped me with that."

He had managed to bottle immortality—sort of—and never thought to tell her? This man in front of her was a virtual stranger.

"What happens if you stop taking it?"

"I will die as nature intended. As we are all meant to."

"Everyone but you, apparently," Finn muttered under her breath.

"I will stop taking the extract when the time is right."

"So, you don't plan on living forever?"

"I plan on living long enough to see my plans through."

Of course he did. His thirst for revenge reared its ugly head once again. He needed to stay alive to ensure his victory—that's how dedicated he was. She understood it—hell, she would have done the same thing if it meant taking down the Reliance—but she couldn't quite tamp down the resentment. It caused her words to leave her in a rush, blurting out every question she'd longed to ask but had never allowed herself to.

"Why do you hate the Reliance so much? Why did you take me in? Why didn't you give me to Iliana as soon as you realized who I was?"

"The best way to answer your questions is to see for yourself." He stretched his large hand toward her and motioned with his horned head for her to take it.

"I can't siphon from people, remember?" She watched his hand like a cobra poised to strike, clinging to the excuse.

"You won't have to. I will show you what you want to see." Grim's eyes flashed with indecision and just a trace of guilt. She understood the former, but the latter confused her. "Khaleerian warriors are not like any other warriors in the galaxy," he said carefully, still offering his hand to her. "We are bred to fight without reason or restraint. Bred to fight like berserkers. Our bodies produce more adrenaline than

any other race. It makes us stronger, faster, and more dangerous. As children we are trained to keep fighting until either
we are dead, or the enemy is."

And yet, he'd spent the last few centuries training himself
to leash his berserker impulses in favor of more controlled
methods of fighting.

"Why are you telling me this?"

"If you take my hand . . . the things you will see . . . I
want you to understand," he stammered. She'd never seen the
Khaleerian so unsure of himself.

Cold fingers of dread latched on to the back of her neck
and refused to let go. Could she really do it? The answers she
so desperately sought were mere inches away from her now.
She had only to close the distance and take them.

Finn shoved one foot in front of the other, closing the
gap separating them. Reaching out with shaking hands, she
wrapped her fingers around his wrist and squeezed.

Everything went dark.

*She stands in the center of a modest cottage. A fire burns in
the stone hearth where several weapons—including a knife
made of bone—decorate the mantel. The wood floor mirrors
the beams crisscrossing above her. The furniture is worn, but
cozy and much bigger than she is accustomed to. Though
the space is sparse, it has been lovingly accented with furs,
ceramic pots painted with patterns of geometric shapes, and
fresh flowers.*

*Grim appears from a room down the hall and walks
past Finn. He cradles a bundle of squirming blankets in his
arms, cooing as he makes his way to a chair by the hearth.
Transfixed by the sight, Finn approaches, curiosity getting
the better of her. She stops behind the chair and peers over
Grim's large shoulders.*

*Round, black eyes with glittering flecks of white—so
much like the spacescape above—stare up at Grim in*

adoration. Golden curls cover the crown of the baby's head, lightly obscuring a pair of dark horns curving around her scalp. Her delightfully chubby face scrunches up and her lip begins to quiver as she brings a chunky fist up to her mouth and sucks.

"Cora!" Grim shouts with a proud smile. The baby startles a moment at the sound before shooting the Khaleerian a toothless grin. "Someone is hungry!"

"Coming!" a female voice calls from somewhere behind them. Cora, as he'd called her, appears at the room's entrance. Her blue eyes sparkle with adoration as she takes in the picture of Grim gently holding the baby in his arms. The Khaleerian's necklace hangs just above the hollow of her collarbone. She brushes stray locks of hair from her face and wipes her hands on an apron.

Moving forward, she reaches out and wiggles her fingers for Grim to hand over the baby. "Come here, my darling . . . my Alice," she croons as she takes the baby in her arms and moves away.

A sudden round of knocks against the cottage door turns everyone's attention—including Finn's—and she jumps before she can stop herself. Grim immediately rises to his full height and assumes a battle stance, his gaze locked on the doorway. Cora's eyes widen to blue orbs filled with terror.

"Let us in, Abaddon. We just want to talk," a voice calls from the other side.

"Take Alice to the back room and lock the door," the Khaleerian orders, whispering harshly. His pupils are already dilating, his muscles taut and straining against the confines of his clothes. He rips the bone knife from the mantel and looks at Cora. "Go!"

Coming unstuck, the woman obeys, hurrying from the room as fast as she can. Grim tucks the knife into the waistband of his pants and opens the door. Several men stand outside and Grim moves aside to grant them entry.

The first man to come inside appears to be in his midsixties with dark hair threaded with silver and eyes that scan the room with keen intellect. They are the same unique shade of cornflower blue as Cora's. He is dressed in a gold, silk shirt, burgundy pants, and a burgundy jacket with the symbol of the Arcturian eye sewn on the lapel. His lean fingers fiddle with the thick, gold band around his index finger. The giant ruby at its center glints in the firelight.

His sharp gaze assesses the Khaleerian.

"Where is my daughter?" he asks impatiently. "I know she's here."

"What do you want, Abraham?" Grim bites out through clenched fangs.

Abraham? Grim knows this man?

The rest of the males outside step through the doorway, filing inside the small space one by one. There are seven in total and they are all human. Each one wears the same uniform of red and burgundy as the first man, Abraham, and each one carries a plasma gun in a holster at their hip.

"I just want to speak with my daughter," Abraham says, clearly lying. On closer inspection, Finn can see that the man's eyes are bloodshot, turning the whites of their depths a bright-red hue. Beneath his fine clothes and haughty expression, his pallor has a sickly yellow undertone to it. He covers it well with his wealth and bravado, but she can see the unmistakable sickness lurking just below the surface. Grim says nothing in response to the man's claim and Abraham's eyes frost over with hatred. He turns to the men accompanying him. "Find her," he orders.

"No!" Grim roars his denial a moment before unleashing his fury on the men closest to him. He grabs one by the arm and throws him, never releasing his hold on the appendage. The arm tears free of the man's body with a sickening squelch, sending a spray of gore onto the walls and furniture. Too shocked to scream, he lands against the

far wall and stares in horror at the stump where his arm used to be.

One of the other men watching comes unstuck and fires off a round at Grim. The laser grazes his abdomen. The trail of blood left behind in the laser's wake only serves to further enrage the Khaleerian. He grabs the terrified shooter by the shoulders and flips his body upside down, slamming him into the hardwood floor headfirst.

The man's neck snaps on impact.

Grim throws two more of the men rushing him and their bodies crash into the furniture, upturning a chair and two small tables in the process. At the combined sounds of bones cracking and glass breaking, Abraham clucks his tongue in disgust and examines his fingers as though supremely bored.

"Cora!" he calls. "Come out and greet your father. Unless, of course, you want your pet to destroy what's left of your pretty little home."

"He's not my pet; he's my husband."

Finn spins to see Cora, her blue eyes shooting fire at her father. At the word "husband," Abraham finally sheds his detached demeanor. His lips curl with revulsion and his eyes glint with unmasked hatred. The last few of his men Grim had yet to kill, retreat to flank him. He glares at the Khaleerian, who is heaving with furious breaths and covered in the viscera of his kills.

"Cora." Grim looks to his wife, panting, and growls deep in his throat, "Get out of here."

The baby in Cora's arms burps and begins to wiggle, drawing their attention. Grim backs up toward them until he is standing between his family and the human intruders, shielding them from harm. Finn keeps her eyes on Abraham, watching the loathing in his stare intensify before he carefully schools his features. His dispassionate gaze flits to the baby.

"I heard rumors, but I had to see for myself." No one speaks for long moments and Abraham sighs. "Darling, you *knew what would happen if you disobeyed me. We came to this galaxy to coexist with its residents, not realizing most of them were no better than animals. They need guidance . . . guidance from their betters. How would it look if the other Arcturians knew my bloodline had been diluted . . . and by a feral Khaleerian no less?"*

Other Arcturians? *Finn can't help the confusion that bleeds into her expression. This man before her can't possibly be an Arcturian . . . he is human.*

"We left Earth because you and people like you made it *uninhabitable," Cora hisses.*

Abraham clucks his tongue in distaste.

"Yet you still chose to join us on the Ark."

The Ark?

Cora soothes the restless baby in her arms and readjusts her hold.

"I joined the Ark to build a better future, not so I could lord over every species in the galaxy like you and your friends, masquerading as innovators of progress."

Abraham grabs his chest and frowns.

"You wound me."

"You can't wound someone without a heart," she returns quickly and without mercy.

Her father swats away the words as though inconsequential.

"You could still help us shape this new Union. If you hand over the mongrel now, we will leave you to play house *with your beast." Grim's roar of fury rents the air at the man's words, but he continues undeterred. "Its existence is an abomination."*

"Never," she hisses, clutching the baby tighter. Little Alice begins to whimper and fuss in her mother's hold.

Sensing the impending danger to his family, the remainder of Grim's control snaps and he launches himself at Abraham and his men. He grabs one by the neck and squeezes until the human's eyes begin to bleed. He drops the limp body to the ground and lunges for Cora's father.

Only inches away from impending doom and not seeming perturbed by the possibility, Abraham lifts his fist to his chin, turns it palm up, and opens his fingers. He blows, sending a cloud of purple dust into Grim's face.

An empty vial drops from his other to the ground and shatters.

The specks of purple begin to glow as they make contact with the Khaleerian's skin. He retreats with a snarl, vigorously swiping at his eyes. When Grim pulls his hands away and blinks rapidly, his feverish gaze is wild. Finn can see his pupils have fully dilated. The black bleeds into his irises until they become twin orbs devoid of light. His face twists, enraged, and he snaps at the air. As he jerks with frenzied movements, he continues to scratch at his eyes.

"What have you done to him?" Cora rushes to Grim's side but he stays her with a shaking hand.

"Stay back," he growls, struggling to get the words out, as though a massive stone has become lodged in his throat. The Khaleerian is on the edge and fast losing control.

Abraham smiles and wipes his hands against each other.

"Undiluted meteor extract. Highly addictive. Through our studies, we've found that in its raw form, the extract can have surprising effects on the different races. I'm going to call it Faze. *Of course, we'll have to dilute the substance before introducing it to the masses." Grim drops to his knees with a roar. He jerks in frenetic movements as his hands clutch his head. Abraham watches him with unmasked glee. "On Khaleerians, this particular mix triggers their berserker rage. Quite a thing to behold, really. When in the throes, they wouldn't recognize their own mother . . . would just as soon slash her throat as clutch her skirt tails."*

Undiluted meteor extract. Purple Faze.

The very invention that kept most of the Outer Rings addicted and malleable. She saw it every day on the Mud Pit staring into vacant eyes as she bypassed countless Mudders

out cold in the gutter, lost in the throes of the intoxi-
cating drug.

Or at least, a diluted version of it. But to consume it in its
purest form? Finn shudders at the possibilities.

"Father," Cora whispers brokenly. Baby Alice begins to
fuss, and her cries grow more demanding. "What have
you done?"

His gaze is cold as it rakes his daughter and grandchild.

"What I must," he told her. "It was bad enough you
bedded the animal, but to let him impregnate you with that
mutt . . . it cannot be allowed to live." His hate-filled stare
moves up from the baby to his daughter. "And given your
disobedient nature, neither can you."

"You're not worried about appearances," she scoffs, a hint
of true fear lighting her eyes before they darken to a determined stormy blue. With resolve, she relentlessly tears into
her father. "You're scared. You're worried that if you allow
the races to mix, you'll lose control of that tight leash you
keep on them."

"Quiet!" he snaps. "There is nothing you can say to change
my mind, Cora."

"You would kill your own flesh and blood?"

Abraham's nostrils flare and his lips twist in a sneer.

"First: that thing, is not my flesh and blood. Second: I'm
not going to kill you. He is."

Grim leaps up from his knees, gaining his feet and coming
at Cora's father in a rush. With lightning-fast movements,
Abraham lifts a square box and presses a series of buttons.
A hard-light shield buzzes to life, forming a protective circle
around him and the few remaining men at his side.

Lost to his rage, Grim slams his fists against the projection,
ramming it with his shoulders to no avail. The baby's wails
become incessant as she fusses in her mother's arms. Cora's
grip tightens around the infant as she desperately tries to
soothe her cries. The sound draws Grim's attention, and he

snaps his head in their direction. His fangs bite at the air. His clothes are torn in places where his muscles have strained too hard against the material.

He sniffs, his crazed black eyes locking on Cora and Alice. Their depths are filled with rage, replacing all traces of recognition. The male's love and compassion for his family have all but disappeared, lost to his animalistic impulse to destroy. As he nears, he regards them like a predator closing in on prey.

Cora stumbles backward as she watches her husband's approach.

"Abaddon, please," she begs. A desperate sob escapes her rosy lips, mingling with the baby's cries. ""Don't do this. You can fight it."

Abraham's cold eyes shoot from Grim to his daughter.

"Goodbye, Cora."

"Please no," Finn whispers. She covers her ears with her hands and slams her eyes shut in horror. When she next opens them, the men have left, and night has fallen. Grim lies prone on the ground—his face turned toward Finn—no doubt dealing with the aftereffects of undiluted Faze.

The Khaleerian's eyelids blink open slowly. His pupils have returned to their normal size and the whites of his eyes are once again visible. Belatedly, they travel over his body and stop on his hands. He assesses the blood there with dawning horror and his breathing increases in speed.

Grim's gaze falls on the bloody bone knife lying at his feet.

He jumps up from the ground as though burned, gaining his feet. He loses his balance and staggers to the nearest wall, nearly snapping the wood support beams in half from the force. As he braces his wobbly legs, his gaze darts around the cottage, widening when they fall on Cora's lifeless body. She lies faceup on the floor a few feet away, her limbs bent in unnatural positions. Her hair is so soaked with blood that it appears to be red rather than its lovely wheat color. Her lips *are tinged with purple, her beautiful face is ashen, and her blue eyes stare unseeing through the ceiling.*

"No!" Grim runs to her and falls to his knees at Cora's side. "No, love. Please wake up!"

His words come out in a broken rush, tears flowing freely down his face. Suddenly, his head swivels and his eyes search the room frantically. Eventually, they fall on a small blanket-covered mound a few feet from Cora's feet.

He scoots over to it and lowers a shaking hand to place it gently on top. When the mound doesn't move, his head bows in immeasurable sorrow. He lifts the blanket and emits a low groan filled with despair. Finn's chest aches but she can't look away. She can't let this great man, brought to his knees by the cruelest of grief, suffer alone.

A moment later, he lifts his face to the skies and releases a gut-wrenching bellow from somewhere deep within his soul.

He takes to his feet and begins to tear through the cottage. As he screams over and over, he throws tables, breaks vases, and punches holes in the walls.

Only when the entire space has been destroyed does he fall to his knees and guttural sobs begin to rack his body.

Finn's eyes snapped open, and she released Grim's arm as though she had grabbed a hot iron. She fell to the mats covering the floor with a thud. The dam of emotion constricting Finn's chest finally burst open. A wave of sobs rose up in her chest as tears streamed in cascading rivulets down her face.

"Why didn't you tell me?"

"*Dhala*—" he whispered brokenly.

"Why didn't you *tell* me!" she screamed.

Fury flashed in Grim's dark eyes, some of the pain there receding in its wake, but it wasn't directed at her. Like Finn, his hatred was purely self-directed. She finally understood Grim on a level so deep, she felt as though she were looking in a mirror.

The Khaleerian's voice came low and filled with fury as he took a step toward her.

"Why didn't I *tell* you that I *killed* my own wife and daughter? When should I have done that, Finn? When you were a terrified child learning to trust again or perhaps these last few weeks when you decided I was an unfeeling, revenge-driven lunatic you despised? When would have the best time to tell you the man you entrusted with your upbringing is a monster?"

"You're not a monster," she whispered immediately.

His eyes drifted shut. When they opened again, they were agonized but determined.

"You are very wrong about that, *Dhala*."

"I would have understood. What they did to you . . ." Finn struggled to push away the horrific images still fresh in her mind. "It's so much worse than I ever imagined."

"The man you saw in those memories does not exist anymore. The things I have done since would have made that man *recoil* in shame."

"They took your family from you in the worst way imaginable," she defended.

"Yes," he allowed. "But I did not show you those memories to elicit sympathy. I showed you because need you to be *prepared* for what must come next."

"We'll get to that," she told him quickly. His eyes softened at her authoritative tone, but she soldiered on as though she hadn't noticed. "You've kept yourself alive all this time to take revenge," she stated. "But why now? Why couldn't you make them pay a century ago?"

"The Disobedients lost the first war because of their haste. I refused to make the same mistake. Besides, the Arcturians are the most heavily protected beings in the galaxy. I had to wait until I possessed *everything* I needed to see my plan through . . . to ensure success." His voice dropped an octave to a low hiss. "Failure is not an option."

If that were true, he was the most patient man in the universe.

Finn thought about the "everything" he needed for success and her voice went flat.

"You needed someone with my abilities," she deduced.

"You and an army of others like you."

Not to mention Tiri. Unique among hybrids, she was possessed of healing abilities and even plant life generation that bordered on miraculous. The little girl and her gifts could ensure the galaxy would never be reliant on anyone for food or air . . . ever again. Though she understood Grim's reasons, his words still stung. She rubbed her chest to alleviate the pain radiating there.

"But I don't understand," she spoke softly, "Who was that man and how is he connected to the Arcturians?"

Grim studied her for a moment. His eyes raked hers with such concentration he appeared to be searching for something in their depths. What, she didn't know.

"Abraham is one of the first Arcturians to arrive in this galaxy and the father of the Union of the Planets as we know it."

How could Cora's father be an Arcturian? The man was human and the Arcturians were majestic alien beings with golden skin and glowing red eyes. Right?

"What are you talking about? That can't be true."

"The Arcturians don't exist, at least not as they've been portrayed by the Reliance. Centuries ago, the planet Earth had become a desolate wasteland, its people nearly extinct. The remaining humans, under the direction of a group of men led by Cora's father, took to space in a ship they called the Ark. They left Earth with thousands of frozen human embryos for repopulation, as well as animals, flora, fauna, food, art . . . the entirety of their culture made it into the Ark. They traveled through wormholes to reach our galaxy, using rare meteor-powered stasis machines to keep them in suspended animation until they reached a habitable planet they could survive on. And they did. Unfortunately, many of the pods were faulty and several of the meteors powering their machines leaked. By the time they reached Tuathan, Abraham and the other human leaders had been compromised by the mechanical failure. Their livers sustained permanent damage, causing sallow yellow skin and bloodshot eyes among other things. Excessive exposure to the stasis chemicals permanently altered the color of their eyes, giving them a diseased hue akin to a festering infection."

Golden skin. Red, glowing eyes.

"The Arcturians are humans," Finn repeated slowly as if in a daze. The words left a foul taste as they left her mouth.

Grim nodded once in affirmation.

"The rest, you know. They stole the Tuathans' tech for their own, weaponized it, and unionized the planets, creating the castes."

"How? How have they managed to keep the lie going all these cycles without ever slipping?"

"The humans spent cycles building a society under their rule, one that mirrored the very worst of their planet's long history. One where the people do not question the authority of their leaders. The Reliance fed into the mystery of the Arcturians, built up the awe until it developed into religious fervor. The Arcturians became gods rather than men. As for the rest, well, if you tell the same lie long enough it starts to feel like the truth. I do not doubt that as the generations continued, the upper-caste humans truly began to believe their forefathers were gods."

"This whole time you knew, and you never said anything." She said the words as an accusation. His dark eyebrows lifted.

"What would it have accomplished?"

Finn came unstuck and began to pace.

"People would know that everything we have and everything we do is built on a lie," Finn held up one of her scarred and ruined wrists, pointing to the slave bands tattooed around each one. "That *this* is a lie!"

He winced at the reminder of her suffering.

"Anyone I told would have been eliminated by the Reliance immediately," he explained slowly.

Finn huffed. The damned Khaleerian had an answer for everything. And yet he had a plan; one he was *certain* would be successful. One that involved a supersecret weapon the Tuathans were currently working on. Would he finally tell her what it was?

She meant to ask, but something else he'd said poked at the back of her brain.

"Wait, you said Abraham *is* one of the first Arcturians, not Abraham *was* one of the first Arcturians."

"He is still alive . . . in stasis with the other original Arcturians, until the Reliance can find a way to reverse the damage the pods inflicted on their bodies. I have no doubt they would kill to get their hands on my meteor formula." Grim stopped his steady dialogue and took in her dazed expression and paling skin. His eyes narrowed with concern. "*Dhala*, are you all right?"

She brought her fingers to her temples and rubbed. Her tone was disgruntled as she bit out, "I find it supremely annoying that you would even ask me that."

By some small miracle, Grim's lips twitched with a trace of humor. Though she liked seeing it—and being the reason it was there—she was too lost in everything he'd just revealed to enjoy it fully. "So, what? You're going to kill him and the others before the Reliance finds a way to heal them? Is that what the weapon Zekiel is working on is for?"

Grim held her gaze for several moments.

"No, Finn, *you* are the weapon." When she continued to stare up at him, frozen and open-mouthed with shock, he took pity on her. "If we get you in the same room with the Arcturians, we can harvest their memories of who they truly are and how they built the Reliance. I take it you saw Abraham's ring in my memories?" Finn nodded her affirmation. "He never took it off; prized it above all things . . . even his own daughter. I am told he still wears it to this day. If I can get you to it, we can use your abilities to upload the memories you siphon and transmit them on loop to every holoscreen in the Union. We can reach every citizen simultaneously. Everyone will know the truth."

"But Zekiel is working on something—"

"Zekiel and the Tuathans are working on a device that will ensure uploading the memories doesn't kill you." Finn's brows drew together in puzzlement. Seeing it, he explained, "The magnitude of what I am asking you to do is ten times that of what you did to Rock in the Dome . . . at least. The strain such a task would put on your body . . . the effects would be lethal."

"But the Tuathans can prevent that?"

"The device will be finished soon."

"This is why you kept me," she declared flatly. "You needed me ready to broadcast the Arcturian's memories to the entire galaxy."

"No," he denied.

"Then the chancellor was right? I'm just some sad substitute for your daughter . . . for Alice." The emotion drained from her—all the life seeping from her veins—and left her cold. She wrapped her arms around herself in a bid to stop the shaking. "It's just a coincidence that I happen to also be the key to winning your war."

Grim took a step closer; she had to crane her neck to see his face. His voice dropped dangerously low.

"Listen to me very carefully, *Dhala*. You are not a . . . replacement for Alice." He almost choked on her name, as though he hadn't said it in many cycles. "She cannot be replaced." His eyes narrowed in on her face before continuing. "After Alice and Cora, I became more beast than man.

For many cycles I wandered the planets in search of death, almost finding it many times. I wanted to join my family, but found I could not allow myself the relief of death. Not until I had punished those responsible. Eventually, the self-hatred turned to rage, and I found my purpose in retribution. I lived for the day I could avenge my family. It was the only thing I dreamed of at night when I slept, the only thing I tasted on my tongue when I ate. *For centuries.*"

"Grim," she murmured, hoping to stop him.

She wasn't sure she wanted to hear more. Already, her chest ached fiercely, and her head swam. She tried to look away, hoping to hide the tears once again pooling in her eyes, but his finger lifted her chin, refusing to grant her mercy.

He continued as though she hadn't spoken.

"The day you stumbled through my doors it wasn't Alice I saw in your eyes. It was *me.*" Surprised, Finn sucked in a breath and searched his face, desperate to know if he spoke the truth. Though his gaze seemed far away and lost in thought, Grim's eyes had softened with affection. "You reminded me of myself. You were so young, yet the pain you had suffered had aged you. It shone from your eyes like a dying star. Before you, I thought I had nothing left inside of me but wrath and the thirst for vengeance. It was not much to live for, but it was enough. Then you came along and parts of myself I thought long dead suddenly came back to life. My purpose changed. *I* changed. Suddenly, revenge and everything I had worked for to ensure it weren't enough. I could kill the ones who had wronged me, but the Reliance would still live on and hybrids like you would always be hunted. *You* would be hunted. The thought of seeking my retaliation, leaving you to live out your days in hiding, became abhorrent to me. I knew I couldn't die until I had made the worlds safe for you."

I knew I couldn't die until I made the worlds safe for you.
Safe for Finn.

A weight settled over her chest, and tendrils of emotions too deep and foreign to name radiated there. The warmth spread, stretching through her body from top to toe and scorching every trace of pain—every scar—it found along the way. Her vision became wobbly as her tears began to fall steadily.

Grim watched them, tracking their movement down her face. The shield dropped from his expression and his eyes blazed with emotion as he took in the effect of his words.

"I should have told you sooner. I realize that now." He looked down, his face pinched tight with regret, and his eyes drifted shut. When he finally looked up at her, their inky depths overflowed with open adoration. She was so used to his habit of concealing his emotions that the sight nearly floored her. He lowered a hand to rest on her shoulder and squeezed. Then he spoke and his words tore her wide open. "You may not be my child by blood, *Dhala*, but you *are* the child I chose as mine."

She couldn't help the surprised sob that escaped her at his words. All this time, he had already claimed her as his own. How could she have ever accused him of using her? This man—the one she respected above all others—*loved* her, had taken ownership over her wellbeing and her future in a way she'd never truly understood until today. Even after everything he'd suffered, he'd chosen a different path, because of a profound devotion to his adopted daughter.

To Finn.

Grim gave her shoulder another squeeze and her hand came up to rest on top of his. At the contact, he took a deep breath and released it as though he could finally breathe fully for the first time in cycles.

The door opened behind them and Iliana rushed in. Her red curls hung in casual disarray around her shoulders and her high cheekbones were flushed. She stopped abruptly when she saw them, sending the full skirt of her purple gown flying behind her from the change in momentum. Finn hastily pulled away and turned. She wiped at her face before her sister could see the tears falling down her cheeks.

"The chancellor?" she heard Grim ask.

"He's still unconscious but recovering in the med ward." Iliana's voice sounded closer than before. Finn finished dabbing at the wetness under her eyes and turned back to the pair. Grim looked relaxed as he watched Iliana's approach.

"Did you get what we need?" he inquired casually.

The courtesan gave him a short nod of affirmation.

"The Arcturians remain on Arcturus. They shipped off decoy pods."

"Good."

Iliana had yet to look at her and Finn released a sigh of relief. She allowed herself to study her older sister for the first time since she'd entered the room.

She stood with her shoulders ramrod straight and held her hands together in front of her so tightly, they appeared to be several shades lighter than her already pale skin. A muscle in her jaw ticked and her indigo eyes burned with intensity.

Iliana looked fit to be tied, like a woman on the warpath.

She finally released the death grip on her hands and threw them in the air.

"How could you bring him here?" she practically yelled. "How could you do that to Finn."

Unimpressed, Grim continued to stare down at the courtesan dispassionately. His stoic mask had fallen back into place and his thoughts were once again unreadable.

"I did it *for* Finn," he told her.

Iliana didn't appear to have a response to that, and she huffed, indignant. As though finally remembering her audience, her gaze flew from Grim to her sister. Her eyes immediately came to rest on Finn's tear-streaked face before homing in on her red-rimmed and puffy eyes. Her eyes narrowed to dangerous slits as she turned back to Grim.

"And a lot of good it did for her! Look at her! You've made her cry!" Before Finn could correct her sister's assumption, Iliana marched into Grim's space and poked his massive chest with a perfectly manicured finger. Grim's eyes fell to where her finger poked him and his eyebrows lifted. Finn blanched. It had most likely been centuries since anyone had dared address him in such a manner. "I don't care if you *are* the Luminary," she told him haughtily. "No one makes my sister cry." Satisfied with the thorough scolding, Iliana disengaged and rushed to Finn's side. She moved so quickly, she missed the humor lighting up Grim's dark gaze. Her worried eyes scanned Finn up and down as she put an arm around her younger sister's shoulders. "Are you all right, Little One?"

Finn wanted to answer, but she'd suddenly found herself alone in a room with the two people who loved her most—who also happened to be her staunchest defenders—and she was momentarily struck speechless. For the first time in her life, she felt something she'd never felt before: Lucky.

"I'm good, Li," she finally managed to push past the lump in her throat. "I'm actually *really* good."

Iliana's lips parted in confusion as she scrutinized every inch of Finn's face. Judging from the barely perceptible widening of her eyes, whatever she saw there seemed to surprise her. The worst of her anger seemed to leave her and her shoulders sagged slightly.

"Of course you are," she proclaimed with confidence. Her eyes hardened to steel and drifted over to Grim as she finished, "And you always will be."

The giant male finally let loose the humor spreading across his face and grinned, chuckling deeply as he did. Iliana didn't seem to care that she'd just earned the Khaleerian's approval. The courtesan turned back to Finn and grabbed her by the hand.

"Come on, Little One, let's get you some tea."

She didn't want tea, but she also found that—for the first time in recent memory—she didn't want to disappoint her sister. Finn reluctantly moved along with the courtesan's tugging, but her face remained turned toward Grim.

She didn't know what to say. She found herself struggling to find words powerful enough to describe what she felt, but they never came. She could only hope he could read the emotion she tried desperately to project.

She knew she'd succeeded when—as Iliana continued to pull her toward the door—Grim did something he'd never done before.

He winked.

After everything he'd just told her, the action seemed ridiculous and out of place on his stern, warlord face. She wanted to laugh, the joyous sound fighting to break free from confinement. It was the most perfect thing he could've done in that moment.

Finn flashed him a wide grin and finally let Iliana drag her from the room.

FOURTEEN

"Thanks for the tea," Finn told Iliana, while struggling to hide a grimace.

Seeing it, Iliana fought a grin and her eyes sparkled.

"You didn't even drink it," the courtesan pointed out.

"That's because it tastes like sewer water," Finn complained. She didn't even bother trying to hide the disgust creeping into her expression.

Iliana finally allowed her grin to spread.

"It happens to be a very coveted brew in the Inner Rings."

"Well, I wish I'd known that sooner. I could've made a killing selling muddy rainwater to the upper castes instead of stealing from them all these cycles."

Iliana's grin became a soft, conspiratorial smile.

"But stealing from them is so much more fun," she admitted on a whisper.

"Careful, Li. You're starting to sound like me."

Rather than sound concerned by the possibility, Finn's voice was more chipper than ever. Iliana laughed, the sound like tinkling bells, and Finn couldn't help but smile.

They'd just spent the last several hours discussing everything Finn had learned during her most recent discussion with Grim. They'd been so consumed with their time together, they'd completely missed dinner.

Now, she lingered in her sister's doorway in an attempt to extend their time together.

"Same time tomorrow?" Iliana asked, her eyes lighting with hope and just a touch of fear. Little did she know, Finn had been wanting to ask the very same thing.

She rushed to answer the courtesan, hoping to alleviate her worry. "I'll be here." As she'd hoped, the fear immediately receded from her sister's gaze and she gifted Finn with another dazzling smile.

"Good. Until then?" Iliana asked.

"Until then," she confirmed

The courtesan finally took her leave and closed the door. Facing the hallway, Finn marveled at how much had changed since yesterday. She still felt like a failure for almost killing the chancellor and forcing Grim to call on Iliana for what they needed, but considering everything that she'd learned since, she couldn't summon the energy to beat herself up over it.

The Arcturians are humans.

Humans who built an entire galaxy on a lie. So much of their Union's values and ethos revolved around worshipping their Arcturian forefathers and the old Earthen way of life, from their art, music, and literature to their architecture and politics.

Those very same humans had spent a century wiping out any other way of life, along with any perceived resistance to their rule, leaving the alien races to waste away in squalor and servitude, while the upper castes lived in a fantasy of riches and affluence.

They'd even crafted a mind-altering substance and peddled it to the lower castes to keep them in line.

What would the rest of the Union do when they found out?

Finn came unstuck, heading in the direction of Conrad's room. Before she got there, she glimpsed white-blonde pigtails coming around the corner. Tiri's green eyes widened when they noticed Finn standing there, and she came to a stop. She wore a bright-green dress that complemented her eyes and the plant-like markings weaving their way across her skin.

The little girl began to twist her small, lavender hands together. Seeing the nervous gesture, Finn felt like the lowest scum in the galaxy. When neither female spoke, Tiri turned tail and began to head in the opposite direction.

"Hey, wait!" Finn called, doing her best to sound casual.

The little girl stopped abruptly and turned. Hope warred with apprehension in her eyes.

"Hi, Finn," she said quietly.

How had she allowed herself to ignore this sweet child for the last few weeks? Spiky quills of guilt nagged at her, but her resolve to set things right far outweighed the discomfort.

Her face set with determination, Finn closed the distance between them with steady strides. Even as she came within spitting distance of the child, her momentum never slowed. The girl's eyes widened to saucers and her mouth opened in confusion.

Finn never slowed until she'd walked right up to the child and wrapped her arms around Tiri's small shoulders. She pulled the girl tight and squeezed. After a moment of shocked hesitation, Tiri relaxed into the hug, bringing her arms around Finn's waist, and squeezing.

A few beats passed before they pulled away. When she released Tiri, the child's eyes shone with joy and her grin nearly ate up her elfin face. Before she could say anything, Finn rushed to apologize.

"I'm sorry, Tiri. I've been a very bad friend. Do you forgive me?"

Though it seemed an impossible feat, the girl's smile widened even further.

"Of course," she chirped happily. "Besides, you're not a bad friend." Her smile faded slightly as she told Finn, "You were just really sad."

Such a simple way to describe it, but no less accurate.

Finn smiled and gave the girl's shoulder an affectionate squeeze. As she looked around the child, her brows furrowed in confusion.

"Wait," Finn said, "Why are you alone? Where's Isis?"

"I snuck out," she admitted, shrugging her shoulders.

"You shouldn't be wandering around alone; it's dangerous," Finn scolded.

"I've been waiting to talk to you for *forever*," the girl defended dramatically. "I wasn't going to miss my chance."

Realization began to dawn. Tiri hadn't approached Finn for weeks. The only reason she would do so now is if she felt certain Finn wouldn't turn her away. And the only way she could know Finn's mindset had changed was . . .

Finn's eyes narrowed with her suspicion. "You've been eavesdropping again, haven't you?"

Tiri's answering smile was unrepentant. "I had to keep tabs on you; you wouldn't talk to me."

"How much do you know?"

"Everything."

"Define everything."

Her mouth set in a line and she brought a finger up to tap her chin.

"I know you've been practicing your abilities, training the hybrids, torturing the chancellor, and Grim finally told you you're the weapon he's been going on about. Oh, and you and Conrad are in *loooove*." She gave the word a few extra syllables for emphasis and wiggled her brows suggestively.

Finn crossed her arms over her chest and glared at the child in an attempt to cover the blush rising in her cheeks. "Kid, we've talked about this."

Tiri waved away her attempts at intimidation. "I didn't need to eavesdrop to know all that stuff, Isis and Grim tell me everything."

They what?

Tiri was just a kid. Shouldn't they be protecting her from the horrific realities of war? Granted, Tiri wasn't *just* a kid. She also happened to be the result of the lifeforce of several Aquariian elders, created in a ritual to bring a supremely powerful being into the world. She could read minds, but she could also heal the land on any planet, making it fertile regardless of the damage it had incurred.

Still, incredible power notwithstanding, she *was* a child, and as such should be protected.

"They don't need to protect me. I told you, I can take care of myself," the child boasted.

"I'm sorry the Arcturians destroyed your home," she told Finn, as genuine sadness pooled within the depths of her eyes.

"They told you about that too?" Finn tried but couldn't keep the horror from leaking into her voice.

"They had to." The child leaned in on a surreptitious whisper. "I'm making sure they can never do it again."

"How?"

"Isis and I have been traveling to the planets in the Outer Rings with Zekiel and some of the Tuathans. Zekiel takes us to places the Reliance can't see, and we plant gardens. I can make them grow really fast," she told Finn in an excited whisper.

"How long have you been doing this?" Finn's voice was whisper soft.

"We've been doing it for as long as I can remember." Her lips tipped down on a sad frown. "I just wish we'd gotten to the Mud Pit sooner."

"So, you really do know everything, don't you?" Finn said the words slowly, as though her brain refused to believe their validity.

"Of course. See, Grim told me you're going to tear down everything the Reliance built, and I'm going to *rebuild* it. Except when I'm done, it's going to be *way* better than it was before."

The child had such a simple way of looking at things, but her candid summary held true, nonetheless.

They both turned after they heard the whoosh of a door opening behind them. Conrad came out into the hall, his big body nearly half the width of the corridor. His electric-blue eyes landed on the pair and narrowed.

"Lil' Bit, what are you doing out here by yourself?"

Completely uncaring that his stern voice had dropped dangerously low, Tiri rolled her eyes and sighed. Conrad stomped over to them. Finn's eyes traveled over him, pausing to study the way his tank top clung to the muscles of his chest. His dreads were pulled away from his face, leaving the runic markings painting his wide shoulders on full display.

"Go back to your room before I summon Isis," he warned the little girl. Finn scoffed at the threat. He'd have to do better than that to intimidate the precocious child.

True to form, Tiri planted her feet and put her hands on her hips. Her adorable face scrunched up as she glared up at Conrad.

As stubborn as the two were, they'd be here all night if she didn't do something. Finn exhaled a little too forcefully, drawing the duo's attention.

"I asked Tiri to stop by for a visit," she explained to Conrad. Judging by the rising glow in his azure gaze, he remained unconvinced. Finn's stare dropped to Tiri as she explained, "She was just leaving."

Work with me, Kid, she thought hard at the girl. Tiri rolled her eyes but didn't argue. Utilizing the child's telepathy, Finn told her, *Don't worry, I'll find you tomorrow after breakfast and we'll catch up. I promise.*

Her vow seemed to placate the girl and she gave Finn a short nod of approval. Her expression turned haughty as she turned and addressed Conrad.

"We'll talk about this tomorrow," she told him, sounding more like a parent addressing a child than the reality. Her words sounded like a threat.

"Whatever you want, Lil' Bit."

Tiri nodded sharply and turned to Finn. She barely had time to catch the child as she hurtled herself at Finn and squeezed. The air flew from Finn's lungs with an "Oof!" Her hold was so tight it was almost painful, but Finn merely held on and squeezed the child back.

"See you tomorrow," she mumbled into Finn's chest.

She pulled away and Finn released her immediately. The little girl shot her one last grin before skipping down the hallway and out of sight, whistling a merry tune the whole way.

Finn shook her head in disbelief.

"Will she be all right by herself?" she asked, still staring at the corner Tiri had just turned around.

"She'll be fine," Conrad responded gruffly. "I heard you both in the hall and called Isis to meet her halfway."

Some of the tension leaked from her shoulders and she finally allowed herself to turn and meet Conrad's stare. She stilled as soon as she got a look at the anger pouring from him in waves. Steam practically wafted from the surface of his ebony skin and his eyes burned with intensity.

"You look mad," she stated the obvious. "Look, as much as I *love* your lectures, this has been kind of an intense day."

A muscle in his jaw ticked. Why was he so angry?

"I know," he told her. He seemed to be struggling to get his emotions in check.

"You do?"

Rather than answer her, he finally came unstuck. One of his hands reached out with lightning speed to snake around her wrist. Before she had time to protest, she found herself being dragged in the direction of his room. Warm tendrils of energy prodded at her feet and the backs of her legs. She realized that in addition to his death grip on her hand, he was using his abilities to push her along in case she resisted.

Finn rolled her eyes but didn't struggle.

Stubborn lunk.

He didn't realize it, but his touch was already doing wonders to calm her frenzied thoughts and frayed nerves.

Once he got her through the door, he dropped her hand and stopped so abruptly, she nearly collided with the hard wall of his back. Fortunately, she managed to stall her momentum before impact. She felt the tingling recede as his power released her as well.

Without giving her a chance to speak, Conrad turned and faced her. The unforgiving glow of his eyes washed over her, making it impossible to read his expression. She blinked away the brightness and opened her mouth to say something . . . anything that might alleviate his unbridled fury.

"I should have come to you sooner, but in my defense—"

He cut her off by grabbing her shoulders and pulling her in for a tight embrace. It was the last thing she'd expected him to do, and her body tensed in surprise. His heat enveloped her, soothing her.

Slowly, the shock wore off. The tension leaked from her and she sagged into his warmth. He said nothing but his grip tightened.

Finn's arms came up and wrapped around his waist as she rested her cheek against his chest.

"This works too," she whispered, savoring her third hug of the day.

If someone had told her three cycles ago that she'd be enjoying this kind of physical contact—even going so far as to seek it out—she would have stabbed them and laughed for twenty minutes straight.

Too soon, he pulled away. Unwilling to sever the contact completely, his hands held on to her shoulders. He brought his face down until it was level with hers. The anger she'd glimpsed in his eyes was no longer visible, having been replaced by concern. The intensity remained, but the glow had receded slightly from his gaze as it roved over every inch of her face.

"Are you okay?"

"What?" She felt her features wrinkle in confusion as she stared up at him. "I thought you were pissed."

"Not at you," he told her. "I've been pacing holes in the floor waiting to talk to you. I heard what happened with the chancellor."

Finn winced, her earlier shame returning tenfold. "So, you heard I screwed up?"

His brows lifted in surprise. "You didn't screw up."

Finn's eyes darted away in embarrassment.

"I beg to differ," she mumbled.

He brought his finger to her chin and applied pressure there until she looked back up. When he had her eyes again, his tone gentled.

"Finn, you're forgetting what happened the day we first met. You gave me your memories of your time with *him*," Conrad's finger moved from her chin to stroke her cheek tenderly. "I felt everything you did . . . the fear . . . the *pain*. I know what that bastard put you through. It was only a matter of time before you snapped. Hell, you lasted a lot longer than I would have."

"Oh, yeah," she grumbled miserably as she remembered their first encounter. He'd merely put his hands on her to calm her, and she'd returned the favor by uploading her worst memories into the poor man for his efforts. "Sorry about that, by the way."

Conrad's full lips twitched but his eyes remained serious. "You never answered my question," he reminded her softly. "Are you okay?"

Finn looked up into his eyes, letting the warmth and adoration wrap around her like a warm blanket. Why had she ever wanted to push this man away?

"I'd be better if you shut up and kissed me."

His answering smile was resplendent. The amused light in his eyes darkened with hunger and Finn's stomach flipped in response. His hand moved from her face to cup the back of her head, his fingers sliding into her hair. She felt his fingers tighten and he tugged gently, pulling her head back and forcing her mouth closer.

"I think I can do something about that," he told her in a gruff whisper.

"Less talking, more kissing."

Conrad's head descended and he happily obliged.

"Wow," Conrad breathed.

Misunderstanding his reverent tone, Finn uttered her unintelligible agreement. "Mmmmm."

"So Grim is over two hundred cycles old?" he finished his thought. If she'd possessed the necessary energy, she would've rolled her eyes and slapped his shoulder in response. Considering her limbs were practically jelly, she didn't give in to the urge.

Instead, she snuggled closer into Conrad's hold and rested her cheek against his naked chest. They lay tangled in his sheets with her upper body resting on top of his and her left leg bent and draping his thighs.

"Your pillow talk needs work," she mumbled against his chest. It began to shake with his laughter, taking her head along for the ride.

In between kisses—and before they'd ended up in bed—she'd told him everything. Apparently, he was still processing.

"I'm sorry it's just . . . two hundred? I had no idea."

"Two hundred and sixty," she muttered through her exhaustion. Her words came out muffled against his skin. "I just told you that the Arcturians are actually measly humans and all you can think about is old man Grim's advanced age?"

Old man Grim. Finn smiled with relish. She couldn't wait to use the nickname on the Khaleerian. He'd hate it.

Conrad's grip around her tightened and his hand squeezed her hip affectionately. He tilted her chin up with his free hand, forcing her to lift her head from the cozy pillow his body made to meet his gaze

"Not that I'm complaining," he told her as a satisfied grin began to spread across his handsome face. "But this feels a lot like cuddling."

Finn dropped her head back down against his chest, nuzzled the rippling, ebony skin there, and sighed.

"This isn't cuddling. I'm just too exhausted to move."

She wondered if the lie sounded as silly to him as it did to her. She had her answer when he chuckled again, the movement shaking her head against him.

She almost laughed with him, remembering the way she'd told him that cuddling was off the table . . . along with anything else that might force her to admit how deep her feelings for Conrad went. She'd needed to keep the lie going—needed to believe that the attraction between them was nothing more than physical.

She may have refused to admit it to herself at the time, but deep down she'd known even then how stupid and fruitless her efforts had been. Nothing between them had ever been casual . . . not since the moment they'd met.

Seeming to read the direction of her thoughts—as was his annoying habit—Conrad's voice lowered to a serious whisper.

"This doesn't feel casual."

As she allowed that full truth to wash over her, she waited for the wave of apprehension that usually followed. It never came.

"I know," she told him honestly.

"Does that mean you're staying the night this time?" He tried to sound nonchalant, but couldn't quite keep the hope out of his voice. His body tensed slightly beneath her as he waited for her to respond.

Finn smiled into the darkness and snuggled closer.

"Don't get too excited," she told him, yawning. Her tone dripped with mock misery and she patted his chest to accentuate her resignation over the great sacrifice she'd be making. "It's too dark to find my clothes and I am not risking a naked walk down a well-lit hallway."

The tension left him and she could imagine his smug smile.

"Probably for the best. Those fluorescents aren't very flattering . . . for anyone."

"We both know I look fantastic in artificial lighting. Now go to sleep before I change my mind," she threatened in a low growl.

His low voice, suddenly serious, cut through the darkness. "Not until you kiss me goodnight."

Heaving a ridiculously dramatic sigh, Finn pushed up and rolled until she lay on top of him fully. She bit back a sigh of contentment at the contact and placed her hands on either side of his face. His hands came to rest low on her hips, his fingers brushing her backside.

While she watched, Conrad's hypnotic blue eyes heated with desire, and his eyelids lowered slightly. They continued to stare at each other, and his breathing quickened, causing hers to follow suit. As though he couldn't help himself, his hands began to move on her, stroking up and down her back from tailbone to shoulders. His fingertips ignited a trail of fire everywhere they touched.

Shivering, Finn finally lowered her mouth to his, tugging on his lower lip with her teeth. He groaned and she took advantage of the opening . . .

FIFTEEN

It felt like they'd only been asleep mere minutes when a high-pitched ringing pierced the air and echoed around the room. Finn shot up in bed, her heart pounding. Conrad mirrored her movements, almost headbutting her in the process. They both brought their hands up to cover their ears in a vain attempt to drown out the sound.

"What is that?" Finn yelled. She could hardly hear her own voice over the blaring sound. Conrad must have read her lips.

"Some kind of alarm," he shouted back. "I've never heard it before."

He threw the sheet off and rolled out of the bed. Snagging his pants from the floor, he slipped them on with hurried movements. Finn followed suit and dressed hastily, wincing at the unrelenting discord blaring from the room's comms. She lowered her shirt over her head and tugged on her boots sans socks. She didn't even bother with the gloves.

Haphazardly dressed, they both ran from the room and rushed out into the hallway, where the earsplitting siren blasted even louder. Iliana and Enyo staggered out of the courtesan's door a few feet away, looking like they'd dressed just as hastily as Finn and Conrad.

Though both women appeared to be frazzled and half-asleep, Enyo stood in front of Iliana—claws fully extended—in a protective stance. The courtesan's wide eyes immediately scanned the hallway and focused on Finn. Iliana came unstuck and headed her way, followed closely by Enyo.

Her sister reached Finn first, snatching up her hands and squeezing them tight.

"Are you okay?" Iliana called out over the screeching alarm.

"I'm fine," Finn yelled back. "What's going on?"

The quartet looked around at each other expectantly, but no one seemed to have an answer. Suddenly, the alarm stopped as abruptly as it had begun. The echoes of ringing still sounded in Finn's ears. Before anyone could speak, Axel tore around the corner and barreled into them.

The large half-Khaleerian's eyes were wide with fear. His horns seemed longer than usual, and his skin had begun to redden slightly, darkening to a shade similar to a bad sunburn. Despite the change in his complexion, he appeared to be keeping his emotions in check.

Finn's stomach sank and her heart began to pound even harder.

"Grim needs you *now*," he told them in a rush, but his gaze remained fixed on Finn.

"What's going on?" Finn asked in a feeble attempt to buy time. Her panic rose so quickly, she was having trouble getting her feet and legs to move.

Axel's face twisted in anger, his fangs elongating before their eyes. "The chancellor escaped," he growled as his skin darkened further with his rage. "And he took Tiri with him."

This isn't happening.

Finn sat in one of the empty chairs in the control room. Her arms wrapped around her middle in an attempt to ward off the chill that had settled in her bones. As soon as they burst through the door, the Tuathans had emptied out, ceding the room to Finn, Conrad, Iliana, Axel, Grim, Enyo, Zekiel, and Isis.

Grim stood before the room's controls. His head was bowed and his shoulders slumped slightly as he watched a recorded video feed of the medical ward. The holoscreens showed the chancellor exiting the bathroom and catching the Tuathan guard unawares. The chancellor struck, taking the alien by surprise before he could utter a cry for help.

He cracked the guard in the head with a nearby chair. The impact sent the Tuathan to the floor. The chancellor straddled the man's torso and continued to violently beat him with both fists. He didn't stop until long after the guard's struggling ceased. A pool of dark liquid began to spread on the floor from the alien's head.

Commandeering the Tuathan's plasma gun, he then proceeded to shoot the remaining guards posted outside of his room. The plasma guns, unfortunately, made little noise, so his escape didn't attract the notice of any other guards.

The holoscreens flashed to different cameras and angles, following the escaped prisoner as he stalked his way down the halls. He made it quite a way down the corridor before running into more Tuathan guards running in his direction.

Hearing the sound of their booted feet approaching, the chancellor darted to hide around a corner. The Tuathans had their weapons pulled and ready, but he had the element of surprise. When they came into view, he shot them just as he had the others, before continuing on his way.

He moved quickly but efficiently, especially for someone who didn't know where he was and had no knowledge of the compound's layout. He remained steady on his trek, inching closer to the docking bay.

Did he realize how close he stood to freedom?

The holoscreens flashed again, this time showing the chancellor as he came upon Isis and Tiri in the hallway. The images from the silent feed were too hazy to make out what words may have been exchanged—if any. Almost as though he sensed her importance, the chancellor struck, hitting Isis over the head with the butt of his gun and latching on to Tiri's small bicep.

He pulled her in front of him and held the gun to her head, using the child as a shield against more advancing Tuathans. When they caught sight of Tiri, they immediately halted, unwilling to risk the prisoner pulling the trigger.

He slowly advanced to the docking bay with the little girl in tow. Finn swallowed hard and looked away.

Enyo, Iliana, and Axel stood against the wall. Each one's face displayed varying degrees of rage and horror.

"Are you sure you don't want me to call one of our physicians?" Zekiel asked Isis with concern. The Aquariian sat in the far corner nursing a cut above her already swelling right eye. She held a towel to the injury to stem the flow of blood trickling down the iridescent blue skin of her face.

"I have told you I am fine," the healer answered sharply. Finn had never seen the woman so close to losing control, and it only served to terrify her further.

Tiri is gone and it's my fault. He has her.

The thought of her sweet little friend at the mercy of the man who haunted Finn's nightmares nearly paralyzed her.

Was he hurting her? Was she scared?

She knew the answer to both had to be *yes* and as that truth settled, she wanted to scream. But she couldn't give in to the weakness. Tiri needed her calm and level-headed.

Suddenly, a roar of fury drowned out their chatter as Grim slammed his fist down and punched the desk beneath him. The metal caved in on itself from the force of impact, nearly breaking the sturdy piece of furniture in half.

Everyone in the room jumped except for Finn.

This is my fault.

Grim had taken a calculated risk bringing the chancellor to Tuathan's safe haven . . . for Finn. He could have taken anyone from the inner sanctum of the Reliance, but he'd chosen Alistair because of who he was to her. In doing so, he'd endangered the Tuathan people and everything he'd worked centuries for . . . once again, for *Finn*.

This is AJ all over again.

Finn ran her hands over her face, scrubbing at her eyes, as though hoping that when she opened them, something would have changed.

Conrad sat next to her, pressing his shoulder into hers. The big man vibrated with rage as he watched the video feed. His hand—clenched tightly into fists—rested on his thighs and his arms shook with the urge to commit violence.

"I know what you're thinking," he told her without taking his eyes away from the screens. *"Stop."*

Finn pushed her weight into him further but said nothing.

Suddenly, Grim took a deep, steadying breath and turned to them.

"Evacuation of the compound has already begun. No doubt, Alistair has already called for backup. Our location is compromised. We must leave immediately."

"Where will we go?" Iliana asked, as she wrung her hands together nervously. The action added wrinkles to the smooth silk of her robe.

Zekiel stepped forward.

"We have always been prepared for any eventuality. There are places we will be safe."

"What about the Arcturians?" Axel growled. "What about Tiri? We have to find her!" As he spoke each sentence, his skin gradually darkened to a wine-red and his breathing became erratic.

"Calm yourself," Grim ordered.

Axel's enraged gaze shot to him. The Khaleerian held his stare and waited for him to rein in his temper. Eventually, his breathing evened out and his skin paled. Satisfied, Grim turned to Finn. He extended a folded piece of paper to her. On it, the word *Dove* had been scribbled in cursive, next to a slapdash drawing of the Arcturian eye.

Dove. The chancellor's nickname for Finn.

Grim unfolded the note and held it out to her. Bile rose in her throat, the saliva returning to her dry mouth. She swallowed down the nausea and reached for it.

Her hand closed around the material as she read the words scrawled inside. A low buzzing sounded in her ears as the wrath built with her.

"What does it say?" Enyo asked.

Finn locked eyes with the feline hybrid and tossed the paper to her. She didn't bother waiting to see Enyo's reaction, already knowing what she would see when she got it opened.

The chancellor's elegantly sprawled challenge had already burned itself into her retinas.

Come and get her.

Finn's jaw clenched and she turned to Grim.

"Please tell me you have a plan," she half-pled, half-demanded.

"Always," he answered easily.

"Wait, how do we know where he's taken her?" Iliana asked. Her eyes were downcast and peering over Enyo's shoulder as she read the penciled note along with her.

Finn stood on shaky legs.

"He's taking her to Arcturus," she told the room at large, though her gaze remained focused on Grim.

The Khaleerian nodded.

"The rest of you are free to go with the Tuathans to safety if you so choose."

"We're not running," Conrad shot back with a low snarl. Across the room, Enyo grunted her approval.

Grim smiled with anticipation.

"I was hoping you would say that." He turned so he could address everyone at the same time. "For those of you who wish to join us, the plan has not changed. We are going to Arcturus to get Tiri back and end this war."

Zekiel rushed to Grim's side, his eyes wide with worry. "But the device hasn't been finished." The Tuathan elder turned to Finn so abruptly, his long gray robes swayed with the movement. "Without it," he told her, "uploading on such a large scale could kill you."

"What's he talking about?" Conrad asked, as he rose to his feet. He looked down at Finn, his blue eyes glowing dangerously.

"Finn?" Iliana questioned. Her brows drew together, and her indigo eyes darkened. She sent a hard glare in Grim's direction. "You never said anything about Finn getting hurt."

Finn had intentionally neglected to mention the dangers involved for her should she use her abilities on such a massive scale. Based on all of the confused faces around the room, it would seem Grim hadn't brought it up either. None of them would ever agree to the plan if they thought Finn might get hurt.

Guilt ate at her, but she forced it down. She looked away and moved to approach Zekiel and Grim.

"We don't have time for this," she told them. "The longer Tiri is with the chancellor, the worse things will be for her. We need to go now, whether the device has been tested or not." Zekiel sputtered while Grim studied her carefully. "Please Grim, we have to go now." She turned to the others. "I'll be okay. I've got this," she assured them.

The confidence in her voice surprised her, but she found herself so desperate to get to Tiri, she would've said anything to convince them. She could deal with the consequences once the little girl was safe.

"Finn—" Iliana appeared to be ramping up to an argument, but Finn cut her off.

"No! Every second we spend talking about this gives the chancellor and the Reliance more time to figure out what Tiri truly is. What she can do. They will kill her when they find out the truth."

She needed them to understand, needed them to mirror her urgency.

"What are you talking about?" Conrad asked. The glow in his eyes receded slightly and they narrowed in confusion.

Having been silent for the entire conversation, Isis finally glided forward and spoke.

"She is Aquariian. Only she is far more powerful than any one of my people combined. She can heal the land and make things grow there faster than they ever would on their own. With her abilities, the Reliance can never again control us with the threat of shutting off their oxygen machines."

Iliana gasped. Enyo cursed under her breath. Conrad ran an anxious hand through his dreads.

"Now you understand the stakes," Grim said. "Finn is right. We don't have time to spare."

"What about the hybrids on *Independence*? We'll need their help," Zekiel added.

"Put the call out to Lex and Jax," the Khaleerian ordered. "We will have to hope they make it in time."

"I must go to the sanctuary and prepare," Isis told the group. Grim nodded his approval and Zekiel escorted the Aquariian from the room.

"The rest of you, go and get changed. Prepare to leave for Arcturus in an hour. We shall discuss plans on the ship."

An hour? Finn's stomach crawled with anxiety at the thought of Tiri alone in the chancellor's clutches for even a second longer, let alone the hours it would take to reach her.

As they exited the control room, Enyo, Iliana, and Conrad all looked like they were chomping at the bit to have a word with her . . . or several for that matter.

She held her hand up and shook her head.

"We don't have time," she stated, before any of them could speak. Though they surely wanted to argue—each one's expression showed varying degrees of anger and worry—they obeyed without putting up a fight. They all realized too much was at stake to waste time on any further discussion.

One way or another, the Reliance's reign would end today.

"Wars are not won without casualties," she whispered the reminder to herself as she made her way alone to her quarters.

Finn didn't know if she'd still be alive when the dust settled, but it no longer mattered. After all, what was one life compared to billions?

She should have felt fear or at least some small amount of trepidation for what lay ahead. Instead, she filled with resolution as Tiri's sweet face flashed in her mind. She didn't know if the child could still hear her, or if she was even in range to read her thoughts, but she projected them as loud as she could regardless.

I'm coming, Kid.

SIXTEEN

Finn sat next to Grim in one of the Tuathan's travel pods. The vessel was much larger than most, seating at least ten comfortably. Like the pods on *Independence*, each one had modifications to its tech in addition to the extra space. Iliana, Enyo, Isis, Zekiel, Axel, and Conrad occupied the other seats forming a semi-circle around the pod's consoles. This transport was merely one in a fleet of twenty currently headed for Arcturus. One held an armory of weapons, while the others transported several of the Tuathans who had been tapped by Zekiel to join them. The Tuathan leader had assured them he'd hand-selected the most competent fighters they had to offer.

Finn ran her hands over the maps Grim had given her of Arcturus. She already knew the planet well from her time there rescuing Enyo. However, this time they weren't storming some half-guarded property of a mid-level religious leader. They planned to infiltrate the most heavily guarded building on the entire planet: a domed structure nestled between the planet's two tallest towers, which served as the council headquarters for Arcturus's most important political dignitaries.

It also served as the resting place for the original Arcturians and their stasis pods.

Movement in Finn's periphery caught her attention. She watched as Zekiel edged closer to her seat. His features softened with compassion as he pressed a small, black box into her hand. He motioned to a series of buttons on the bottom side.

"You'll need to activate the device before you begin siphoning," he instructed. "The code is 020220."

"What does it do?" Finn asked. As her bare hands squeezed the box, her mind swatted away the buzzing pull of memories left behind by the Tuathans who had built it. She felt Grim lean in closer at her side to listen in.

"Simply put, it's meant to keep you alive," he said with a strained smile. When neither Grim nor Finn spoke, the smile faded. "But more accurately, it was created to boost the signal."

"The signal being me?" Finn asked, feeling Grim tense next to her. Zekiel nodded.

"You'll be using your abilities to upload the memories you siphon to the entire galaxy. Without a limiter to stem the tide, broadcasting the memories on such a massive scale would almost certainly have devastating effects on your body. The device will act as a conduit between you and our network of surveillance throughout the Union. With the device, any damage you sustain will be much less severe and much easier for Isis to heal. That is, if it works."

"It *will* work." Grim's low hiss sounded like a vow, one that promised pain to anyone who dared to break it. Zekiel paled slightly and swallowed. Finn took pity on the man and offered him a soft smile.

"Thank you, Zekiel. I'll keep it close," she assured him, as she tucked the small device into the harness she wore strapped to her chest. It joined ranks with the hard-light shield and several knives also strapped there, as well as the two plasma guns holstered at her hips. The elder Tuathan returned her smile and gave her knee a gentle pat before moving away.

Finn ducked her head and finished siphoning from the maps on her lap. When she was done, she folded them up and handed them back to Grim.

The Khaleerian took them and tossed them aside. He turned to her fully and arched a brow. His dark eyes flashed with indecision and the barest hint of worry he tried to hide.

"*Dhala*, are you sure about this?"

She wasn't, but it was far too late for her to waver on her decision now.

"This was always the plan," she told him with feigned confidence. "Don't get squirrelly on me now."

"The plan never included putting you in more danger than was absolutely necessary."

"They have Tiri, Grim. It *is* absolutely necessary."

A war waged behind his eyes as he struggled to accept the truth of her words. She took pity on him and changed the subject.

"What will you do when this is all over?"

A careful mask fell over his features. The cold fingers of foreboding latched on to the back of Finn's neck and refused to let go. She sat up a little straighter in her seat, suddenly desperate to hear his answer.

"I planned to stop taking the meteor nutrient," he told her quietly.

"What!" She didn't mean to yell, but she hadn't been able to stop herself. The sound bounced off the pod's walls, causing every head within to snap in their direction. Finn lowered her voice to a harsh whisper and leaned in closer to him. "That's it? You're just going to save the galaxy and then *die*?"

"I have surpassed my lifespan several times over, *Dhala*."

"So?" she shot back. She crossed her arms at her chest and her face twisted into a sullen frown.

Seeing it, he smiled.

"So, it is my time," he explained gently. "I can rest knowing you will finally be safe."

"That's the stupidest thing I've ever heard." Hearing the casual insult, his brows slammed together, and his smile faltered. She'd never spoken to him in such a way. No one had. The Khaleerian looked like he couldn't decide whether to be flabbergasted or enraged. She didn't care either way. "Less than twenty-four hours ago, you told me that I'm the daughter you chose."

"You are."

"Well, the feeling is mutual! And now you just want to leave?" She threw her hands out dramatically, drawing attention from the other passengers again. This time, she was too lost to fury to bother lowering her voice. "I barely remember my biological father. I had nothing . . . *nothing* until you took me in. You may have chosen me, but I chose you right back." He froze next to her. She was too far gone in her rant to notice. "I didn't realize I had to spell that out for you," she finished on a huff, falling back against her seat with a thump.

Grim barely reacted to her theatrics or increasingly snotty tone. Instead, his mouth hung slightly agape, and his shining eyes searched her face.

"I will keep taking it," he whispered immediately.

"You will?"

"For as long as you want me to." His emphatic confirmation soothed the worst of her anger.

"Good," she grumbled. "Glad that's settled."

Zekiel went to the ship's controls and strapped himself in. The fish marking on his cheek began to glow as he fiddled with the buttons there.

"We're preparing to travel through the wormhole. Please make sure to engage your safety harnesses."

Fortunately, the Tuathans monitored several wormholes outside of the Reliance's interplanetary transit system, allowing them to travel freely without having to stop at any Reliance checkpoints.

At least now they would have the element of surprise.

Conrad took the seat on Finn's other side and strapped in. She mirrored his movements, giving her harness a few extra tugs for good measure. While necessary, wormhole travel wasn't exactly her favorite pastime.

Conrad leaned over as far as his harness would allow.

"Hey," he whispered. His eyes shone with emotion and his grave tone dripped with sincerity. Finn tensed in response. "If something happens to me down there—"

"No." She bit the word out through clenched teeth.

"No?"

"No," she confirmed abruptly, refusing to look his way.

"Hellion—" he started.

Finn turned her head stiffly and snapped, "Conrad, I love you, but maybe save the conversation for a time when we're not about to hurtle through space."

He stilled next to her. His shocked whisper reached her a moment later. "You love me?"

"Conrad, if you don't stop talking, you're not going to have to worry about something happening to you down there, because it's going to happen to you *up here*."

Unconcerned by her threat, the fingers of Conrad's right hand wrapped around Finn's left and squeezed. His warm smile grew until his dimple made an appearance."I love you too, Hellion."

Even as joy burst through her chest at the proclamation, she kept the glare firmly in place on her face.

"You're still talking," she pointed out. "Why?"

Conrad chuckled and intertwined their fingers. In Finn's peripheral vision, she glimpsed Grim listening in on their whispered conversation. "Eavesdropping is beneath you," she told the Khaleerian on an eye roll.

His dark eyes rotated between Conrad to Finn. Looking down at her, the severity in his expression faded. "I approve."

Finn pretended to huff in annoyance as the warmth in her chest began to spread, burning away any lingering fear. "I don't recall asking."

The Khaleerian smiled before returning his gaze to the far wall.

Soaking up the comforting presence on either side of her, Finn closed her eyes and breathed deep.

The wormhole spat them out into Arcturus's orbit and Zekiel reminded everyone to remain strapped in. He activated several holoscreens. Three-dimensional images of Arcturus' surveillance feed began to take shape above the pod's console. Zekiel fixed his gaze on them while his fingers tapped away at the ship's controls. He studied the transitional images and ordered their small group to prepare for landing.

Half of the remaining Tuathan fleet came through another, smaller wormhole near the planet's eastern hemisphere. The other half of the Tuathan pods waited behind on the other side for the go-ahead to make their way through the wormhole to Arcturus.

Finn tracked the tiny dots in the distance, counting each one until reassured the first wave had all made it through without incident. Zekiel eyed the other group's descent on Arcturus and continued his pod's trajectory in the opposite direction.

"Incoming," he murmured.

Suddenly, three large Reliance ships appeared mere kilometers from the descending Tuathan transports and bore down on them. The Reliance spacecrafts' heavy artillery began to fire at the small convoy of pods. Soundless beams of red shot through the sky, annihilating two of the ten vessels.

The resulting silence was deafening.

"Come on," Zekiel whispered to himself.

Two more pods exploded in a brilliant flash. The debris traveled away from the explosion point too fast for their eyes to track, leaving a spherical fireball in their wake.

Zekiel activated the pod's comms, his marking glowing so bright she had to shield her eyes from the luminosity.

"Now!" he yelled.

The waiting Tuathan pods propelled through the wormhole close to the fray and took the Reliance spacecraft by surprise. Their gunfire changed directions toward the new threat, but before they could fire on the newly arrived vessels, another, unexpected large mass shot through the wormhole at the Tuathans' rear.

A huge bulk of space debris careened behind the pods, following the spinning magnets that had been activated on their exterior. The second wave of Tuathans closed in on the Reliance ships—debris in tow—and released the magnets as they neared. The Tuathan pilots engaged their abilities to squeeze every ounce of power from the engines, and they veered off in opposite directions, giving the Reliance fleet no time to escape as the space debris came hurtling toward them.

The resulting collision lit up the sky like a supernova.

They lost another group of pods too close to the explosion to make it out unscathed, leaving a total of eight Tuathan ships—including the one carrying their weapons cache—unscathed. The remaining transports continued their descent to Arcturus.

"I can't believe it worked," Axel whispered in awe. His excitement faded slowly, and he sobered as he took in the somber mood of the pod's interior. Blushing, he slumped back in his seat.

Zekiel programmed their transport for landing and bent his head in silent prayer for the fallen. Though the Tuathans had known they were volunteering for a suicide mission, it still didn't lessen the sting of their sacrifice.

Finn's throat ached as she fought back tears. Conrad's hand squeezed hers tighter.

Eventually, Zekiel raised his head. "Prepare to land in ten minutes," he told them.

To her right, Iliana's worried gaze caught Finn's. A stoic mask fell over her features—no doubt for Finn's benefit—as she nodded once in reassurance.

Enyo sat next to the courtesan. Her head rested against the back of her seat; her eyes were closed in the picture of relaxation, but Finn noticed the way her nails cut into the ends of her armrests. The warrior hated flying. Iliana's pinky finger snuck out to stroke Enyo's furry, claw-tipped hand, and the female's nails receded slightly.

Finn's lips twitched as she shook her head. Some of her anxiety left her at the sight. Leaning back in her chair, she closed her eyes and prepared for their descent.

SEVENTEEN

Finn stepped out of the shadowed alcove shielding her from view. Grim kept pace beside her while the others in their group—made up of Conrad, Isis, Axel, Iliana, Enyo, and Zekiel—followed closely behind. She kept her right hand resting on the plasma gun holstered at her hip and wore a modified hard-light shield on the other. The small device encircled her middle finger like the band of a ring and hummed, vibrating against her hand.

The city around them had erupted into chaos. The chancellor—in all his smugness—had obviously assumed the enemy would never make it past the fleet of spacecraft mustering in wait at his behest to obliterate them upon entrance through the wormhole. He hadn't even bothered to evacuate the planet. Above them, a riot of ships and escape pods took to the air in a frenzied swarm as the panicked upper castes escaped Arcturus.

In the distance, explosions tore through the air and lit up the sky. The flames leapt toward the fleeing masses, their heat kissing the underbelly of the runaway transports. The surviving Tuathans had landed. Triggering several explosives from their weapons cache, they proceeded to unleash holy hell on the Reliance soldiers waiting for them on planet.

The ensuing pandemonium served as the perfect distraction, allowing their small group to enter the city unnoticed. They wound a path past the countless sweeping glass skyscrapers and through the abandoned streets lined in gold.

Holoscreens flashed panicked messages, alerting Arcturus's inhabitants of the impending danger encroaching from the east.

A deafening roar sounded as a Reliance gunship blasted past them and headed into the distant fray. The vessel flew so low to the ground, the engine's heat caressed the skin of her face. Finn halted the others with her hand until it had passed fully.

She motioned with her head toward the planet's two tallest towers in the distance and the giant Arcturian eye nestled between their peaks. Grim's eyes followed the direction of her gaze and narrowed. They signaled the others back into movement and the group continued their trek to the council headquarters.

Finn adjusted the comm device at her ear.

"Where are they?" Iliana whispered the question from behind her.

They'd yet to hear a peep from *Independence*. Lex and Jax had never responded to their distress signal or the constant stream of communication from the Tuathans. Finn refused to allow her mind to focus on what that silence could mean for the twins and the rest of their friends. She needed to stay centered and concentrate on the plan . . . on getting to Tiri.

"It doesn't matter," Finn told her sister. "We have to keep going without them."

The sky lit up with orange flames as another huge explosion sent at least three of the Reliance ships careening to the earth below. The fiery vessels dropped from the sky, their impact causing multiple secondary explosions. The earsplitting booms hit their group a second later.

Finn signaled to everyone behind her, and the group increased their pace. They headed deeper into the hub of the city. As they did, the skyscrapers around them seemed to grow in size the closer they got,.

"Eleven blocks left," Finn muttered. She took a deep, steadying breath as her eyes scanned the streets. The sounds of several booted feet pounding the road echoed from her left and grew louder with each passing second. Hearing it, the group stayed their approach. Following Finn's lead, they hurried down the nearest alleyway and waited.

At least a dozen armed Reliance soldiers sprinted around the corner of a synthetic flower boutique on the opposite side of the street, followed by a small squadron flying several feet above the ground in hover pods. The soldiers were dressed for war in their anachronistic steel-toed jackboots, high-collared, red waistcoats bearing the Arcturian eye, golden leather gloves, and holsters across their chests and at their hips.

Finn's pulse pounded in her ears as she waited for them to pass. She felt Conrad tug on her sleeve from behind.

"Incoming," he whispered.

Finn turned toward the mouth of the alley behind them. A small group of soldiers had entered the space at their rear, forming a wall of red and gold as they searched the area for threats. They had a Sirian in their midst and the massive alien's lupine snout twitched and sniffed at the air. Eventually, either more would join their ranks, or Finn and the others would be pushed through the mouth of the alley and into the streets, leaving them open and vulnerable to attack.

The Sirian's yellow eyes scanned the length of the alley until they fell on the group of hybrids.

Enyo growled low in her throat. Finn's eyes dropped to the female's hands and watched as her nails elongated to small, pointed daggers at the tips of her fingers. The Sirian soldier snarled, drawing the attention of the others.

"There they are!" one shouted.

Finn engaged the hard-light shield, just as the soldiers began to open fire. Blasts from plasma guns bounced off the shield and into the buildings on either side of them, shattering the glass and sending the shards raining down on them. Finn increased the shield's radius with the flick of her finger and the hard-light projection formed a dome around their group.

The soldiers approached slowly, maintaining formation. Some of them fiddled with comms, no doubt alerting the other patrolling squadrons of their location.

The Sirian broke away from the rest. His enraged yellow gaze remained lasered in on Enyo. Suddenly, he fell to all fours and charged them. The beast snarled and snapped at the air and his claws scraped against the gold-flecked concrete as he tore down the alley.

The soldiers followed his lead and rushed the group.

Enyo crouched low in a ready battle stance.

"Lower the shield," the hybrid growled. Her tawny eyes never left the approaching Sirian as she tracked his movements.

"Not yet," Finn told her.

The soldiers continued to fire plasma and stunner blasts, but as their frenzy to reach them grew, the shots became wild, bouncing in all directions.

"Finn," Iliana whispered as the soldiers neared. Finn's hand wrapped around her plasma gun. Her indigo eyes tracked their movements as she silently counted down from three in her head. When she reached one, she turned to Conrad.

"Now!" she yelled.

The glow of Conrad's azure gaze washed over them. Before the soldiers had time to shield their eyes, their forward momentum halted mid-step. Their hands flew in the air and the plasma guns were ripped free from their grips. The weapons hung midair as though held aloft by ghostly specters. Mouths agape, the soldiers' shocked and confused expressions remained fixed above on the floating guns.

Gritting his teeth, Conrad's eyes began to glow brighter than she'd ever seen them. The result was blinding. Finn squinted away the brightness and watched as the guns twisted in on themselves, their forms crumpling from an unseen pressure. Completely useless now, they dropped to the ground at the soldiers' booted feet. Shortly after, the stunner gloves were torn free of their hands. They went flying through the air and several feet around the alley's corner until they disappeared from sight.

Conrad, his mouth set in a hard line of concentration, breathed heavily from the exertion of manipulating so many people and weapons at once. He would need time before he could use his powers on such a large scale again.

Finn released the hard-light shield and the projection around them disappeared. She pulled her plasma gun and began firing, removing the shield and tossing it to Isis. The Aquariian slipped it on. Now she would be protected as she followed closely behind them to heal their fallen.

Finn knew the Aquariian wouldn't be able to heal them repeatedly without fatiguing and eventually burning out. She only hoped they could keep the injuries to a minimum and reserve the healer's strength until the time they reached the council headquarters.

Enyo set off in a blur of motion as she crouched down to all fours and sprinted toward the Sirian soldier. Finn cursed and immediately removed her finger from the trigger, afraid to hit the hybrid now sprinting directly in her line of fire.

When only a few feet separated them, both Enyo and the Sirian launched into the air. Their bodies collided and the male lashed out to slash the hybrid with his claws. Enyo grunted, but her movements never faltered. She wrapped her limbs around the soldier and sank her fangs into the tendon connecting his neck and shoulder. The male roared in pain as blood sprayed from the wound.

Finn lost sight of them as the rest of the soldiers shook off Conrad's abilities. They came unstuck—pulling the heavy reinforced wooden staffs from their belts—and began to advance. Grim moved from Finn's side and approached the onslaught with slow, steady strides.

They smiled as they took in his unhurried pace, incorrectly assuming him to be less of a threat because of it. Those smiles faltered and their eyes widened with surprise and terror when he began to snatch them from his path and throw them in the air like sacks of wheat. The Khaleerian's rhythmic, calm breaths never increased, even as he sent the men flying into buildings. Their bodies hit the concrete with sickening thuds and their screams of alarm died on impact.

The hybrids behind Finn began to move, running to meet the remaining soldiers head-on. Axel roared. Though his skin had darkened to an angry red, his eyes remained clear. He appeared to be maintaining control as he grabbed the soldier closest to him and ripped out the man's throat with minimal effort. The human's hands came up to clutch the ragged, bleeding wound as he fell to the ground. He thrashed and gurgled for a few seconds before his movements ceased.

Iliana followed the path Grim cleared as he shot out calculated kicks at soldiers' chests and sent them flying. Every now and then, one would slip through and Finn watched with pride as her sister squared up and took them out.

Dropping her shoulders and raising her fists, the courtesan ducked out of the way of an impending blow from a soldier's staff and spun back to face him. She blocked a hard left her opponent tossed her way. Using the man's momentum to her advantage, she wrapped her arm under and around his bicep and flipped him to the ground.

More soldiers began to flood the alley and Conrad refocused his efforts on disarming them with his abilities. She worried he was tapped out, but only a moment passed before more plasma guns and stunner gloves went flying. Though he tried to hide it, his heavy breathing and the lines of tension around his eyes showed his fatigue.

"Isis," Finn called. When the Aquariian turned to her, she motioned the healer over to Conrad with a nod of her head. The female hurried over to the big man, disengaging her shield to pull him close and then re-engaging. Her cyan blue hands began to glow as she placed them on Conrad's chest and closed her eyes.

Finn was surprised to see Zekiel running in front of the duo and taking out any soldiers who broke through with a brutal efficiency that belied his advancing age. Every so often he would turn to Isis and Conrad—fully protected by the hard-light shield. Once satisfied with their safety, he would return to the bedlam.

Finn darted out of the path of a wooden staff heading toward her in a downward arc. She spun around behind the soldier wielding it and launched a hard kick to the back of his knees. The man collapsed to all fours just as another soldier came running at her from the left. She pointed her plasma gun at the back of the former's head and squeezed. He collapsed to the ground in a motionless heap, the hole in the back of his head still smoking as he did.

Finn turned just in time to take the impact of the latter's body as he side-tackled her to the ground. As they rolled, he ended up on top, and she took a hard punch to the jaw. She fought past the blinding stars filling her vision and lifted her hips. All the while, she dodged the ensuing rain of frantic punches to her face.

Wiggling her lower body, she displaced the soldier enough to get her feet up and kick him off. She rolled to stand and charged him before he could recover and gain his footing. Pulling one of the knives free of its strap, she fell upon the dazed soldier and sank the blade into his neck, severing his jugular.

His eyes bulged with terror and his hands came up to his throat. Finn heard a yell behind her and turned just in time to see Enyo soaring through the air. She fell upon a soldier who stood with his staff raised in the air and seconds from bashing in the back of Finn's skull. Enyo took him to the ground and straddled his hips. He screamed for mercy as she brought her claws down and slashed violently at his face and throat.

"The Sirian?" She asked Enyo, whose only response was a bone-chilling, bloody grin.

Finn nodded her gratitude to her friend and moved on to square off with two more soldiers sprinting her way. Conrad appeared at her side and intercepted one of them. The soldier held a long blade in his hand and slashed at the blue-eyed hybrid. Conrad pulled his abdomen back and narrowly avoided being sliced wide open. He straightened and blocked his attacker's forearm on a downward arc. He followed up with a sharp headbutt, connecting just above the man's nose.

Finn returned her attention to the other soldier heading her way. He paused mid-sprint and gaped as one of his brethren sailed over his head and landed headfirst on the ground with a sickening crunch.

Thanks, Grim.

Taking advantage of the distraction, Finn holstered her plasma gun and charged. She unsheathed two wicked blades the length of her forearm and sprinted at the man. He didn't even see her coming until she sank both knives into his neck. As he dropped, four more soldiers came at her from the left. Finn briefly skipped backward and forced them into a funnel. The closest two rushed in with their staves raised. Just as they came within striking range, Finn flicked her wrists and splashed the fallen soldier's blood from her blades into their eyes. The act blinded them long enough for the pair to stumble.

She reversed the grip on her knives and shoved them through the men's exposed throats. Twisting, she yanked hard and sprayed gore in an arc. One fell to the ground instantly and she shoulder-checked the other, sending him tumbling over his compatriot.

The remaining two soldiers hesitated slightly before attacking. One of them yelled, spurring the other past his indecision, and they both came at her with renewed grit.

Finn stood to her full height and waved them over with a long blade. They at least showed more sense than the cooling corpses at their feet and spread out to flank her. Both attacked her from opposite sides. One used the staff of the fallen soldier below him and staggered his attack pattern to keep her on the defense.

A heavy boot to the ribs sent her reeling, and she rolled to her side, struggling to breathe. Faster than he had any business being, the larger of the two swung his staff in an attempt to cave her skull in. At the last second, she raised her blades in an X to deflect the blow. They shattered on impact.

She rolled in desperation, and when she got the distance she needed, she drew a pair of smaller blades. Each curved hook extended from the bottom of her grip with a blade as long as the width of her palms. She leapt and dug them both under the soldier's ribs. Savagely, she ripped outward, disemboweling him.

The last remaining soldier surprised her by throwing his staff at her head and sprinting straight toward her. She raised her arms to defend against the flying wooden weapon and it connected with her wrists, knocking the knives from her grip. He rushed her before she could reclaim the weapons or unholster her gun.

Using her abilities became her only choice.

As he neared, she wove, dipped, and evaded. Slipping every strike, her opponent finally relented for a brief moment to reset. Finn struck, placing her bare hands on either side of his face. For a split second, the unexpected movement stunned him.

"Ever wonder what two decades of pain feels like all at once?" she asked him quietly. Finn triggered her powers, sense memories flooding from her fingertips into the soldier. An overwhelming torrent of agony racked his brain and overloaded his nervous system. By the time she removed her hand, he was frothing at the mouth and unable to stand.

She let him fall into a heap and jogged back to the group. She headed straight for Isis and allowed the Aquariian to heal any damage using her abilities so forcefully may have inflicted.

"There's too many of them," Iliana yelled to her from across the fray. More soldiers began to flood the alley from both sides, closing in on their group and preventing any means of escape. They now outnumbered the hybrids five-to-one.

Axel stood closest to the opening, and a handful of newly arrived soldiers attacked him simultaneously. They latched on to the red giant's arms and legs. Another one leapt onto his back and wrapped thick forearms around his neck. Enraged, Axel bellowed to the skies. Before he could dislodge and throw them off, they began to beat him with their staffs.

Grim fought to get to the young Khaleerian hybrid, but a wall of soldiers stood between them. He slashed out at them, knocking back several violently, but two more stepped forward in their place.

Finn unholstered her gun and aimed at the crowd, hoping to create an opening for Axel. Before she could squeeze the trigger, she heard Isis yell from behind the wall of hard light. Finn followed the direction of the Aquariian's gaze.

Overwhelmed by a three-person attack—two in front and one behind—Iliana took a hard kick to the midsection and doubled over. The soldier at her back sent a violent kick to the backs of her legs and sent her staggering forward to the ground. Enyo roared her rage, but a new line of soldiers blocked the path between her and the courtesan.

No! As Finn took in the wall of enemies between them, her mind screamed, and her heart raced with panic.

There was no way she could reach her sister in time.

Finn began firing in vain on the line of soldiers separating her from her sister. One by one, she left smoking holes in their chests and heads. As they dropped in succession, several more rushed forward to take their place.

Finn shouted her rage when a barrier formed in front of her, and she lost sight of the courtesan. Suddenly, crossfire from a soldier's plasma gun grazed her right wrist. The wound cauterized on contact, but the surprise and ensuing sting of pain caused her to drop her weapon.

Holding her injured wrist, she bent to pick it up. A shadow fell over her and she ducked just in time to avoid a killing blow from the enemy's wooden staff. Her eyes landed on a loose staff lying on the ground. She toed the staff and kicked it into the air, catching it on its descent. As her opponent's weapon slashed through the air a second time, she raised her staff with both hands to block it. Ignoring the sting from her injury, she held fast and shot her foot out to kick him in the groin. When he hunched over on impact, she brought the wooden staff down on his spine.

She continued to beat back the encroaching soldiers until she finally got Iliana back in her line of sight. The courtesan was struggling to remain upright. Blood poured from a gash above her eye. Her hunched shoulders and heavy breathing highlighted her fatigue. She blinked away the blood trickling into her vision. Distracted, she never saw the soldier behind her . . . or the plasma gun aimed at the back of her skull.

Finn screamed her sister's name.

As she did, time seemed to slow down. Iliana's pain-filled gaze found Finn across the fray and filled with resignation. Tears streamed down Finn's face, mingling with the sweat and dirt there.

As she watched, frozen, smoke began to waft from the top of the head and hands of Iliana's attacker. Belatedly, the man seemed to register the temperature change. He shrieked with pain and he became engulfed in blue flames. One by one, the soldiers around Iliana burst into flames. The individual fires remained strangely contained—never spreading—and went out as soon as each soldier fell to the ground and ceased flailing.

Finn's chest squeezed with hope. More soldiers around her began to drop as smoke filled the alley. Her eyes lifted and searched the sky. She caught sight of giant, talon-tipped wings soaring in the air above them.

Mace.

The winged hybrid swooped down until he flew a few feet above the ground. As he neared, Finn realized he was carrying something. His smooth features were pulled tight with exertion and the muscles of his arms pulled taut. They stayed that way until he let go of the weight and shot straight back up into the air. A dark figure fell to the cement ground of the alley and landed on his booted feet. The newcomer stood to his full height and lifted his bald head.

Aedan's dark eyes found Finn in the crowd, and he began throwing carefully aimed balls of fire at the soldiers surrounding her on either side. The flames engulfing his hands made him look like an avenging angel. Once he'd taken out the attackers in her immediate vicinity, he moved with calculated strides and carved a pathway over to Conrad.

Sweat glistened on Conrad's body as he fought a brutal battle of five against one, holding his own despite being outnumbered. He alternated between using his abilities and hand-to-hand combat.

Aedan launched more fireballs at Conrad's opponents, sending them to the ground aflame and shrieking with agony. Conrad looked up from the blazing semi-circle surrounding him to see Aedan. After a long moment, Conrad grinned and closed the distance between them.

Aedan watched his approach warily, his head cocked to the side with confusion until Conrad extended his hand to the firebrand and clapped him on the back. "Welcome to the fight!" Conrad shouted over the noise of the fray. The two exchanged a smile before they squared up back-to-back and returned their attention to the conflict around them.

A crush of soldiers slowly closed in on them, their bodies forming an imposing circle around the duo.

"We outnumber you ten to one," the squad leader shouted to Conrad and Aedan. Nervous sweat covered his forehead. "Surrender now and your deaths will be quick."

"Ten to one?" Aedan asked casually, as he tossed a predatory grin to Conrad behind him. "You definitely should've brought more guys."

The soldiers were so startled by the hybrid's casual dismissal of their numbers, it took them a moment before they came unstuck and attacked. Conrad lunged at the closest soldier, grabbed a combat knife from the holster at his hip, and buried it in the man's neck.

Behind him, Aedan tackled one soldier into another. Standing, he smashed the first soldier's head with the heel of his boot and repeatedly punched the other in his face until he went limp. As the fiery giant rose to address the next two in range, a wet squelch distracted him. Aedan spun in time to see a Reliance soldier fall to the ground with a blade jutting between his eyes.

Aeden grinned and gave Conrad a nod of approval for his kill. "Nice one."

Conrad's eyes gleamed with blue fire and his expression filled with menace as he held off a new squad of attackers.

"Thanks," he called over to Aedan.

The two hybrids lost themselves in a dirty ballet of violence, each using brute force and sheer overwhelming power to reduce the opposing force's numbers in short order.

One soldier grabbed a fistful of Conrad's dreads and pulled hard enough to loosen one. Conrad roared from deep within his chest. He grabbed the offending hand in one of his own, grabbed the man's wrist with the other, and rolled. The motion pulled the soldier to his knees and set him off-balance. He then wedged a boot into the man's throat and yanked hard, crushing his windpipe.

Above them, Mace returned. Once again, he flew low to the ground, and dropped two more newcomers into the melee. Raven landed on a soldier, knocking the man to the ground, and rolling with him. Jax dropped a few feet to her left. His ambers eyes sought out Axel. When he found the red, giant, he grinned. He sported multiple bleeding wounds, but it was obvious that whoever gave him those wounds got even worse.

Mace dove low and extended his wings, taking out a line of soldiers. His talons sliced into the humans' skin, sending a fountain of blood spraying in his wake.

As Mace flew up, a stray beam of plasma tore through his right wing, leaving a smoking hole in its wake. He flailed in the air. The wind whipped and tore through his wing, sending him toppling to the ground. He landed and rolled, curling his wings around himself to soften the fall.

Mace shot to his feet and brought his fists under his chin. He pivoted on his feet to address the approaching threats. Using his good wing as a weapon, Mace spun low to the ground and kicked out the feet of the soldier nearest him. As he moved, his wing swung out in a semi-circle. The row of deadly talons at the wing's tip shot out in an arc, decapitating the nearest row of Reliance soldiers.

"Sorry we're late," Lex called through the comm in Finn's ear. The mischievous pilot's chipper voice had never sounded sweeter.

Engines roared above them and *Independence* came into view. Hot wind slapped at their faces as the vessel hovered several meters above the ground. The ship's underbelly opened wide, and more figures began to pour out from within. They dropped from ropes and descended the ship's metal ladder in a wave.

Madam Califax was nearly unrecognizable in her cargo pants and a long-sleeved shirt. The upper-caste female's brown hair had been pulled away from her face, set with determination as she stood on the roof of a nearby building and eyed the enemy through the sight of a plasma rifle. Mr. Green—the stylish announcer from the Dome— dropped down to the roof next to her. The upper-caste male had traded his glittery makeup and flamboyant clothes for combat boots, a simple shirt, and tactical cargo pants. Like

Madam Califax, he eyed their group from behind the sight of a plasma rifle.

More and more people Finn didn't recognize began to rush to their aid, including a small group of hybrids she'd never seen before. The fight began to pour out into the street as the rapidly increasing number of allies joined the battle.

Finn caught Grim's gaze. His dark eyes softened with relief for a moment, before he went back to snatching soldiers up and throwing them through the air.

With renewed energy, she turned back to the soldiers nearest her. They were busy staring into the distance at Raven, watching as she squared off with another row of soldiers. Her mouth opened, and she released a low-frequency cry.

The noise never reached Finn, but she could see the sound waves in the air where the hybrid's shriek had left her lips. They shot out in a concentrated mass of energy. The force of the reverberation sent the soldiers soaring backward as they clutched their bleeding ears.

Using the chaos and the soldiers' inattention to her advantage, Finn took them out easily with brutal hits from the wooden staff she still clutched in her right hand.

Even more soldiers fell to the ground around her in a growing heap and Finn looked up to see Madam Califax and Mr. Green. With brutal efficiency, the duo perched overhead and picked the enemy off one by one from behind the sights of their rifles.

Isis remained concealed behind the safety of her hard-light shield. She left a freshly revived Iliana and ran between the battling groups looking for more injuries to heal. Zekiel followed closely behind. The Aquariian's blue skin had paled, and her silver eyes were dark with fatigue.

How much longer could she keep up with the demand for her abilities?

Jax and Axel worked together, clearing a path through the alley and out into the street. Axel swung both arms out and violently clotheslined multiple soldiers at once, while Jax picked off anyone who managed to break through. The pilot looked around until his eyes landed on Finn.

"Let's go!" he shouted. "We need to get you to the headquarters."

Finn motioned to Grim. The Khaleerian immediately gathered their group—made up of Enyo, Iliana, Isis, Zekiel, and Conrad—and ushered them through the alley. Axel, Jax, and Aedan followed closely behind. Together, they sprinted down the street, dodging the plasma fire of pursuing soldiers as they did. Conrad and Iliana kept pace on either side of her.

"We're almost there," Jax shouted from behind her.

The council headquarters came into sight straight ahead, looming above them. Their feet pounded the pavement as more and more smoke filled the sky above them, and glass from the skyscrapers shattered and fell to the ground around them. Several times Finn just barely managed to dodge huge shards of glass that could have decapitated her.

When less than four blocks separated them from their destination, the earsplitting sound of approaching engines stopped them in their tracks. They ducked and covered their heads, watching in horror as a massive Reliance gunship shot through the sky toward them. The bulky, modular vessel painted an intimidating picture. Dimly, Finn thought it looked like a giant gun covered in more guns. It stopped abruptly and hovered above them.

Conrad's eyes began to glow. His muscles tensed as he focused his concentration on the enemy vessel.

"I can't hold their fire for long," he told her through gritted teeth.

The group stood open and exposed in the middle of the street. In the distance, *Independence* and her allies remained locked in battle and unable to break away to assist them.

There was nowhere to run . . . nowhere to hide.

More Reliance aircraft joined the gunship. Conrad began to shake and sweat broke out on his brow.

Finn locked gazes with her sister and grabbed her hand. On her other side, she reached out with her free hand and interlaced fingers with Conrad.

They'd come so far, only to get this close and fail.

The gunship's weapons whined low as they prepared to fire.

Finn felt Grim's stare, and her eyes flitted over to him. His gaze filled with regret as he watched her. She squeezed Conrad's then Iliana's hands and closed her eyes.

"Incoming!" The shout coming from the comm in her ear jolted Finn and her eyes shot open. The gunship above them took several direct hits from enemy fire, sending pieces of shrapnel flying off. She tilted her head up to Conrad and found his glowing gaze had widened with surprise.

"That was Shane," he told her, surprise filling his voice. He pressed a finger to his comm and smiled wryly. "Did you have to wait until the last second?" he asked his brother through the device.

A barrage of fire rained down on the Reliance gunship above them, forcing the vessel to turn and face the new threat head-on.

"You know me, I like to make an entrance," the captain of *Independence* quipped. Through the smoke, dozens of smaller Reliance gunships shot through the sky, continuing to rain fire on their brethren. At least half of their numbers raced off to aid *Independence* several blocks away, while the other half warred with the ships above Finn and her companions. Finn released her hold on Conrad's and Iliana's hands.

"Those are Reliance ships," Finn breathed as she pointed to the newcomers. "Why is the Reliance firing on its own people?"

Conrad glanced down at her and began ushering her further down the street as he spoke.

"Shane has made a lot of allies over the cycles. He's not the only member of the upper caste who disagrees with the way the Reliance is running things."

Finn remembered Shane's argument with Grim. *There are innocent people out there in the Inner Rings . . . good people who don't agree with the Reliance.*

The group maneuvered further down the street.

"This is why he left without a fight," Finn stated in amazement. "He always planned on gathering allies."

Conrad nodded.

With the addition of Shane and the gunships, the opposing sides were finally evenly matched. The diversion allowed their group to traverse another two blocks toward their destination.

Several of the ally ships lowered, dropping ground support as they did. Dozens of soldiers and hybrids swarmed the streets, flanking them on either side. Sasha—looking every bit like her Supersonic alter ego from the Dome—led the charge, zipping around and disarming enemy soldiers so fast, she became nothing more than a blurry dot in the distance.

Behind her, a wall of hybrids in every shape and size—ranging from a handful of Kreetian hybrids to half-Saosin hybrids like Mace. Even a few half-Goslans that must have been grown in a lab followed the trail Supersonic blazed, taking out soldiers with poisoned tentacles as they did.

"Look at all of them," Finn breathed.

Conrad tugged her into motion, following the rest of the group.

"It looks like my brother has been busy," he told her quickly, but with no small amount of pride.

Finn didn't get a chance to digest his words. An explosion tore through the street next to them, shattering the glass of the buildings on either side of their group. The force of the blast lifted them from the ground and sent them all flying.

The impact knocked the air from Finn's lungs and left her gasping. She barely registered the muffled sounds of running and screaming through the intense ringing in her ears. She coughed, wincing at the fire in her ribs the movement elicited. She forced herself up to her hands and knees and wiped at her eyes, struggling to see through the dust and smoke. When she pulled her hand away, blood coated her fingers.

Feeling around for injuries, her fingertips brushed over a cut just above her temple and she flinched. Her hands reached out and she ran them blindly over the ground until she felt a hand. Finn latched on and crawled over. She found Iliana staring up at her with a faraway look in her eyes.

"Li," Finn whispered between coughs. Her sister's indigo eyes drifted over to her and blinked slowly . . . too slowly. Finn's voice became urgent as she scooted closer. "Li?"

Iliana lifted a hand to her younger sister's face, but it dropped weakly less than halfway to its goal. Dark-red blood pooled below her abdomen, staining her shirt and dripping down to the gold-flecked cement beneath them. Finn's eyes frantically searched her sister's body, finding shards of glass had embedded themselves in her chest and stomach.

"No," Finn moaned, and the sound became a low wail as it left her lips. "Help me!"

As the battle waged on both above and below, Isis and Zekiel dropped to their knees at her side. Grim, Aedan, and Conrad formed a barrier of protection between the huddled quartet and the violent combat taking place behind them. Isis's lean body sagged into Finn. She felt the Aquariian's shallow breaths as she worked Iliana's shirt up and got started on the worst of her wounds.

"Isis," Zekiel warned. "You can't take much more."

The healer waved him off with a tight smile.

"I will be fine, my friend."

"Isis—" Finn began. The dual sides of her brain warred with one another. If they lost the healer, they would be flying into the lion's den without a safety net. But if Isis did nothing, Iliana would die.

"It's all right, Finn," Isis cut her off. "Just hold your sister's hand."

Numb and shaking, Finn did as she said.

Isis reached out with trembling hands and placed them on Iliana. A blue glow began to emanate from her fingers. The radiance gradually spread, washing over Iliana, and shrouding her in light.

Ever so slowly, the courtesan blinked. She gazed up at Finn and took a deep, gasping breath. She sat up—so quickly, her head almost slammed against Finn's chin—and threw herself into her little sister's arms. Holding her tightly, Finn turned to the Aquariian at her side and her eyes went wide with horror.

"Isis!"

The healer fell into Zekiel's waiting arms and collapsed against him. Her already shallow breaths became ragged. Zekiel traced his fingers gently down her cheek as tears welled in his amber eyes. Finn dove to the Aquariian's side and grasped the alien's slender blue hand in her own. Isis squeezed weakly as her lids drooped.

"Isis," Finn cried as she rambled. "It's going to be okay. Just tell me what to do. Tell me how to help you." Tears streamed down her dirt-streaked cheeks.

"There is nothing. I am exactly where I am meant to be and I have no regrets," she told Finn between wheezes. "Now . . ." With a final burst of strength, she pushed Finn away and her steely eyes narrowed. "Go and get our girl."

Finn choked on a sob as the others closed in from behind. Grim pulled her to her feet and into his arms. She kept her eyes on Isis, watching as the Aquariian's eyes closed with one last rattling breath, and she went limp in Zekiel's arms.

"We have to go," the Khaleerian told her as he spun her away from another falling ship's shrapnel.

Finn nodded and swiped at the tears under her eyes. Enyo helped Iliana to her feet and pulled her in for a tight embrace. The courtesan's lip quivered as she stared at Isis's lifeless body. Finn held her sister's eyes until her breathing steadied.

Zekiel finally released his hold on the Aquariian and gently placed her fully on the ground. He stood, whispering a prayer under his breath as he did. When he finished, his eyes roamed over the group and narrowed.

"Let's go."

EIGHTEEN

Finn held her ribs and trailed the others as they sprinted the rest of the way to the council headquarters. A line of soldiers waited for them, guns drawn.

"There's another entrance around the side of the tower," Finn told Grim between pants.

Several of the soldiers began firing. They sent the plasma streams from their guns straight into the group.

Too many injuries slowed her movements and before she could dart out of the way, Finn found herself staring down an incoming beam of plasma aimed at her chest. In a fruitless bid to protect herself, her hands shot up. Just before the plasma could smoke a hole in the center of her chest, a blur of movement shot in front of her.

Sasha's dark eyes widened and froze on Finn as the beam tore through her midsection from behind and came out the other side to graze Finn's arm. She dove forward to catch the speedster as the woman's legs folded and she collapsed.

Using his abilities, Conrad halted the remaining streams midflight. He strained from the monumental effort, sweat pouring through his dredlocks and down his face.

Finn gently brought Sasha to the ground.

"Pretty sure . . . you . . . have to . . . forgive me now," Sasha rasped, choking on her own blood between words. She gasped then, and the pupils in her eyes dilated. Finally, she went limp.

With a guttural yell, Conrad reversed the plasma rays' path and sent them back into the line of soldiers. They barely had time to shout their surprise before the beams tore through them. Aedan shot fireballs at another group and Axel and Enyo charged the rest on foot.

"Go!" Conrad yelled to them. "We'll hold them."

Finn locked eyes with him. Her gaze screamed her denial. If he continued to use his powers without inhibition, he'd be leaving himself weak and vulnerable.

As they held hers, his glowing eyes softened almost imperceptibly. He nodded once for her to make her escape and returned his focus to the melee ahead.

Enyo dove and tackled a soldier to the ground, slashing his throat as they landed. Another soldier ran at her from behind but stopped short when Iliana stepped into his path. She cracked him on the side of the skull with a staff, taking him by surprise. His head snapped to the side and he collapsed.

One of his comrades grabbed the courtesan from behind and wrapped one arm around her middle and the other around her throat. Rather than panic, Iliana reached out a hand behind her, feeling around until she caressed his cheek tenderly, as though they were lovers.

The man's eyes widened and his mouth opened in a silent scream. His arms released her. She spun out of his grip in time to watch the male scratch at his eyes and crumple to the ground in a broken heap.

Jax ran to Finn's side. His face was covered in dust and soot, giving his dark complexion a gray hue.

"What are we waiting for? Let's go!"

Before she could move, one of the smaller Reliance gunships dove low overhead and began firing on them. Grim picked her up and threw her out of the line of fire, before diving in the opposite direction. She had precious seconds to brace for impact. She took the brunt of the fall on her right side, jarring her injured ribs more than she would have liked, but not enough to incur further damage.

Finn rolled and stumbled her way to a standing position. The gunship was headed on a straight trajectory for Jax, who stood alone and exposed in the street. The beams of plasma tore through the cement closer and closer to the young hybrid and sent a spray of concrete shooting into the air like fireworks.

A roar sounded behind her and Finn turned to see Axel charging across the roof of one of the shorter buildings nearest Jax. His skin had turned a dark crimson and his face twisted in unbridled rage. His barrel chest heaved as he sprinted from one end of the roof to the other and dove off.

Despite the sheer mass of his body, he practically flew. Time stood still for a moment as Finn watched Axel sail through the air and land on the hood of the gunship firing on Jax. On impact, the vessel tilted and wavered from the added weight. Before it could right itself, Axel began pounding his fists into the cockpit, shattering the glass, and causing the plasma guns to fire wildly in all directions.

Jax watched the action unfold with dawning horror.

Axel slammed his fists down one last time, sending both the vessel and the hybrid careening into the nearest building.

The ensuing explosion shattered the glass and shook the ground.

"Axel!" Jax screamed and ran toward the fire, but Zekiel tagged the back of his shirt and pulled him into his arms. The elder Tuathan whispered something against the struggling hybrid's tear-streaked cheek and Jax's shoulders sagged. Soon, they began to shake with sobs. Zekiel squeezed his biceps and whispered something else in his ear and Jax's shaking ceased.

"We need to go!" Grim shouted. He grabbed Finn's wrist and tugged her toward the building's side entrance. Zekiel released Jax and the pair followed close behind.

Grim dispatched the steady stream of stray soldiers that crossed their path with minimal effort. Finn tried to breathe around the pain in her ribs as she struggled to keep pace with the others.

They made it to the building's side entrance and pushed their way through the doors. Stepping inside, golden, marble floors covered with shiny, red geometric shapes filled their view. Each one had an Arcturian eye painted in its center. Red, velvet rugs carved a path up a golden double staircase leading to a row of gilded elevators. A towering Arcturian statue loomed between them.

Unable to help herself, Finn's wide eyes scanned up past the glittering, gold-flecked columns and matching walls covered in full-length mirrors to the red, velvet drapes mounted atop sweeping glass windows framed in gold, and matching crystal chandeliers. When her gaze reached the ceiling, her mouth dropped open in shock. The aureate arched ceiling was covered in breathtaking gold leaf and bas-relief; she'd never seen their equal, not even in one of Grim's books.

"Holy Gods," Jax muttered in awe. "We could break down this building and feed the Outer Rings for a decade."

Zekiel placed his hand on the young man's shoulder and urged him toward the staircase. "A wonderful idea we should revisit when we're not in imminent danger," he said.

Finn unfroze and followed her companions to the staircase. Though each step set her aching ribs on fire, she managed to climb them without too much issue. When they reached the top, three soldiers waited for them—one in front of each elevator—with guns drawn.

"Fire!" one of them shouted.

Before they could do so, though, the guns were torn from the men's hands and sent airborne. They landed at the foot of the stairs where Conrad stood panting, his eyes glowing brightly.

His expression was forbidding as he motioned with his head for Finn to get moving.

Jax turned to her, eyeing the immobile soldiers, and cracking his knuckles.

"You go ahead. We've got this."

Ending the conversation, Grim strode forward and punched the nearest soldier so hard the impact of his body dented the elevator doors. He picked the man up by the collar of his waistcoat and sent him soaring through the air. The dead soldier landed with a thud just as the elevator opened. Zekiel, Grim, and Finn filed in and the doors closed on Jax and Conrad engaging the other two soldiers.

The seconds it took to ascend to the highest floor of the building felt like an eternity. When the elevator finally stopped and the doors opened, plasma guns immediately began firing on them. Finn dove behind the corner of the elevator. One by one, she and Zekiel used their plasma guns to pick off the line of soldiers waiting for them with cold accuracy. Grim took out any stragglers with the throwing knives he'd strapped to his thigh. Once the threat had been eliminated, the trio rushed out from within and froze.

The chancellor stepped out from the shadows and into the center of the corridor, radiating menace and blocking them from their destination. Tiri stood in front of him, wincing at the painful grip the man's left hand had on her little shoulder. In his other hand, he held a plasma gun to the girl's head.

"Put it down. Both of you," he ordered, motioning to Finn's weapon.

Tiri's green eyes widened to orbs when she caught sight of her trio of rescuers. Finn gave the child a brief glance to assess her wellbeing and kept her focus on the chancellor. The fact that she was still alive and unharmed meant he hadn't discovered her abilities or true origins.

Finn holstered her gun and held her hands up in supplication.

Finn! You came! The child's relieved voice filled her head. Her blonde curls swayed as she looked behind them expectantly. *Where's Isis?*

Finn kept her expression neutral and locked eyes with the chancellor. They darted wildly between her, Grim, Zekiel, and the explosions lighting up the sky outside, making him look slightly more deranged than usual. His hand around the gun trembled.

She'd been right before. He hadn't expected them to make it this far.

Keep still, Kid. We'll get you out of here.

Tiri's brows furrowed, but she stilled her movements and remained quiet.

"Let her go, Alistair," she told him. She kept her hands raised and moved slowly in a semi-circle so as not to spook him. He tracked her movements, taking in the way she favored her right side and the blood still caking her face.

His skin reddened in anger and his eyes shot fire.

"Why won't you die?" he screamed at her, spittle shooting from his lips and dotting his grotesquely scarred face as he did.

"I could ask you the same thing," she quipped, trying to keep his focus and rage on her and only her. Grim prowled to his left just out of the chancellor's eyesight. If she bought him enough time, Grim could incapacitate the chancellor and free Tiri from his hold. It was a risk, drawing the wrath of an already crazed man, but Tiri was too important to risk. She continued baiting the chancellor, to hold his attention. "I won't waste my breath. We both know you're more cockroach than man."

The chancellor's eyes glittered dangerously. He removed the gun from Tiri's head and pointed it at Finn. Despite the new danger to herself, Finn's shoulders sagged infinitesimally with relief. With painfully slow, calculated steps, Grim continued to close the distance between himself and the chancellor.

"And you're nothing but a dirty street rat. Fortunately, I know how to exterminate vermin," he told her as his finger slid over the trigger. "Did you really think you could beat us?" Grim took another silent step. Suddenly, the chancellor glanced back at the Khaleerian and clucked his tongue. "You really don't know when to quit do you?" he asked the horned alien. "You had your chance to stop this, old man. Now you lose everything. Again."

Grim moved so quickly that the chancellor didn't have time to prepare. The Khaleerian dove the rest of the distance separating them. The chancellor's smile faltered as the Khaleerian collided with him. He managed to fire off a round before impact. As he fell, his finger continued to squeeze the trigger and the plasma gun fired several more times. A stray beam hit Finn squarely in the chest and she flew backward, dropping to the ground. She felt nothing but the fire's excruciating heat from her neck down.

"Finn!" Tiri screamed and ran toward her.

"No!" Grim's agonized bellow reached Finn a second later. Turning her head, she brought her gaze from the arched ceiling to the Khaleerian.

She had a clear view of the side of his face twisted in rage. His massive chest heaved with fury. He stood over the chancellor, watching him gasp and struggle to recover from the impact of the Khaleerian's horned head. Grim reached down with his hand, grabbed the chancellor's jaw, and lifted him, holding him aloft.

The chancellor fired two more rounds before the Khaleerian wrapped his other hand around the chancellor's and squeezed, crushing the bones of his hand to dust.

The Khaleerian turned his other giant hand where it held the chancellor under his jaw and wrapped his fingers around the sides of his head. His palm covered his nose and mouth, and the chancellor's eyes shot wide as he tried to breathe. Grim leaned in until their noses almost touched and hissed, "For my daughter."

The chancellor's face registered his confusion for a moment, before his eyes fell on Finn and realization dawned. Then,

Grim's hand closed around the chancellor's face and squeezed slowly. He continued to squeeze, ignoring the cracking of bones and guttural choking sounds coming from his victim as he crushed the man's jaw, teeth, and soft palate. The blood vessels of Alistair's remaining good eye popped, giving it the same red hue as one of his beloved Arcturians.

Grim finally released him and the chancellor fell to the ground with a loud thud. He landed facing Finn. Her gaze remained locked on his, taking in the macabre picture of the bloody, broken lower half of his face. Eyes on Finn, the chancellor took one last, wet, rattling breath before finally leaving this world for good.

Dimly, Finn registered Zekiel crouching above her with sobbing Tiri at his side. The elder Tuathan's face pulled taut with concentration as he slapped at the sparks emanating from her chest.

Sparks?

Finn looked down and noted the smoke billowing from the coin-sized hole in the chest of her jacket. Zekiel tore the garment open to reveal the smoldering prototype device she'd tucked into her inside pocket earlier that day.

"It worked. The limiter absorbed the plasma's energy." Zekiel told her with relief, as he pried the device from her clothes. "It saved you."

At his ministrations, Finn cried out in pain. A tear below the neck of her shirt revealed a shallow, ragged wound surrounded by severely burned skin. Her eyes teared and she gritted her teeth. Still, she'd recover. The injury wasn't nearly as bad as it could have been.

Grim stomped slowly to her side. Relief had begun to seep into his gaze until he scanned her body, and the anger swiftly returned. His jaw tightened when he saw the wound. Tiri's hand clung to hers as tears streamed down her face.

"It's okay," Finn told them both. "I'm okay." Zekiel helped her sit up. Finn's eyes roved Tiri from top to toe before she reached for the girl and pulled her close. "What about you? Did he hurt you?"

"No," Tiri mumbled into Finn's shoulder.

Grim fell to his knees at her side and she finally took note of his ragged breathing and pained expression.

Finn sat up straighter.

"Grim?" The Khaleerian's eyelids drooped as he looked down at her. A second later, he collapsed from his knees and fell fully to the ground. "Grim!"

The searing pain in her chest and ribs stole Finn's breath, but she ignored it to dive to Grim's side. He landed on his back, his breathing shallow, and stared up at the ceiling. Finn leaned over him, putting her face in his line of sight. His dark gaze fell on her and he blinked slowly. Panicked, she scanned his body frantically, gasping when she glimpsed the holes piercing his chest and stomach.

"He's been shot!" she screamed a Zekiel. The elder Tuathan looked down at them in horror but remained frozen. "Do something!"

"I—I can't," he stammered.

Finn's hands shook as she placed them on his wounds and applied pressure in a feeble attempt to stem the flow of blood.

"The—The extract," she stammered to Zekiel. The elder Tuathan's eyes brimmed with sadness and his tone gentled.

"It cannot heal injuries like this."

Grim's hand covered hers on his chest and squeezed weakly.

"Everything is all right, *Dhala*." He expelled a wet cough and blood began to trickle down from the side of his mouth.

"Please, Grim," she sobbed, holding the side of his head with her free hand. Panic rose in her chest, making breathing an impossible task. "Please don't leave me. I can't do this alone."

Behind them, the elevator beeped, and the doors began to open. Finn tensed, tightening her hold on Grim's hand. Zekiel raised his gun and aimed. The doors opened fully to reveal Jax and Conrad. Dirt streaked their faces and blood oozed from various injuries, but the duo looked no worse for the wear. Seeing her on the ground, Conrad charged out, running down the corridor, and sliding to her side.

Grim took in the people surrounding him and released her hand to cup her cheek with his big palm.

"You are not alone." His eyes flitted to Conrad next to her and then returned to Finn. "You have your family now."

"*You're* my family," she told him desperately as her tears choked her.

"And you, Finn," he struggled to speak as his breathing became more ragged. "You will always be *my child*."

Finn wept freely and dropped her forehead until it touched his. Her tears fell onto his face, intermingling with his own. She wrapped her arms around him and held on tight. Several more coughs racked his body. When they eased, he turned his face toward her and whispered in her ear.

"Finish it."

Finn swallowed the wail desperately trying to escape and nodded. Grim wheezed one last time and his body went limp. His hand sagged, falling away from her face and dropping to his side.

He was gone.

She felt Conrad's hands at her back and turned into his arms. He held her tightly as she struggled to rein in her sobs. Several moments passed with nothing but the sounds of the war waging outside and Finn's weeping to break the silence. When her breathing had slowed somewhat, she pulled from Conrad's embrace and stood.

He watched her, his lips parted in confusion, as she limped away from them.

"Where are you going?"

She paused to look back at him over her shoulder.

"To finish this."

NINETEEN

Finn took in the Arcturians' resting place and quietly seethed. A row of at least a dozen stasis pods lined the walls of the room, beeping steadily and displaying each one's vitals on a line of holoscreens mounted there. The pods were connected to a console in the center of the room monitoring the machines and displaying the security feed from outside the doors.

The door leading to the Arcturians and their stasis pods had been locked and armed; guns mounted above the doorframe waited, ready to dispatch trespassers. Fortunately, her Tuathan companions had made short work of disarming the door's security and gaining entry without triggering the security measures put in place by the Reliance.

Much like the rest of the building, the room had been decorated in pure decadence, with several burgundy chaise lounges, golden wall sconces, countless paintings in gold frames, golden floors covered with red, geometric area rugs, and various sculptures.

"Finn, the plasma gun destroyed the conduit. We have no way of minimizing the damage your powers will inflict on your own body," Zekiel reminded her for the third time. "And there is no Isis to heal you."

Ignoring him, Finn searched the pods, peering through each glass viewing window until she found what she was looking for. She took in the sagging yellow skin and gaunt cheeks. The face on the other side appeared sicklier than it had in her memories, but she recognized him all the same: *Abraham.*

"This is the one." She pointed to the stasis pod and waited for Zekiel to join her. Instead of moving, he continued to stare at her, disbelieving. "Finn, if you go through with this without the limiter, it will kill you."

"That's not an option." At the sound of Conrad's angry rumble, Finn turned to see he and Jax had joined them inside. The Tuathan pilot didn't seem to be paying attention to their conversation if the far-off look in his sad eyes was any indication. Conrad's glowing blue eyes searched Finn for injuries. When they fell on the wound at her chest, he said, "You're already injured. If Zekiel says you can't do this safely without a limiter, then we're not taking the risk."

Finn walked to him and took his hand in hers. She motioned to the corner of the room where they'd set Tiri up on a lounge outside of earshot. The girl clutched a pillow to her chest and kept her eyes on the holoscreens above. Finn pled with her eyes for him to keep his voice down.

"We don't have a choice," she whispered.

Conrad clenched his jaw in stubborn defiance.

"We've already lost too much, Finn."

"That's exactly why I *have* to do this."

Before he could argue further, Jax joined their huddle and waved his fingers in front of his chest.

"Did somebody order a limiter?" he asked.

"Not now, Jax," Conrad growled.

Finn studied the pilot. Despite the jest, both his tone and facial expression were uncharacteristically subdued. The grief of losing Axel had cast a shadow over his eyes, tinging them with somber resignation. It was so out of character for the half-Tuathan, the stark contrast jarred her.

Finn turned to Zekiel to find him already watching the trio. His mind worked rapidly behind his eyes.

"Would that even work?" she asked him.

After a beat, he raised his gaze to her. "It could." Before any of them could react to his assessment he said, "It could also kill you both."

"Come on, we all know I'm too awesome to die." The pilot's halfhearted boast did little to inspire confidence. "Besides," he continued, "I'm the most powerful half-Tuathan in the room."

Conrad ran a hand through his dreads in vexation.

"You're the *only* half-Tuathan in the room." His blue eyes shot to Zekiel. "You're not actually considering this, are you?"

"Jax is right. He is more powerful than any Tuathan technopath. With his unique abilities, he could serve as a signal booster and keep Finn from overusing hers."

"And what if you're wrong?"

Zekiel said nothing. Conrad shook his head and looked at Finn. His eyes began to fill with panic as he took in the resolute glint in hers. On this, she would never relent, and he'd finally begun to realize it.

He brought his face close to hers and held her gaze in desperation. "I can't lose you too."

Finn's tone gentled as she squeezed his hand and swallowed the lump forming in her throat. "You won't."

She didn't know how, but she managed not to choke on the lie.

Conrad's shoulders sagged in defeat. He released her hand to wrap his arms around her and pulled her in for an embrace. His lips rested against her forehead as he whispered, "I love you, Finn No Last Name."

Finn's heart ached. She leaned away from him, getting enough distance between them to meet his gaze. This moment meant too much. Every cell in her body screamed for her to ease his worry. She settled for telling him the truth instead.

"I love you, Conrad Marthox." His eyes drifted shut at her words. Her lips lifted in the ghost of a smile as she waited for them to reopen. When they did, she said, "You're not such a bastard after all."

Conrad sighed and shook his head in disbelief.

"How many times do I have to tell you—"

"I know, I know. Your parents were married."

Near them, Zekiel fiddled with a small black box and pressed a few buttons.

"If we're going to do this, we need to do it now."

Finn nodded and pulled away. She followed Zekiel over to the stasis pods while Conrad went to sit with Tiri and watch. Jax came up next to Finn and leaned in to whisper out of the side of his mouth. "You know we're probably going to die, right?"

They reached the side of Abraham's stasis pod and Finn stopped moving. She turned to the half-Tuathan fully and placed her hand on his shoulder, touching him for the first time since they'd met.

"Thanks for doing it anyway," she whispered back.

"For Axel," he said. "And Grim, and AJ, and every other hybrid these bastards took from us."

Zekiel held up the box he'd been fiddling with and handed it to Jax.

"Take this. It's already programmed to broadcast whatever Finn uploads to every holoscreen in the Union."

Jax took the box in his grip and closed his eyes. Slowly, tendrils of electric blue energy began to slither down his forearms past his wrists and shot from the tips of his fingers into the device. When his amber eyes next popped open, they appeared distant and unseeing. The fish marking on his cheek began to glow brightly.

"I'm in."

Zekiel ushered Finn forward and motioned to the stasis pod. "Once we open the pod, we won't have a lot of time. I'll keep him alive as long as I can outside of stasis. Upload everything you siphon into Jax. We'll take care of the rest."

"Got it."

Zekiel put his hands on the keypad connected to the pod and typed in a code. Like Jax, the fish marking on his cheek began to glow and his eyes slid shut in concentration. The stasis pod released a low hiss of air and the lid slowly opened outward, revealing the man inside.

Thanks to Zekiel, the machines connected to Abraham continued to work away, pumping oxygen and fluids into his husk of a body. Finn reached inside without hesitation, grabbed the ruby ring circling Abraham's index finger, and slid it off. Clutching it in her fist, she reached out and withdrew one of the fixed blade daggers from his belt.

The room fell silent as its occupants watched to see what she would do next. Finn bent over the pod and leaned close to hiss against Abraham's cheek.

"This is for Cora and Alice."

She brought the tip of the blade down to his chest. With deliberately slow movements, she continued to push down until it pierced the skin. Gradually, she increased the pressure until she'd sunk the entire thing into his chest. As the hilt of the blade hit him, and the steel pierced his black heart, his red eyes shot open in surprise and pain. Finn released her hold on the knife and brought her hand up to cup his cheek. With her head still close to his, she whispered again.

"And this is for my father."

She let the memories drift from her fingertips into his cheek, showing him the worst of Grim's pain at his expense. His eyes widened and blood trickled from the corner of his mouth. His mouth opened in a silent scream.

Whether it was the memories or the knife that ultimately killed him, she'd never know. Zekiel looked down at the dead human with dispassion before returning his stare to her.

"What about the rest of the pods?" he inquired.

"Leave them. When this is over, they'll answer to the rest of the galaxy."

Finn straightened and walked to Jax's side. His cheek still glowed brightly and the tendrils of energy connecting his arms to the black box swirled with activity. One of his eyes popped open at her approach.

"You ready?" she asked him.

The left corner of his mouth tilted up and his open eye sparkled with a morose combination of humor and sadness. "It was nice knowing you, Sexy Stowaway."

Finn rolled her eyes at the nickname and gripped Abraham's ring in the palm of her hand. Then she wrapped the fingers of her other hand around Jax's bare forearm. He gave her one last nod before closing his eye and returning his focus to the broadcast. Taking a deep breath, she let the memories attached to Abraham's ring flood her. As Finn siphoned each one, she uploaded it to Jax.

The humans boarding their Ark.

Abraham and the others becoming ill from the malfunctioning stasis pods.

Their landing on Tuathan and subsequent poaching of the alien species' technology.

The decision to name themselves Arcturians and rule the new galaxy of planets they'd stumbled upon as gods.

One after the other, they flashed behind her lids and she pushed them out into Jax.

The creation of the caste system. The enslavement of the other races masquerading as salvation. The manufactured meteor extract and its distribution to the Outer and Inner Rings, designed with the sole purpose of keeping the masses weak and pliable.

Every moment of violence, every act of cruelty laid bare for the world to see.

She finished with her own memories of the Dome and Grim's memories of Abraham and the night Cora and Alice had been taken from him so cruelly.

One by one, the scenes played out above them on the holoscreens like movies. Lastly, she focussed on her memory at the callous extermination of the Mud Pit and its people.

Finn let the memories rush through her and straight into the homes and lives of every inhabitant of the Union. The room around her spun and lights flashed behind her eyelids. Ignoring the fatigue, she continued to upload anything and everything, afraid to miss even the smallest detail.

She kept a tight grip on Jax's arm, even as they both fell to the ground, their legs too weak to support them.

Her eyes drifted shut . . .

Somewhere in the distance, she heard Conrad's shout of alarm and Tiri's panicked shriek. Hearing them, Finn tried to force her eyes open.

It was the last thing she did before her last reserve of strength gave out and everything around her went dark.

TWENTY

The sound of muffled laughter stirred Finn from a deep sleep. Her lids felt too heavy to open. She remained still, listening as the sounds became clearer. Laughter and soft chatter intermingled with the steady, rhythmic beeps of machines nearby.

It took long, exhausting moments, but she managed to blink her eyes open slowly.

She immediately regretted it.

Bright light flooded her irises and she struggled to blink away the stinging tears it induced. When her vision finally cleared, she allowed her gaze to flit around the room.

The arched ceiling above her had been painted with fantastical images of the Arcturians and their arrival in the Union. Disgusted, she turned her head and saw golden walls and floors.

Everywhere she looked, she saw evidence of the Reliance.

Had it all been for nothing?

Medical machines lined the floor, their displays beeping with vitals. Finn lifted her arms to find several tubes pumping fluids and plasma into her veins.

"Hey, she's awake!"

Her eyes sought out the owner of the voice and scanned the room until she found Jax lying in the bed next to her. Like her, several tubes connected his arms and chest to the machines around them, feeding him a steady stream of fluids and plasma.

His amber eyes danced with humor as he took in her dazed expression. Next to him, Axel perched on the side of the mattress, his large hands enveloping Jax's. Finn squinted at the pair in confusion.

"Axel?" Finn winced at the roughness in her voice. The horned hybrid shot her a shy smile.

"Hey, Finn."

Given that the last time she saw him, he'd been riding a gunship into the top floor of a building, the red giant looked no worse for the wear. He wore a white silk shirt and cotton pants, and his dark horns were so shiny they looked polished.

"Am I dead?" she asked the room at large.

"Dead? You're a freaking *legend*!" Lex twirled into the room in a blur of pink and purple braids. She came to a stop next to her brother's bed and squeezed into the tiny open space on Jax's right side. She grinned around a lollipop and watched Finn expectantly.

Finn eyed the three of them in bed together and carefully lifted her hand so as not to disturb the tubes there. She massaged her aching temple with a finger.

"So, I'm in Hell," she muttered under her breath as she glared at the gold surrounding her on all sides.

Lex leaned into her brother, cupped her hand, and stage-whispered. "I see she's still as pleasant as ever."

Yep, definitely in hell.

"Thank Gods, you're finally awake." Iliana rushed into the room then. Her older sister was a vision in a sweeping blue gown embroidered with purple flowers. The courtesan's heels clacked against the floor as she ran over to Finn. She sat on the edge of the bed and took her little sister's hands. "How are you feeling?"

"Where are we?" Finn probed.

"We're still on Arcturus. You and Jax were too weak to be moved, so we brought you to the council's medical ward."

"That explains all the gold," Finn grumbled.

"You and Jax have both been in medically induced comas for weeks," Axel added.

"Weeks?" she repeated in disbelief.

Finn tried to sit up on her own, but she found her muscles were weaker than they'd ever been. Iliana helped her up, fluffing the pillows around her as she did.

Weeks?

She had so much she wanted to ask, she was having trouble getting started. Before Finn could verbalize the countless questions forming in her head, more and more people began to file into the ward.

Conrad came through first, followed by Zekiel, Enyo, Aedan, Raven, Mace, and Tiri. All too soon, the room became crowded with visitors and Finn sighed in relief to see them all alive and well. Aedan stood back against a wall, watching Finn with a mixture of relief and pride. Walking past him, Enyo flashed her fangs in a wide grin and joined Iliana.

Finn waved weakly, but she only had eyes for Conrad. His blue eyes anxiously sought out hers. When he saw her sitting up and conscious, he immediately rushed to her side. He appeared to be freshly showered, his dark skin still glistening with moisture. He'd pulled the dreads away from his face and had chosen an all-black ensemble, from his shirt to his shoes. She noted the lines of tension painting his handsome face and frowned.

Careful not to disturb her tubes, he sat opposite Iliana and pulled Finn ever-so-gently into his arms. She breathed in his scent and reveled in the feel of his strong arms wrapped around her. After long moments, she pulled away, letting her gaze drift up to his. The lines of tension eased with his relief as his glowing eyes drank in the sight of her.

"Did it work?" she asked him.

His lips twitched slightly, and he turned his head to look across the room at the far wall. Finn followed his gaze, finally taking note of the holoscreens mounted throughout the ward. Each one flashed between different memories she'd siphoned and uploaded and footage of the "Arcturians" and their stasis pods being removed from the council headquarters, while masses of enraged bystanders threw objects and screamed profanity.

More live newsfeeds showed upper-caste reporters out in the streets of the Outer Rings as they interviewed lower-caste aliens of all races.

"It's been playing on a loop every day since the broadcast," Conrad told her quietly.

Finn grinned up at him.

"We actually did it."

She returned her stare to the screens, eager to see more. It took her a moment to finally notice the list of names flashing on the upper corner of each display. Each name had an image of either an alien, human, or hybrid next to it.

Iliana noticed what had caught her attention and her lower lip trembled.

"The fallen," she said quietly.

Enyo placed a hand on the courtesan's shoulder.

Countless names and faces flashed on the screens, including several Finn recognized: Madam Califax. Mr. Green. Sasha. Isis.

One by one, she scanned their names and faces as a lump began to form in her throat. Next to her, Tiri sniffled as Isis's name and picture faded from the screen. Finn took the girl's hand and pulled her onto her lap. Once settled, Tiri buried her face in Finn's shoulder and kept it there.

Suddenly a still shot of Grim filled each of the holoscreens. In large font, the words "Khaleerian heralded as hero" flashed next to his image. Her chest tightened and tears began to form at the sight. Finn's eyes shot to Conrad. Seeing the shock and hope warring together on her face, he nodded his head and smiled gently.

"It's true. He's become the face of a new revolution."

Finn let that news settle, the tears flowing freely down her cheeks. The screen flashed again. This time, a silver-haired reporter with violet eyes stood next to a soldier in full uniform.

"Hey, I know him!" Lex shouted excitedly.

She froze when the man's name appeared on the screen. *General Shane Montgomery.*

The captain of *Independence* looked dapper and clean-shaven wearing his full uniform. Finn tore her eyes from the screen to look at her companions."General?"

Someone shushed her and increased the volume on the screens. Conrad smiled and mouthed the word "promotion."

Finn watched in awe as Shane discussed the drastic changes being made to the Reliance government, which included the elimination of the caste system and the return of plant life and oxygen to the planets.

Finn gazed down at the back of Tiri's head.

Such a big job for such a little girl. Seeming to hear her thoughts, Tiri turned her face and gazed up at Finn with big green eyes.

I'm scared, she told Finn telepathically. *Isis was supposed to be here to help me. I don't know if I can do it by myself.*

Finn gave Tiri a reassuring squeeze and rested her cheek on top of the girl's head.

It's okay to be scared and it's okay to be sad, but you're not alone. I'll be with you every step of the way.

Tiri's little body tensed in her arms and she pulled away to meet Finn's gaze.

You will?

Finn smiled.

You can try to get rid of me, but I'm telling you right now . . . You're stuck with me, kid.

Tiri's answering smile was resplendent. The room erupted in chatter as the group continued to watch Shane's interview. The little girl sagged back into Finn's hold and sighed.

Later that night, Finn lay in her bed. Though her body had fatigued, her mind didn't experience the same exhaustion. Instead, it raced. Conrad sat next to her on the left. He had yet to leave her side since she'd woken, as though he feared if he took his eyes off her, she might disappear. On her right, Tiri snuggled into her side under the covers and slept soundly. Jax and Axel also slept peacefully, intertwined in the bed next to them. Lex, Enyo, and Iliana had fallen asleep in nearby chairs.

Conrad's finger rubbed soothing circles on her wrist.

"What happens next?" she whispered into the dimly lit space between them.

"We make sure the change sticks, like Grim would've wanted."

"And then?" she pushed.

She'd been so consumed with Grim, war, revenge, and everything in between, she'd never allowed herself to think about the after. Now, for the first time in a long time, peace was within reach.

What were they going to do with it?

Sensing her growing anxiety, Conrad squeezed her hand. Rather than answer, he reached into his pocket and withdrew a small item. Taking her left hand in his, he slipped the object onto her ring finger. Finn looked down and her mouth dropped open as she got a good look at the silver band now encircling her finger. She caught sight of the Khaleerian gemstone from Grim's necklace glittering at its center and her wide eyes shot to Conrad. He smiled and pulled her face close to his.

"For starters, I'm thinking it's about time we got you a last name."

EPILOGUE

Gliese
Ten Cycles Later

Finn sang softly under her breath and cradled the baby wrapped snugly in blankets in her arms. The gentle creak and sway of her rocking chair soothed the infant's squirming. Her chubby little fists rested beneath her chin and her blue eyes began to drift shut slowly.

Finn breathed deeply, inhaling the scent of fresh-cut grass intermingling with the flowers Iliana had planted in her garden. From her spot on the porch, she watched the green blades sway in the breeze and listened to the delighted shrieks of the children playing in the backyard. The sun had just begun to set on Gliese, streaking the sky with brushstrokes in a myriad of pinks, oranges, and purples.

The door opened behind her and Finn turned carefully so as not to disturb the baby. Tiri emerged from within the house carrying a bottle. Her round face had matured and slimmed with age, and the vine-like markings decorating her lavender skin only served to highlight her elfin beauty. Her long, white-blonde curls flowed freely down past her shoulders and nearly reached her waist. She'd grown into her round, green eyes and they filled with affection as she gazed down at baby Alice from beneath a fall of heavy lashes. She shot Finn a dazzling smile and motioned for her to hand over the little one.

Finn shifted Alice, wrapping the blanket tighter around her small body, and transferred her into Tiri's waiting arms. She took her seat in the remaining rocking chair opposite Finn and began to move slowly, humming a cheerful melody as she did. Alice immediately latched onto the bottle and began sucking hungrily.

"Mommy! AJ used his powers on me again and got mud all over my clothes!"

Sophie, Finn's eldest, came darting around the corner from the backyard and ran straight for the porch and her mother. Sure enough, the girl's lovely floral dress sported dark splotches of brown. The muck even caked the dark-red ringlets on the left side of her head, matting them together there. She climbed the steps one indignant stomp at a time and turned to Finn, blue eyes fuming.

Finn shared a knowing look with Tiri. Her sweet Sophie hated getting dirty. The child was much more at home surrounded by flowers and pretty things. More and more every day she reminded Finn of Iliana at that age.

"And where was your father while all this was happening?" Finn asked the irate little girl as she fought a smile. While she waited for an answer, she licked the pad of her thumb and began wiping at the dirt marring the light-brown skin of the child's cheek.

"He was laughing," Sophie groaned, rolling her eyes.

Tiri giggled across the porch, earning a glare from the frustrated little girl. She quickly rearranged her features to look contrite, then she got up from the rocking chair—still cradling baby Alice—and knelt to Sophie's eyeline.

"What do you say we go and get you changed? After I put Alice down for her nap, you and I can have a tea party."

Her anger forgotten, Sophie's expression immediately brightened, and she gave Tiri a soft smile of adoration.

"Can I wear your green dress?"

"Absolutely," Tiri answered immediately.

The little girl squealed and jumped up and down before turning to her mother. As was her way, Sophie threw herself into Finn's arms with abandon and hugged her tight.

"Are you coming too, Mommy?"

Finn squeezed before releasing the child, noting the mud that had transferred from her the girl's dress to her blouse with humor.

"I'll be up after I have a chat with your brother," she promised. Satisfied, Sophie grinned and skipped ahead of Tiri into the house.

The little boy in question came tearing around the side of the house just as Tiri and Alice disappeared inside. He made a beeline straight for Finn as fast as his little legs could carry him. Conrad trailed behind him, smiling so brightly she could see his dimple, even at this distance.

"Abaddon Jax Marthox!" she called, struggling to make her voice sound stern. The boy's cherubic face and clothes were covered in mud, even more so than Sophie's had been. The dark coils of his hair bounced as he ran. As he neared, she noted the slight glow fading from his indigo eyes.

In his haste to get to her, he tripped on the second step. He righted himself and grinned, exposing the dimples on either side of his cheeks. When he'd scaled the porch fully, he threw himself onto Finn's lap, knocking the air from her lungs. AJ climbed up fully to perch on his knees and placed his little hands on either side of her face, forcing her to meet his serious gaze. "I didn't do it," he told her in a grave voice.

"Do what?"

His solemn eyes narrowed as he leaned in and whispered, "Whatever Sophie said I did."

Conrad joined them on the porch just in time to hear the boy's murmur. His eyes sparkled when they met Finn's and soft laughter shook his large chest. Finn shot her husband a halfhearted glare and focused on her precocious middle child.

"Would you like to tell me why you're covered in mud?" she asked him.

"I was trying to catch one of the piglets."

"They weren't cooperating," Conrad added cheerfully.

"Yeah, they weren't cop'erating," AJ defended in his adorable little boy vernacular. "I had to use my powers."

Finn tapped the boy's button nose.

"And how did your sister end up covered in mud?" she asked him.

"She wasn't cop'erating either."

"Well, be that as it may," she whispered against his soft coiled locks. "You still owe her an apology."

"Okay," he said in defeat.

Finn gave him one last hug and kissed his forehead. "Go on now. She's upstairs having a tea party with Tiri."

"Is she wearing the green dress?"

"Yes."

She took in the boy's crestfallen expression and tilted his chin up with her finger. "Auntie Li left a trunk of old gowns in my room the last time she visited."

AJ perked up at the news and leapt off her lap. He ran for the door, nearly bursting through it in his haste, and rushed inside. His heavy footfalls stomped up the stairs until they could no longer hear them.

In the newfound silence, Conrad's eyes found hers and he crooked his finger at her.

Finn rose from her seat and walked into his waiting arms. She rested her head against the hard wall of his chest and tilted her face up to watch the sun as it began to disappear below the horizon. The pastel sky began to darken as night fell and brought a peaceful stillness with it.

"We did good, Hellion," he whispered against her hair.

"We also did *well*," she told him, grinning.

He pulled her away slightly to look into her eyes. The glow of his gaze washed over her, warming her from the inside out.

"I love you, Finn Marthox."

"And I love you, Conrad Marthox."

Finn smiled at the irony. After all this time, she finally had a last name.

She lifted her mouth to press against her husband's. His arms tightened around her in response, and he reciprocated by deepening the kiss. Inside the house, the children shrieked with laughter upstairs. Moments later, the sound of something breaking, followed by Tiri's uninhibited laughter, echoed against the walls.

Finn groaned and sagged into Conrad's arms.

"Did that sound like something important?"

Another crash sounded above them, followed by Sophie's lividly shrieked, "AJ!"

The noise was finally too much for the sleeping infant in the next room and Alice's cries soon filled the house.

"No, but that did," Conrad mused.

"When are Iliana and Enyo coming again?" she asked him, her voice brimming with hope.

"Not soon enough," he answered with a chuckle.

As night fell fully on the Marthox farm, her husband sighed in contentment and kissed the top of her head.

Hand in hand, they happily joined the chaos inside.

THE END

ACKNOWLEDGMENTS

I'm still struggling to accept the fact that after a decade of dreaming, plotting, dreaming some more, and writing, the Reliance trilogy is complete. It's been so amazing (and surreal) to hear all of the wonderful feedback from you readers. I think a part of me has been afraid of finishing the series. I mean, the third book in a trilogy is by far the most important, and the fear of screwing it up has been (only slightly) paralyzing.

Thankfully, I have a publisher that kept me on track and motivated, while also being extremely patient. I also have a husband who is currently on payroll as my biggest and most enthusiastic cheerleader. I could not have done any of this without him. Thank God he accepts kisses and new chapters as currency. Speaking of my husband . . . Jack, I want to thank you. Not only did you take on extra household duties with our toddler so Mommy could have time to write, but you have always played an integral role in giving me the courage to do the things I'm afraid of . . . like finish a book series I've been lovingly crafting for over a decade.

And, if you like the fight scenes in this book, they are an amalgamation of my imagination and Jack's, along with his vast knowledge of combat. Both proved invaluable in the creation of many scenes within this book.

So, Jack, thank you once again for being the best partner I could ever ask for.

Finally, thank you to all of you beautiful readers out there who have stuck with the trilogy since the beginning. Thank you for loving these characters and this story as much as I do.

And for those who didn't like it . . . thank you for the constructive criticism. In your own way, you too have made this trilogy better than I ever dreamed it could be.